THE LAST S

The Last Straw

Stress Needn't Make You Ill

Peter G. Campbell

Arlington Books
King St, St James's
London

THE LAST STRAW
First published 1990 by
Arlington Books (Publishers) Ltd
15–17 King Street
London SW1

© Peter G. Campbell 1990

British Library Cataloguing-in-Publication Data
Campbell, Peter G.
The last straw: stress needn't make you ill.
1. Man. Stress
155.9042

ISBN 0–85140–784–6

Typeset in Great Britain by
Inforum Typesetting, Portsmouth
Printed and bound in Great Britain by
Redwood Press Ltd, Melksham, Wiltshire

'Sensible people will see trouble coming and avoid it, but an unthinking person will walk right into it and regret it later.'

        Proverbs 22:3 [Today's English Version]

Dedication

To my wife Honor (who put up for so long with my use of the computer), and to my son James (who taught me how to use it in the first place).

Acknowledgements

While I acknowledge assistance from many sources, I am particularly grateful to the following persons and organisations, either for permission to use their original material for quotations and research purposes, or for their advice and encouragement which has enabled me to finish this book:

Mr M. Budd,
Mr B. Butler,
Dr B.M. Childe,
Mr G.H. Davies,
Dr H. Howell,
Mrs J. Hampton,
Dr K. Miller,
Mr A. Scott-Morley,
Dr C. Smith,
Mr S. Stock,
Dr V. Wheelock,
Sunday Telegraph,
The Watchtower Bible & Tract Society of New York Inc.

Contents

Introduction		xi
Chapter 1.	The Changing Pace of Modern Life	1
Chapter 2.	Our Food Supplies	10
Chapter 3.	A Balanced View of Food Additives	27
Chapter 4.	Our Water Supplies	40
Chapter 5.	Stresses From Our Social Way of Life	56
Chapter 6.	Stresses of a Biochemical or Medical Nature	67
Chapter 7.	Chemical Stresses From the Environment	83
Chapter 8.	Electromagnetic Stresses from the Environment	95
Chapter 9.	Choosing the Right Foods & Remedies	117
Chapter 10.	Kinesiology – A Way to Check Your Sensitivities	136
Chapter 11.	What Else Can We Do?	151
Useful Names and Addresses		161
Index		171

Introduction

This book contains the essence of many experiences undergone whilst working within the food industry, and latterly running my own business over a number of years; during this time it has been my privilege to be able to offer help, generally related to food & diet, to many extremely pleasant and intelligent people whose health regrettably has been affected in some way by the twentieth century. Although I have sometimes been called a 'boffin' I consider myself a pragmatic person and so if an idea or a suggestion works in practice then I feel that others should be given the opportunity of knowing about it and finding out if it helps them too.

While there is certainly a growing concern about what we are doing to the environment, and many well-qualified specialists are devoting all their time and energies to the subject, relatively few seem to have considered so far the details of what the environment is doing to *us* (though this is primarily the result of what we did to it first!). The intention, then, is that this book should benefit in a practical way to anyone who has a genuine interest in this subject. To add weight to the views expressed, some of which are bound to be personal to an extent, I have included a large number of extracts from scientific literature which are all related to stress in some way, and would recommend serious readers to try to follow up at least some of them.

Prior to founding the Foodwatch service for allergy sufferers in 1982 with my wife Honor I had spent over twenty years dealing with various technical aspects of our food supply; after a spell in teaching, followed by cosmetics research and development, I worked on product and process development with the Milk Marketing Board, after that for the largest producer of artificial food colourings in the U.K., and finally for a large frozen food company

xii *The Last Straw*

where I was responsible for all technical matters. Consequently I feel that I should be reasonably well qualified, both academically and from practical experience, to collate together in this book information which any interested person can utilise to benefit the health and quality of life of both himself and his family. However I can claim only to have 'scratched the surface' of the subject, and any of us can add to the store of useful knowledge – we do not all have to be Einsteins.

I must emphasize at this point that the book is in no way intended to be scaremongering, but it does reveal that there are many issues affecting us all to which we should pay more than the usual attention. It is my hope that it will serve to redress the balance a little, considering (a) the 'over the top' attitude so often reflected in media coverage of any subject and (b) the opposing stand frequently adopted by official sources that we, the public, have no need to become concerned about the potential dangers of any scientific and technological innovation as the scientists have everything under control.

Many thinking persons now realize that the huge increase in general malaise that we see all around us today has two prime causes: firstly the contamination of the environment, which affects the purity of our food and water supplies, and secondly the dramatic increase in stress levels imposed upon our bodies in this twentieth century by the multiple and rapid changes in lifestyle that we are trying to accommodate. I support the theory, although it is really now more than a theory, that ill-health strikes when the individual's immune system is stretched so much by the unrelieved circumstances of life that it is no longer able to cope with the load of stress; hence 'The Last Straw'.

Naturally I hope that you will agree with most of what is said in the book, but inevitably there will be points of disagreement, which is really a healthy situation as no-one can be right all the time. I would certainly welcome any constructive criticism. Genuine progress in understanding life, as in science, comes first from the presentation of observations, then logical discussion and reasoning followed by further experimentation to confirm or modify the original views.

But it is common sense that concerned individuals who are prepared to take an active interest in the workings of their body, their

Introduction xiii

food supply and their environment can achieve a great deal towards better health, and a more fulfilling life within their families and the community at large. My intention is above all that now you have taken the trouble to open up this book, you will continue to read it and find it both stimulating and helpful in a practical and down-to-earth way in your daily encounter with the environment.

Chapter 1
The Changing Pace of Modern Life

How many of us can put hand on heart and say that we enjoy really good health today? Some of us may be fortunate in this respect, but the plethora of books on health care that have been written in recent years would seem to suggest that many of us are still looking for some improvement.

It is true that modern medicine has put an end to a number of killer diseases, but in their place we keep on hearing of the increase in allergy, heart disease, cancer, AIDS and so on, and many of us may wonder how much influence we can have on our health in today's modern industrialized society. As the pace of life quickens, it seems as if we have to expend ourselves more and more just to keep up, and many are finding that scientific advances have brought with them some unexpected problems and complications.

For many centuries prior to our own, life proceeded at a somewhat slower pace and individuals' expectations from it were less. So for all of us caught up in today's frantic world (whether we like it or not), it can be enlightening to talk to those people in their eighties and nineties who can still recall the time when there were no radios or televisions, no aeroplanes and very few motor cars. Although I suppose many of us look back wistfully to the days of our youth, those of that particular generation are only too pleased to confirm that the Edwardian era at the beginning of this century was more leisurely and one in which the prospects for a better quality of life seemed more encouraging than ever before, largely due to the promises held out by science and technology. Television and film dramas set in that period, such as *Upstairs, Downstairs* and *Flambards*, have cleverly and effectively evoked the special atmosphere of this era. Then in 1914 came the Great War, known as the 'War to end all Wars'. It is important for us to recognize that

2   *The Last Straw*

irreversible changes to society followed the war, just as many well-known historians and others have admitted.

For example, Harold Macmillan said: 'Everything would get better and better. This was the world I was born in. . . . Suddenly, unexpectedly, one morning in 1914 the whole thing came to an end.' Randolph Churchill, in a review of a book about his father Sir Winston Churchill, made this comment: 'The shot which was fired on June 28th 1914 in Sarajevo had shattered the world of security and creative reason. . . . The world has never been the same place since. . . . It was a turning point, and the wonderful, calm, attractive world of yesterday had vanished, never again to appear.' The philosopher Bertrand Russell said in 1953: 'Ever since 1914, everybody conscious of trends in the world has been deeply troubled by what has seemed like a fatal and predetermined march toward ever greater disaster.' In fact World War 1, which in itself was responsible for the deaths of up to 18 million souls, was followed in 1939 by another even more widespread conflict which had claimed some 55 million lives by the time it ended in 1945.

Dramatic changes

Who can doubt that the world is in a period of dramatic change, politically, economically, environmentally, socially and morally? The recent and sudden changes in Eastern Europe and certain Third World countries demonstrate this well. What must concern us all is that these people, who have as much right to a reasonable standard of living as we do, are looking to the West as their role model, and hoping to achieve a higher material standard of living and with it greater happiness and freedom. While we would all agree that great improvements are long overdue, we have to ask ourselves if the West is in fact a desirable role model, or have we not rather gone 'over the top'?

Is it not our responsibility to see to it that these countries do not make the same mistakes that we have made? This will not be easy: we may have enjoyed the benefits of relative material prosperity at the expense of the environment, and realised just in time the longer-term damage we have caused, but how do we dissuade them from copying us too closely? As *Awake!* magazine said recently [1]: 'Now the rich nations, in effect, propose saying to the

The Changing Pace of Modern Life 3

poor ones: 'We've already got our rich life-style. Suddenly we have become very concerned about the environment. We're sorry, but you can't have what we already have. You need to be 'wiser' than we were. You can't use all this cheap energy as we did. You're going to have to use more expensive energy and grow more slowly, make your people wait longer to have the life-style we tell them they should emulate.' How is that likely to go over in the Third World?

Each year seems to bring its own new crop of problems, wherever we may happen to live. Those in the third world at present remain desperately short even of the basic necessities for life, whereas we do not starve, although other issues and responsibilities of a more complex nature plague us. It seems that many of life's surprises are unpleasant ones, and that as a result our lives become rapidly more stressful as time goes by; many, yearning for a simpler way of life, have opted out of society in one way or another. Of course, 'green' is the 'in' word in politics, and we have yet to see how effective the movement will be; however history tells us that whereas many individuals enter politics with the very best of intentions, most find in due course that, however sincere they are, they cannot beat the system. We can now see the long-term results of tampering with our environment in ways never possible before this technological age, and Rachel Carson's book *Silent Spring*, which may have seemed far-fetched to many when published in 1963, is proving to have been a remarkably accurate prediction of today's state of affairs environmentally.

Science and a stable society – are they compatible?

So we could well ask if science and a stable society are compatible. Certainly I would not like to answer an unequivocal 'yes' to that question. Man by nature is inquisitive, so as our knowledge of science and the world around us has increased we have begun to exploit that knowledge, although our discoveries have not really uncovered anything very new; frequently they result from observing nature and attempting to copy it in a very imperfect way, in the 'invention' of electricity, sonar and aeroplanes, for example. The splitting of the atom, however, was quite another matter as no living creature other than man is known to have attempted, let alone achieved, such a feat! While everything developed by man is

4   *The Last Straw*

essentially neutral from a moral standpoint and could be used for benefitting the human race if so intended, in practice it is often used to make possible the more effective killing or poisoning of other humans, animals and plants. We can now harness the atom for peaceful power, and we can send men into space, but many persons have asked themselves what have been the real benefits, if any, of all that effort and expenditure? Is scientific research merely an expensive form of escapism?

The historian Arnold Toynbee commented: 'It is tragic to think that we have been so successful in the technological field, whereas our record of moral failures is almost immeasurable.' How sad that, just at a time when we could have been making such great strides forward with our new-found knowledge, we see only too clearly the signs that relationships within families and between human beings in general are becoming more fragile. No wonder that more people are turning to alcohol, tranquillizers and other drugs in an attempt to alleviate the stresses of life that they feel so strongly.

One wonders if our lives are meant to be this way. Could it be that without being consciously aware of it, we are all influenced by the certain knowledge that one day our lives will come to an end? Could this explain, at least to an extent, the way we try to cram as much as we can into each day whilst there is still time; to acquire as many possessions as we can afford (or ill-afford); or to reach the top in our chosen field of work? The result is that we create for ourselves an even more stressful existence.

And yet, however long we might live, we could never know or do it all. A person could spend his entire working life studying one specific subject, such as the structure of water, black holes in space or the life cycle of the butterfly, only to find out after fifty years or so that although he knows more than when he started, he has an even greater number of deeper questions that remain unanswered. We could, perhaps, compare our area of knowledge to the area inside a circle, the circumference of that circle representing the boundary of our knowledge and hence the contact with the un-known. Just as the area within the circle will increase as we expand our knowledge, so the circumference too will extend as we realise that our contact with the unknown is greater than it was. The more we know, the more we realise that we don't know! For most

The Changing Pace of Modern Life   5

people who enjoy living, this realisation can be frustrating, because just as we feel that we may be getting somewhere our body or mind reaches such a stage of degeneration that we can do little more before our life ends. Although many of us can expect to live to a reasonable age today, the real expectancy of life has not really changed for thousands of years, so that even if we do achieve the age of eighty, ninety or more, how many of us can find real pleasure and fulfilment in the evening of our lives? There is a French proverb which, roughly translated, means: 'If only youth had the experience, and old age the ability!' Or consider the words of Moses recorded in the Bible[1]: 'We have finished our years just like a whisper. In themselves the days of our years are seventy years; and if because of special mightiness they are eighty years, yet their insistence is on trouble and hurtful things.' Nothing much has changed! Yet, even if more and more people can be given the opportunity to live longer by being technically cured of cancer, heart disease, arthritis or multiple sclerosis, where is the money going to come from to pay for these treatments?

Our generation – why so stressful?

Even our response to everyday necessities like eating and drinking can be affected by the levels of stress that we are coping with. A person who is forty years old, and has eaten three meals a day since babyhood, will by now have chewed his way through no less than forty thousand meals! Yet, however many meals we eat, we never get bored with eating (although perhaps we cannot say quite the same about the washing up), so obviously eating was intended to constitute one of the simple and recurring pleasures of life. How sad it is that for many of us this no longer holds true, as we are only too well aware that, if we eat certain foods, we can suffer with any one of a wide variety of symptoms.

But why us? Why our generation in particular? Could there be something inherently wrong with us as individuals, or is the problem far broader than that? I believe that it is not unreasonable to suggest that the state of our health depends not only on our inherited genetic make-up but also on the demands made on us by our society and other aspects of our physical environment. As I am a food technologist by profession you will understand my main interests being in food, diet and health (we are indeed what we eat),

6 *The Last Straw*

and it struck me recently that one of our most regular and very personal encounters with our environment occurs each time we sit down to a meal. So perhaps it could be enlightening to examine in more detail the nature of our dietary practices.

Eating patterns

In western society we tend to eat a rather unvarying diet based largely on dairy produce, refined wheat and refined sugar. If you are sceptical, just run through in your mind the foods which you commonly eat which have one of these as an ingredient, either major or minor. It is true, and should be emphasised, that as the result of education we now eat as a nation more fruit and vegetables, more wholemeal flour, and less fatty red meat, but it is a fact that only about ten years ago the United Kingdom held the dubious title of 'the most constipated nation on earth'! A lack of fibre, particularly soluble fibre, slows down the passage of food through our digestive system, resulting in the accumulation of toxins; so could our national predilection for sweet, fattening and relatively fibre-free foods be a prime cause of the accelerating increase in food-related disease? Many nutritional experts believe this to be so.

Compare our situation with that in many third-world countries, where the diet may be extremely monotonous, being based on such cereals as rice, maize or millet. As the media have shown us so dramatically in recent years, these millions of human beings may be severely malnourished and are in danger of death from starvation (recent figures indicate one such death every eight and a half seconds approximately) yet western-style ailments such as constipation, heart disease, cancer or allergy do not appear to be endemic; this is fortunate as, if these people became allergic to their staple food, their health would be in even graver danger than it already is.

In a report to the *British Medical Journal* about ten years ago, doctors investigating the Tswana tribe in South Africa found that in many cases the elderly coloured people had arteries that were in as good condition as those of white youngsters, and that there was an absence of coronary heart disease. They noted that 'Rural South African blacks live on a diet high in fibre and low in animal protein and fat.' So it cannot be just eating the same foods regularly,

The Changing Pace of Modern Life

whether they are refined or not, that we have to blame for food-related disease, although it is one factor that must be taken into consideration along with our western way of life with its great expectations, and consequently its high levels of stress.

Ironically, there could be enough good food for everyone; the director of the United Nations Office of Inter-Agency Affairs and Coordination said some twelve years ago that, if the agricultural potential of the earth can be maximised, at least 38 billion people could be fed (that is about seven times the number of persons alive today); this would, of course, necessitate much better international cooperation than we have at present. And in 1984 the U.N. Food and Agriculture Organisation maintained that with moderate improvements in agricultural methods, the earth would be able to provide food, even in developing areas, for up to nine times the population forecast for the year 2000[3]. At a yet more recent conference of the World Food Council (a UN agency), delegates were told that although at least half a billion people in the world are going hungry, global food production is still about 10% higher than it need be to feed everyone. Yet because of complacency, neglect and incompetence we still have food surpluses in some places and severe shortages in others. Way back in 1937 the *Boy's Own Paper* published a cartoon which is just as apposite today as it was then; it showed two characters, one emaciated and the other with a huge paunch. In simple terms, the fat man said to the thin man 'You look as if you've been in a famine', to which the thin man replied 'Yes, and you look as if you caused it!'

'Stop the World!'

Back in the sixties the musical show *Stop the World – I Want to Get Off!* reflected the disillusionment felt by younger adults, and the various peace movements of the time attracted many, although the solutions they offered were not always practical ones. In the late seventies, some fifteen years later, was there anywhere left in this crowded and polluted world where people could lead a simpler, less stressed yet meaningful existence? High in the Himalayas north of Kashmir lived the Hunza tribe, with a simple yet healthy lifestyle. Much of their food was raw, most was vegetarian, their water and air were clean, and they took plenty of exercise; it was not uncommon for the Hunzas to continue active lives to the age of

8   *The Last Straw*

a hundred years or more. These people had become well adapted to their way of life over many generations; they had no great ambitions, they did not expect to jet-set around the world or pull off dramatic multi-million pound business deals, yet traditionally they were a content and healthy people. In the late seventies, researchers writing in the UNESCO magazine *Impact of Science on Society* on the subject of cancer distribution throughout the world reported that this was the only place in the world that was free of cancer. The reason for this distinction was given as their frugal yet healthy diet, their lack of industrial pollution and lives free from stress. The report went on to say that the highest cancer rates exist in 'countries which have the greatest industrial density', and that the increases in cancer were 'constant, undeniable and alarming'.

Yet only two years later, *Wall Street Journal* columnist Ray Vicker wrote a disturbing article indicating that things were changing fast for the Hunzas. A spectacular new road, the Karokoram highway, which runs between Sinkiang, in China, and Pakistan, passes through the valley where the Hunzas have always lived out their remote existence. With the road has come 'civilisation' of a sort, with all its concomitant problems. As Ray Vicker reported: 'At one lunch stop on a hike from Baltit, the Hunza guide lunched on a can of Heinz baked beans. . . . He topped this off with half a dozen caramels eaten with one . . . mouthful, then lay on the grass smoking cigarettes until the hike resumed. Told that smoking is bad for the wind on a hike, he shrugged, "Now we have bus. Not necessary to walk so much anymore." '

What about our expectations?

In stark contrast with the traditional Hunza way of life, just consider our expectations. We live in an increasingly competitive society, in which we are encouraged from a very early age to be winners and not losers. Obviously not everyone can be a winner, but losers are often made to feel a great deal more inadequate than they really are, especially as chance circumstances such as an accident can change a person's fortunes in a split second. As we have seen, stress affects all of us to an extent, but we can create our own problems if we expect too much of ourselves or life in general. There is certainly much scope for disappointment and stress in

The Changing Pace of Modern Life

today's world, but surely no-one in his right mind, even if he considers himself a loser, should think of giving up. I have always found it helpful to try to see things the way they really are and to be realistic about life; then there is an opportunity to understand the problems involved and maybe overcome some of them, which can be very satisfying – most of us enjoy a challenge if there is a reasonable chance of success. I remember once seeing a notice in a statistician's office which read: 'Do not adjust your mind: there is a fault in reality.' I thought at the time, and I still do, that although this was meant in jest it was in fact a very astute observation of people's attitudes in general. Surely if we are that concerned about life, not just for ourselves but for others too, we *should* be prepared to adjust our minds and our way of looking at things, because there is certainly no fault in the reality of the world around us.

The first section of this book will now continue looking in more detail at the sources and effects of the different types of stress factors that go to make up the composite load of stress that we all carry to differing extents; the second section looks at the ways in which we can learn to unburden ourselves of at least some of these stress factors which can be potentially so harmful to so many of us, and hopefully enjoy a healthier and more fulfilling life as a result.

REFERENCES
1. 'A Global Solution', *Awake!*, 8 September 1989.
2. *The Bible, (New World Translation)*, Psalm 90, verse 10.
3. *Land, Food & People*, U.N. (F.A.O.), Rome, 1984, pp 16–17.

Chapter 2
Our Food Supplies

In a better world than our own, anyone interested in horticulture would likely have the space, time and energy to grow most, if not all, of his food supplies. After all, the planting, harvesting and preparation of food is an occupation which still takes up much of the day in many parts of the world, and the bartering of surplus supplies is one way of ensuring variety in the diet.

However, as we know only too well, this world is far from ideal. In many areas, the main activities of each day have to be concerned with working to make ends meet. This way of life produces its own high levels of stress, but in addition it makes it almost impossible for the average person to be self-sufficient, although some people who feel that life should not be ruled by the profit motive find it a goal sufficiently appealing for them to try.

Under conditions of greater world stability and prosperity, we would probably tend to rely on natural methods of growing food, without recourse to the artefacts of a chemical industry. In fact there are signs that the views of the 'green' consumer are going to become more important to industry and politics in the future, especially as members of the Royal Family have publicly affirmed their support for natural agricultural methods. Increasing numbers of those who have gardens or allotments are following the advice given on television and in books to grow 'organically' as far as possible, in an attempt to (a) halt the pollution of the countryside, and (b) improve their health by not consuming foods which have been adulterated in any way.

Natural foods – are they safe?

Before looking at the various ways in which the quality of our staple foods may have been changed by mass production methods,

Our Food Supplies

it might be enlightening to consider some of the properties of 'natural' plants to see just how safe or otherwise they can be. An excellent reference book in this regard is *Food for Free* by Richard Mabey[1]; he starts his introduction by saying 'The first time I was offered a whole dish of wild vegetables I was frankly scared . . . To be embarking upon such a strange and risky eating venture seemed – dare I say it – *unnatural*.' He continues: 'It is a sad and not a little remarkable how thoroughly we are all constrained by modern attitudes to food . . . it is those foods that are grown furthest from our sight that seem to be the most popular. There must be no hint of the dirtiness or the ups and downs of the growing process. The produce must be attractive, shapely, regular – all the things that plants rarely are in the wild . . . If plant breeding has . . . sacrificed much for the sake of convenience, those old robust tastes, those curly roots and fiddlesome leaves, are still there for those who care to seek them out . . . I wrote this book because it seemed sad to me that this enormous storehouse of free, wild food is now all but ignored.'

It would take a lot of courage for those of our generation, so used to the prepackaged presentation of so much of our food, to experiment with potentially new food sources. We tend to have implicit faith in the system that we have grown up with.

To be fair, quite a number of 'natural' foods can have unexpectedly unpleasant properties. The Sunday Telegraph Magazine carried an article by Terence McLaughlin some years ago entitled 'Eating Dangerously' which showed that it wasn't just man's added chemicals which made some foods unsafe to eat; nature could produce her own hangovers, hallucinations or deaths too! Several sections of the article have been reproduced here and are quite revealing about the nature of some food plants:

> If you like things spicy, . . . go easy on the nutmeg. It contains a drug called myristicin, with effects similar to those of LSD – hallucinations, a feeling of exhilaration, and later on a very nasty hangover. It also lowers the blood pressure, which could be dangerous if you already have a tendency in that direction. All these effects have occurred with as little as a fifth of an ounce of the spice.
>
> Over-ripe bananas have the opposite effect: the blood pressure increases and the mind races with over-activity, due to a material called serotonin that develops in the fruit. Some serotonin is essential for

12 *The Last Straw*

normal brain activity, but too much can cause over-reaction, irritability and quite irrationally violent responses to the most innocent actions or comments.

Several foods contain cyanides – not enough to kill you unless you eat vast amounts, but quite enough to make you feel and act as if you had been at the gin. Lima beans, familiar in Britain as dried butter beans, often contain cyanides: some varieties may secrete so much that as little as a quarter of a pound of the beans is a fatal dose. Fortunately the varieties that we get in the shops are selected for freedom from poison, but many cases of illness occur every year among the peasants in Central and South America. Mild doses cause the symptoms of drunkenness, so it is perhaps significant that botanists call the beans *Phaseolus lunatus.*

One pulse, khesari dhal, (*Lathyrus sativa*), which is widely grown in India and the Middle East, is so notorious in its effects that doctors have the special name lathyrism for the symptoms. . . . Those who eat it (regularly) . . . lose all sense of time and their muscles refuse to obey them. . . . They may develop permanent paralysis. Khesari and the related pulses are what the Bible calls 'tares', and the effects of such a diet may explain the bitter condemnation in St. Matthew of 'the enemy who sowed tares among the wheat'.

Plum and peach stones, almonds and apple pips also contain cyanides, and . . . the poison can be extracted by some processes . . . Professor Arnold Bender . . . has found substantial quantities of cyanide in the rougher varieties of (the) Yugoslav (liqueur) slivovitz, . . . produced from plums.

Honey too can have hazards. When bees collect nectar from poisonous flowers, particularly members of the rhododendron family, the poison does the bees no damage; but human beings who eat the honey get intoxicated.

Lettuce . . . contains a material called *lactucarium* that was once used as a substitute for opium in sleeping draughts. Garden lettuce produces very little of the drug, but wild lettuce is quite a good source, and can be quite soporific when eaten (a piece of information apparently known to Beatrix Potter, and introduced into *The Tale of Peter Rabbit*).

Even potatoes remind us that they are members of the same botanical family as deadly nightshade by producing a drug called solanine, which causes dizziness and raises blood pressure in small doses, and can actually kill. 'As recently as 1959 four people were killed by solanine,' says Professor Bender. 'A hotel proprietor and four of his family had jacket potatoes which were sprouting. He didn't eat the skin and survived, but the others died.' The rule for preparing potatoes, then, is green for danger.

Our Food Supplies 13

(The) fungus ergot grows on rye and other cereals as 'rust', and can have terrifying hallucinatory effects if eaten – not surprising, as the material is the parent substance for LSD. People who have eaten rye bread made with ergotised grain often believe that they can fly or walk on the water, and thus injure or kill themselves.

The author concludes: 'If there is a moral to all this, I think it must be that you really cannot trust Nature in matters of food. Apart from all the well-known hazards like deadly nightshade, henbane, monkshood, laburnum, hemlock, thorn apple, foxglove, meadow saffron, yew, and so on, there are countless other traps for the unwary diner, and many of these have direct effects on the brain and nervous system.'

Reading the whole of this well-researched article may make us wonder how any humans ever survived in far-off days to tell their families that a particular plant was safe (and good) to eat! Today we are fortunate in having not only centuries-worth of knowledge to draw upon, but also the results of countless tests carried out by plant-breeders, Research Institutes and so on, which together go to convince us that, in general terms, what we have grown to accept as food is in fact safe to eat.

What is 'fresh'?

There are various practices in agriculture which could perhaps alter in some way the nature of the food being offered to us. The foremost of these surely must be the quantity of chemicals which are used in food production, ranging from the pesticides, herbicides and fungicides through to hormone treatments, preservatives and sterilisers, flour treatments and so on. We talk glibly about 'fresh' food but how fresh is most of it today?

To satisfy the year-round demands for seasonal foodstuffs such as fruit and vegetables, supplies have to be resourced and flown in from all over the world and this becomes apparent from looking at labels in the supermarket. Although the film-wrapped packs of fruits and vegetables look clinically clean and inviting, how can a prospective purchaser know how much time has passed since they were first harvested?

Irradiation

The fresh appearance of some foods is certainly due largely to

14 *The Last Straw*

refrigerated storage and an efficient transportation network, but many people are concerned by the recent government decision to permit the use of irradiation to extend the shelf life of 'fresh' foods by killing off harmful bacteria and perhaps delaying ripening processes; this is a contentious subject indeed, and one which may sometimes be treated more emotionally than it should be, but certainly one of the side-effects of irradiation is to induce specific chemical changes in the composition of the food which could in themselves be potentially harmful to humans; Indian research some years ago showed that changes in the chromosomes occurred when rats were fed irradiated wheat. Most major U.K. supermarket chains have decided (at the time of writing) not to stock foods that have been irradiated, and at least three U.S. States have banned them, with a number more likely to follow suit. But what about ingredients in processed foods, such as herbs and spices? How are we to know about them unless the industry is completely honest with all aspects of food labelling?

Many food experts are concerned that irradiation is a completely unnecessary process; it has been called 'a technology looking for a use', and suggestions have been made that it is the interests of the nuclear industry that are at stake rather than those of the consumer or even the food industry itself. Of course if the foods in question were truly fresh and free of contamination then irradiation would be quite unnecessary.

At present there are no routine tests available to establish whether a food has been irradiated; there are several under development, but so far they are expensive and time-consuming. Contrary to some uninformed opinion, the food itself is of course *not* radioactive!

Growing your own

A keen gardener or producer will recognise that commercially grown produce can seldom compare either in taste or nutritional value with that which has been freshly picked from a garden or allotment. In former days people used to have to make do with what was available locally, and we have learned from the two excellent BBC television series *The Victorian Kitchen Garden* and *The Victorian Kitchen* what a little ingenuity could achieve, even if it was only the privileged few in days gone by that were able to

Our Food Supplies 15

enjoy the benefits of employing full-time gardeners. Now society demands an ever-wider range of goods all the year round and there may be a price to pay in that we cannot expect all this imported food to be in prime condition. Anyone who has ever tasted a ripe orange plucked from a tree and compared it with one from the local greengrocer cannot fail to appreciate the difference. And indeed there are differences that can be detected chemically: fruits picked whilst unripe and then ripened off the plant apparently develop a higher proportion of sucrose to fructose than fruits allowed to ripen naturally.

Many commercial crops are grown on soils whose fertility is artificially maintained in the short term with chemical fertilisers rather than by being bolstered for the longer term with plenty of organic matter. It has been suggested that as a result many of our staple fruits and vegetables contain less in the way of vitamins and minerals than they used to; maybe there is a good reason for taking all those supplements after all!

In a society as preoccupied as ours with making money and spending more and more time on recreation, it is not surprising that many people do not have the time or inclination to grow their own produce, and some market gardeners and farmers have realised that a 'pick-your-own' facility is a good compromise, as it can provide not only fresh food but healthy recreation for the family, whilst the reduction in labour costs means lower selling prices. So there can be benefits for all with this system, but of course the produce that you take home with you, although undoubtedly fresh, may have been treated with agricultural chemicals and it is best to check whether they have been used if anyone in your family is known to be chemically sensitive.

Deep down most people will acknowledge that there is nothing to compare with the quality of homegrown produce, and so it must be significant that gardening as a leisure industry has blossomed in recent years. However today's houses have such small gardens that most of us have to be content with a limited supply of home-grown food, but all over the country there are areas of land set aside for allotments which are not being used to anything like their full potential. If these areas are not taken up, there is a danger that the local Council may release the land for building yet more houses, and then the allotments will be lost for ever. Allotment growers

16 *The Last Straw*

will often tell of the camaraderie, and sometimes the competition, but would not consider giving up the privilege for the world until the ageing and aching back becomes just too much to bear! And even then 'no-dig' gardening techniques can be resorted to.

Organic growing

Anyone who has a genuine concern for the environment as well as for growing food will seriously consider growing organically without any artificially introduced chemicals, and this can be a really satisfying challenge. A good introductory book on the subject is Successful Organic Gardening by Geoff Hamilton, well-known for his programmes on BBC TV[2], and he says in the introduction: 'My aim is to make a productive, beautiful, interesting and enjoyable garden that provides an alternative habitat for wildlife of all kinds, gives me a happy, healthy and absorbing occupation and provides me with food that tastes like nature intended and that I know is free from pollution.' Now that the Prince of Wales, who grows organically at Highgrove, has officially endorsed the organic movement, it should receive even further momentum. The Henry Doubleday Research Association, under the direction of its President, Lawrence D. Hills, and its dedicated staff must take much of the credit for reawakening the public's interest in these matters.

Added chemicals in foods

When chemicals are used in food production or treatment, what can end up in the food that we buy? For a full discussion of the more important aspects of this subject, essential reading is Stephanie Lashford's book The Residue Report[3], especially the section on 'Politics of Food Residues'. If you know that you are sensitive or 'allergic' to foods and chemicals, bear in mind that often it is not the food itself that affects sensitive individuals but some treatment that has been given to it. A few examples have been chosen below for discussing in more detail:

Oranges and other fruits

Regrettably we cannot grow oranges here in our climate, or we would all know what they should really taste like! Commercially they are normally picked green and ripened under controlled conditions so that they appear to be just at peak condition when we buy them. When an orange is past its best it tends to grow mould on the surface and turn brown inside, and this has to be inhibited as far as possible to prevent wastage. So a selection of chemicals, including diphenyl, may be sprayed onto the skin to give a waxy protective coating, and this is probably why the larger types of orange in particular, such as Jaffa, seem to keep so well. Smaller varieties like satsumas and clementines may not always be chemically treated. Lemons tend just to shrivel as they dry out, although if stored in humid conditions they will sometimes show mould growth; one supermarket chain is now selling untreated lemons. If you think that you may be sensitive to citrus fruits, it is worth bearing in mind that many allergic people have found to their surprise that, although they cannot eat oranges when at home, they can enjoy them with no ill effects when they are on holiday, in Spain for example.

Some persons appear to be sensitised to citric acid itself, which is the natural acid principle found in all fruit of the citrus family. It seems that the underlying reason may be the increasing use of commercially-produced citric acid (thousands of tons annually) for use as a food additive; it is included in so many manufactured food products that there is a danger that we are overdosing ourselves with it. Interestingly, malic acid (which occurs naturally in other soft fruits such as apples) does not seem to be having any similar effects.

Many imported apples and pears are likely to have been sprayed or dipped in solutions containing chemicals such as ethoxyquin, benlate or thiophanatemethyl, which protect them against moulds, rot etc., so they should always be peeled before being eaten, although even this precaution may not be entirely effective as these chemicals can leach through the skin and into the flesh of the fruit.

Dried fruits (sultanas, apricots etc.)
If dried fruit is juicy and bright in colour, then without a doubt it will have been treated with sulphur dioxide; this chemical acts both as a preservative and to retain the natural colour of the fruit, and is widely used in vine fruits (particularly sultanas) and other dried fruits such as apricots, pears, peaches, mixed peel, glace cherries etc. Sulphur dioxide is potentially a powerful irritant to the respiratory system, and can cause asthma and other breathing problems.

18 *The Last Straw*

As an example, one supervisor in a food factory in which I worked was overcome by the fumes when opening a container of fresh diced apple treated with sulphur dioxide, and had to receive medical attention urgently as he could hardly breathe.

You might think that buying dried fruit in a Health Food Store might be the answer, but regrettably this is not so. A few years ago, one nationally known chain of health food stores went so far as to make available to its customers a leaflet extolling the virtues of dried fruits, and encouraged them to select those which did not contain any preservative; sadly there was not a single dried fruit product in the store which lived up to that claim.

Even the fruit and nut bars promoted as healthy snacks do not reveal on their labels whether the fruit used contains sulphur dioxide; usually it does.

Potatoes

Some people find that, whilst they can eat potatoes without ill-effect throughout the summer and into the autumn, they cannot do this during the winter. If this has been your experience, you may be one of those who are affected by a commonly used practice in the U.K. for preserving main-crop storage potatoes in bulk, that of dusting them with a hormone called tecnazene, which prevents sprouting and also has a fungicidal action. The symptoms can be varied but seem commonly to include severe stomach pains. However, smaller growers do not always use tecnazene, and so you may well find a reliable source of supply locally. Interestingly, the levels of tecnazene officially permitted in potatoes were increased threefold in 1989, from 0.01 mg/kg body weight to 0.03 mg/kg body weight. The Advisory Committee on Pesticides, after considering new data submitted, concluded that an Acceptable Daily Intake could be set several times higher than that set by the WHO on a precautionary basis in 1983.

Of course potatoes are renowned for 'cleaning up' the ground and are often grown for that purpose, so it should not be surprising that many people find themselves sensitive to them in some way. Even growing your own potatoes does not guarantee that they will not upset you as most seed potatoes have themselves been chemically treated. Genuine organically grown potatoes are definitely the safest source, although the season lasts for only a few months.

Our Food Supplies 19

Beware also of 'new' potatoes, which are imported from many different sources; in order to reach the early markets and thus command the highest prices, the development of potatoes is often encouraged by heavy fertilising of the soil, and residues can of course remain in the crop after harvesting. It must also be repeated that on no account should potatoes with green patches on them be eaten. One of the hidden dangers of irradiating potatoes would be that they would not look green but might still contain the poison solanine mentioned earlier.

Surprisingly, some varieties of dried potato, potato crisps, frozen chips and croquettes are better tolerated by some individuals who are aware of their general sensitivity to potatoes; this may be because the potatoes are processed whilst still extremely fresh, but as far as I am aware no one has investigated this in detail.

Dairy Produce

Milk has been consumed in various forms for several thousand years, but mostly as sheep's or goats' milk in times gone by; historically the consumption of cows' milk is a relatively recent phenomenon. Since the 1960s we have all been encouraged to 'drink a pinta milka day'; in fact this sales 'target' was never reached, a peak figure being 5.8 pints per person per week in the late 1960s. Nevertheless the campaigns to perpetuate this particular drinking habit have persisted as consumption has gradually declined (down to 4.05 pints per person per week in 1987), and a variety of new 'added value' milk drinks have been introduced to encourage sales further.

I remember reading somewhere that about 5% of the world's population is allergic in some manner to cows' milk. The allergy specialist G. Davies claims in his book[4] that between 75% and 90% of his patients are milk-sensitive, and that American figures indicate that '58% of those of ethnic extraction and 18% of whites are allergic to milk.' Many medical professionals are beginning to question whether cows' milk is in fact as good, or as necessary, for us as we have been led to believe; certainly very little of the calcium it contains remains in a form available to the body once the milk has been pasteurised, as the enzyme necessary to promote take-up of calcium by the body is destroyed during heat-treatment. Much intolerance to milk is due to the absence in the gut of an enzyme called lactase which would normally break down the lactose sugar content of the milk; this is said to be especially prevalent amongst Asians although not confined exclusively to them. But milk is such a complex food that an individual could be sensitive to any one of many aspects of it. For example, it frequently appears to be the whey proteins (lactalbumin and lactoglobulin) that cannot be digested; the casein protein and the fat are tolerated relatively better.

There are probably several reasons why many people can tolerate goats' or sheep's milk so much more successfully, but an intriguing theory is that, because the size of these animals compared with cows is so much closer to that of humans, their milk will be better digested by us. There may well be some truth in this and it could be related to the enzyme systems of the animals; certainly enzymes from the cow can produce very potent effects in humans as the following example will show.

It has been observed in a number of allergy clinics that the vast majority of those patients who are allergic to the dairy produce of cows can eat, without any ill-effect, 'vegetarian' cheese and rennet-free cottage cheese, although they are made from cows' milk. Why should this be? I can put forward only my own theory at present. When cheese is made, the whey containing most of the lactose and the whey proteins is drained off, leaving primarily the casein and fat behind. This might in itself be then acceptable to many milk-sensitive persons, but then calf rennet is added, consisting of a preparation derived from the contents of calves' stomachs; because of its powerful effects the cheese produced is now no longer suitable for such sensitive people. To make a hard 'vegetarian' cheese such as cheddar, the curd is treated, not with the traditional calf rennet but with a vegetable coagulating agent derived from a form of harmless mould (usually *Mucor miehei*), with the result that the final cheese looks, smells and tastes just the same but is far better tolerated. Some dairy-sensitive persons also find that they can eat certain cheeses from abroad without ill-effect, such as Gouda, Edam or Emmental; why this is so is not clear, but it must presumably have something to do with milk quality. Bacteriological contamination by *Listeria monocytogenes, Coliforms* etc. is unlikely to be a problem with these hard cheeses.

Sometimes it is found that canned evaporated milk can be tolerated but not fresh milk: this may be because the natural enzymes in

Our Food Supplies 21

the milk (complex biologically active proteins which can cause immune system reactions) are denatured by the heat-treatment process and hence rendered ineffective.

So the reasons for milk sensitivity are not as simple as might first appear, and the whole issue is complicated even further by the way in which our dairy industry is now organised for efficiency and profit. To be fair the Milk Marketing Board has effectively fulfilled its primary function, that of guaranteeing a market for milk instead of farmers having to pour a lot of it away as they did prior to the 1930s; surplusses in recent years have been largely due to European Community policies not always in harmony with those of the UK, and with the quotas currently imposed there is now a milk shortage both within the UK and the rest of Europe.

The Board's routine testing procedures are both thorough and frequent, but of course it is impossible to test everything; there will always be the occasional farm where, due to either carelessness or unscrupulousness, small amounts of such contaminants as cleaning chemicals, antibiotics and other drugs, excessive bacteria etc., can be present in the milk as it leaves the premises. And due to the practice of treating the cows' feeding pastures with fertiliser, it is not uncommon for milk to contain measurable quantities of nitrates.

Thirty years ago contamination of milk supplies was not so great a potential problem. Before the advent of the bulk tankers, milk used to be filled into churns which were then put out for collection by the milk lorry. On reaching the dairy, each churn was unloaded onto a conveyor belt, and as it passed along the lid was lifted and the milk inspected. The man responsible for this most important of quality screening responsibilities was known as the 'sniffer', and he was usually an elderly employee who had worked at the creamery for many years and hence knew from experience when milk was satisfactory and when it was not; indeed it was on his decision that milk was either accepted for processing or diverted to the laboratory for a proper examination. A quick visual examination would reveal the presence of blood, foreign matter, evidence of clotting etc., while a sniff would detect the likelihood of staleness, excessive numbers of bacteria or chemical contamination. In this way the potential public milk supply enjoyed an expert though subjective assessment before it was ever allowed into the dairy for processing.

22 *The Last Straw*

But what is the situation today? Firstly, the milk is put into bulk tanks on the farm; it is then transferred to a bulk tanker where it is mixed with milk from other farms. On arrival at the dairy it is then added to the existing bulk supply ready for processing. And if any milk is surplus to the day's requirements, it may be held overnight and mixed with the following day's intake. Despite the undisputed improvements in technical know-how which make for rapid and accurate laboratory testing, these tests cannot reflect the quality of individual batches of milk as they used to. So any error, misjudgment or malpractice on the part of a farmer or farm employee has the potential for contaminating far greater amounts of milk than ever before, possibly with profound implications for us all. This is the price of what we call progress, and who is to say whether there is any connection between the increasingly large number of cases of antibiotic drug sensitivity in humans and the possibility that we have all been sensitised by ingesting in our daily pinta a minute but finite amount of antibiotic residue?

Wheat Flour
It is generally agreed by nutritionists that wholemeal flour, and preferably stoneground, is better for your health than white flour, partly because of the fibre content. However, there is a somewhat cynical view that the 'F-Plan' diet which has proved so popular with doctors and public alike was initially dreamed up by marketing agencies who were keen to promote the sale of bran at inflated prices; formerly, the bran removed from the increasingly-popular white flour would likely have been fed to animals as a by-product, hence generating little if any profit, but here was a chance to increase the profitability of the flour-milling industry, by ensuring that bran was consumed by humans and not animals. We should perhaps be grateful that there is not an alphabetical successor to the F-Plan diet as it might have entailed us consuming our furniture!

A disadvantage of wheat bran is that the particles are very rough and jagged, as can be seen if they are examined under a microscope; it should not therefore be surprising that they can irritate the digestive system. Some people with severe stomach cramps have traced down the cause to bran. Also unless the bran comes from organically grown wheat, there is another hazard in that

Our Food Supplies

when the wheat is sprayed, most of the chemical residues end up on the outside of the wheat grain, which is then promoted as healthy dietary fibre. The method of milling used is also significant; stone-grinding produces a flour that is more suitable for the digestion than does roller-grinding.

So what about white flour? This is not, as one might expect from recent publicity, purely a junk food; far from it, although it does, of course, lack much of the fibre of the original wheat. But, because of its refined nature, it does tend to be metabolised by the body far more quickly than does wholemeal flour, and for some diets (e.g. for arthritis, diverticulitis and candidiasis) it would not therefore be recommended. There is another aspect of white flour, however, which is implicated in causing a variety of health problems.

Many allergic people who go abroad on holiday, to France for example, find that they feel a lot better and can eat almost anything, including the local bread; yet when they return home their symptoms start up afresh. What is so different about French food, and especially the bread? We all appreciate that the French, and indeed most Europeans, consider the quality of their food supply as one of the most important things in life. As Geoffrey Cannon said in his book *The Politics of Food*[5]:

> The British value food less than people on the Continent, because we have been trained to think that food is good just because it is cheap. This nonsensical attitude has been reinforced by industry: food is now the only major commodity usually advertised in terms of its cheapness. As a nation we have learned to value high quality clothes, cars, carpets and computers, but still shop around for 'penny-off' food.

The French, then, do not add anything to their white flour, in common with most of their neighbours. In the U.K. millers are obliged by law to make certain additions, a legacy of wartime Britain when it was considered that certain vital nutrients might be lacking in the nationally restricted diet; in fact those who survived the war were probably fitter than the majority of us today. These additives comprise calcium carbonate (chalk), iron (often added as iron powder, only about 1% of which can be used by the body anyway!), Thiamine (Vitamin B1) and Niacin (or Nicotinamide)[6].

In addition to this legal requirement, a large proportion of white flour supplied in the U.K has had 'improvers' added to increase the

24

The Last Straw

performance of the flour in breadmaking; this practice stems, at least in part, from the cheaper cost of European grain compared to the 'hard' Canadian wheat which was traditionally used for making the British-style white loaf. Much research has been carried out in recent years to find ways of using higher percentages of the 'softer' European wheat in our bread. For example, the use of potassium bromate results in a more consistent crumb texture in both white and brown breads, although it has not been used in wholemeal breads. After its oxygen content has been released by the heat of the oven, potassium bromide remains (chemically identical to the well-known sedative). But now the MAFF has ordered that it be struck off the list of permitted improvers as laboratory tests have linked its residues in the final product with cancer (in rats, at least). In practice the larger bakeries are now favouring the use of Vitamin C (ascorbic acid), which is hopefully safe enough.

Bleaching of flour is carried out either with chlorine dioxide, benzoyl peroxide, or a combination of the two; these chemicals are capable of modifying the structure of the protein of the flour as well as whitening it. Chlorine dioxide is a toxic gas in its own right, and benzoyl peroxide has a peculiar claim to fame: it is the same chemical that is used for 'curing' fibreglass, i.e. it is the main component of the thick liquid that you squeeze from a tube and mix with the powder to harden it! Both are hazardous because of their high oxygen content, which, if released by heat, could cause a fire.

Benzoyl peroxide has been implicated in a number of apparent 'allergies' to flour and wheat, and can cause symptoms of arthritis, rhinitis and asthma, amongst others. When I was responsible for a private food company in the early eighties, I championed the return to unbleached flour for this reason for several years, but a small voice is seldom heard in a crowd and it took media pressure to encourage the large plant bakeries to begin using unbleached flour in 1986. The ingredients list on most supermarket loaves now indicates that unbleached flour is used. Although a number of private bakeries used unbleached flour for a while, most did not continue to do so as to them there did not appear to be any advantage, and have now reverted to using bleached flour. So if you are concerned (as you should be), check with your baker what he uses and if his bread is made with bleached flour try to persuade him to revert to unbleached flour for the sake of the health of all his customers.

Our Food Supplies

Health food stores

Are health food stores really that different from supermarkets? Shops, like any other business, are concerned primarily with making a profit, and the profitability of many health food stores has suffered in recent years since the supermarket chains introduced health food sections (which begs the question as to the quality of the rest of their produce). Because of superior buying power the supermarkets were able to undercut the retail prices in the health food stores in many cases; many of these stores now make more of their profit from the sales of vitamin and mineral supplements than they do from the sale of food, and this is why there is currently such an outcry about the proposed new EEC regulations for 1992; certain European countries consider vitamins and minerals as medicines and hence to be sold only through pharmacies, whereas in the UK they have always been considered as foods and have therefore been more widely available. It has been reported in the trade press that up to eighty per cent of health food stores might be forced out of business if the UK does not get its own way in this matter.

Of course there are many such shops owned and staffed by individuals who care a great deal about their customers' well-being, and who will do anything they can to help; many who do not get the sympathy and hearing ear that they feel they have the right to expect from their G.P. tend to gravitate towards the local health food store. Many minor health problems can often be cleared up in this way, and there are instances in which, if a shop is fortunate enough to have sufficiently qualified and caring staff, the local people with health problems will tend to go there first before considering their G.P. Busy doctors have reason to be grateful to such places.

But just because there are such shops, this does not necessarily mean that the foods they stock, and which you as a customer will select, are automatically free of certain ingredients or additives. In 1983 the New York City Department of Consumer Affairs (the equivalent of our Trading Standards Department) attracted wide publicity by reporting that foods sold in so-called health food stores were identical to those in ordinary supermarkets, at double the price, with unchanged quality and having identical levels of

26 *The Last Straw*

pesticide residues. Could it be that the U.S.A. is the only country where such practices occur? Surely that is extremely doubtful.

The moral surely is that, wherever you choose to buy your food, it will benefit you to be highly selective, as not all food may be as good for you as you have been officially led to believe. With knowledge about food comes the responsibility to shop wisely for the sake of your health.

REFERENCES
1. Mabey, R., *Food for Free*, Fontana/Collins, 1975.
2. Hamilton, G., *Successful Organic Gardening*, Doring Kindersley, 1987
3. Lashford, S., *The Residue Report*, Thorsons, 1988, pp. 166–173.
4. Davies, G.H., *Overcoming Food Allergies*, Ashgrove Press, 1985, p. 26.
5. Cannon, G., *The Politics of Food*, p. 388.
6. *The Bread & Flour Regulations 1984*, S.I. 1304, Schedule 1.

Chapter 3
A Balanced View of Food Additives

What an emotive issue the subject of food additives has turned out to be! Hardly a day goes by without it being aired either in the press or on the television. Indeed, so much has been said, and so many opinions from learned sources offered that the average consumer can well be excused for feeling extremely bewildered by it all. Fact has even been transmuted into fantasy. Otherwise why would people say, as they often do: 'I won't eat anything with an E number in it'? Obviously they do not understand that the list of food additives allocated E numbers is supposed to indicate additives that are safe to consume in reasonable daily amounts and not those substances that are potentially lethal.

The food industry's view

Even the food industry itself has recognised the existence of the 'health lobby', and a recent article in the trade press[1] discussed the public's reaction to E numbers, which, it reported, 'were aimed at simplifying label declarations and to reassure the public as to the ingredient's safety. In fact it appears to have had the reverse effect. . . . ' While the existing food labelling regulations allow for manufacturers to declare food ingredients and additives by either their name, their E number (if allocated) or both, many manufacturers are now consciously choosing to declare all ingredients by name only, omitting any mention of E numbers at all; this seems to be the result of a recognition by the marketing executives concerned with maximising sales that 'the public do not want E numbers in their food'. Surely we should aim to have a more balanced view of matters, and when the whole subject of health and additives is looked at as dispassionately as possible, the truth emerges that, whilst the vast majority of permitted food additives are quite

28 *The Last Straw*

harmless when ingested in the usual small amounts, there are a few categories, particularly flour treatments, artificial colourings and preservatives (whether based on benzoates, sulphur dioxide or nitrites and nitrates) which are proving to be more harmful to a far greater number of people than has ever been admitted by any official source. This is evident from the findings of many well-established allergy clinics, and indeed it would seem that a large number of allergies to food are in fact more likely to be sensitivities to chemical additives, either intentional or unintentional.

Much criticism has been levelled at the food industry in recent times, but to be fair it fulfils admirably, in general terms, its weighty responsibility to ensure that we are fed safely and well at reasonable cost. There can be no doubt that if it was not for the many technical advances made in food processing during the past fifty years, we would not have anything like the choice of fresh or manufactured foods available that we have today, with the convenience of prolonged shelf life and reasonable retail price levels. How unfortunate then that the credibility of the industry seems to have been undermined somewhat in recent years, partly due to its misunderstanding of the nature and potential severity of the additives problem.

In the foreword to the booklet The Chemistry on your Table, published by the Chemical Industries Association Ltd., the comment is made that 'words like 'additive', 'processed', 'chemical', 'emulsifier', 'antioxidant', 'monosodium glutamate' and the various E numbers have become the best appetite suppressants since cod liver oil.' This surely must be a gross overstatement: many people are either still blissfully unaware of the potential problems or they are not prepared to consider changing the eating habits which they have developed over a lifetime; there are similarities here with the smokers who will not even try to break the habit, even though in this case they cannot fail to be aware of its dangers, as they are stated in large print on every packet purchased. Maybe, just as regular smokers are addicted to nicotine, so we have become addicted in some way to some of the artificial chemical substances added to our food.

As mentioned earlier, it is currently a good marketing strategy to declare the names of ingredients on a food label in such a way that it appears that the product contains no E numbers, and definitely no

A Balanced View of Food Additives

artificial colouring or preservatives; however, common sense tells us that this does not automatically guarantee that the food is of high nutritional quality or that it actually does us any good. Also we might question the motive behind declaring, for example, that a powdered gravy mix contains no artificial preservatives when (a) from the nature of the product none should be necessary anyway, and (b) it can be seen from the label that it does contain several artificial colours.

A few years ago an editorial comment in one of the food trade journals said[2]:

> As the food industry faces increasing criticism on matters relating to diet and health, the time has come to present the other side of the argument. Misconceptions about food and its ingredients have been fuelled by one-sided and often biased reports by the media and popular press and the targets for their attacks have ranged from red meat and dairy products to fat, salt, sugar and additives. . . . In the past two years, the reputation of the food industry has been damaged to such an extent by the campaigns of food extremists that *logical and balanced explanations will not be enough to rectify the current situation* [my italics]. Concrete plans of action must be decided upon and implemented immediately, particularly as some processors have already announced plans to remove artificial additives from their products, which can only add to the current confusion and frustrate the efforts of . . . the rest of the food industry.

The majority of the public, who are consumers but not manufacturers (although every manufacturer is also a consumer) might well be forgiven for being somewhat alarmed by reading statements such as these: if 'logical and balanced explanations' are not enough, what will the food industry do next to make its point?

The attitudes of food companies to artificial colourings in particular seem to reflect a reluctance to admit that there are any real problems resulting from their use. A spokesman for a large food colour manufacturer in the U.K. was recently quoted as follows[3]:

> Throughout their long history of use synthetic food colours have been subjected to extensive toxicological testing, not only in the U.K. but also in Europe, USA and Japan. [We] carried out tartrazine feeding studies in man as long ago as 1911. No detrimental effects were noted as a result of consuming up to 10,000 times the normal daily intake.

30   *The Last Straw*

What the writer has not taken into consideration is that during the past 75 years or so the overall toxic load on our bodies has increased by such dramatic amounts that we could not necessarily expect those results to hold true today. And indeed he goes on to say:

> Recent food trials have suggested that some synthetic food colours may cause allergic reactions. This is a very complex subject, but it is important to place the matter in its true perspective. Some possibility of allergic reactions to tartrazine, which is a salicylate, has been indicated, although *the level of the response is very low* [my italics]. In addition there is a suggestion that some food additives, including synthetic colours, may be involved with hyperactivity in children. The various trials have given different results. More controlled trials are required to assess the scale of the problem, but *the evidence so far indicates that only a very small percentage of the population is likely to be affected.* [my italics]

The medical view

This view is sharply in contrast with the practical evidence now accumulating at allergy clinics, which indicates that a very high percentage of patients known to have food allergies are sensitive to tartrazine (and often other artificial colours too). Although it might then be argued that the total number of persons attending allergy clinics is a minute and certainly atypical portion of the population as a whole, we should recall the point made by Dr Richard Mackarness some years ago in his famous book *Not All in the Mind*[4] that '30% of people attending G.P.'s have symptoms traceable exclusively to food and chemical allergy; a (further) 30% have symptoms partially traceable to this cause.' A more recent book[5] suggests that other experts now believe that this figure is indeed correct. So on that basis, there could be literally millions of people in this country alone who are now suffering from the effects of what has been done to our food supply, either directly or indirectly. What about the countless man-hours lost in industry and commerce, the huge sums of money paid out in sickness benefit and the chronic misery caused to countless individuals? Why do the Department of Health, and indeed so many individuals in the mainstream of the medical profession, still seem to show such little interest in the potential there is both for improving the quality of life and saving money and resources too? Happily there are many

A Balanced View of Food Additives

signs that the food industry itself has responded and is beginning to do the right thing by the consumer, but maybe more out of commercial considerations than altruism.

Despite the scathing comments about allergy still made even in some medical circles, there is evidence from properly constituted scientific studies about the effects that can result from the ingestion of colours and other additives. In 1959, the first reports of urticarial reactions to tartrazine were published and since then many patients who cannot take aspirin have been found to be sensitive to tartrazine as well (there are similarities in chemical structure between the two). Interestingly, a further paper in 1978[6] dealing with urticaria found that the naturally derived colour annatto was tolerated even worse by the subjects than the artificial colours (more than twice as many were sensitive to annatto than to tartrazine). Other studies on urticaria have shown up positive results when patients are challenged with the antioxidants BHA and BHT, the benzoate preservatives, yeast and aspirin. In the late 1950s an outbreak of what was termed 'Dutch Margarine Disease', which caused coloured eruptions of the skin, was attributed to the use of a novel emulsifier.

Aspirin has been known since 1919 to cause serious reactions with some asthma patients, so it is not surprising that tartrazine has a similar effect in some cases. A paper published in 1976[7], in which 140 asthmatic patients were checked for any sensitivity to aspirin and tartrazine, showed that most who reacted to one also reacted to the other, and that about a third of the patients were already aware that they were sensitive to colours in foods. Some asthmatics have also been found to react to sulphur dioxide. A case history concerning the possible effect of tartrazine on the heart follows shortly.

However, it remains difficult to obtain accurate figures for the frequency of sensitivity for any of these additives, because as Adrian Hill has said[8]: 'most of the evidence comes from isolated case reports or studies of highly selected populations from which extrapolation to the general population is difficult.' He makes the tongue-in-cheek observation at the end of his article that 'the only way to ensure absolute food safety is to eliminate food.'

But one only has to meet persons afflicted in this way to recognise how real the suffering can be. Many have been housebound or

32 *The Last Straw*

not fit enough to hold down a job before they took themselves in hand and found a sympathetic medical practitioner. Many parents suffer sleepless nights for years on end because the behaviour of their children apparently cannot be controlled, even during the time they should be asleep. Thinking and caring parents are beginning to recognise that there are ways in which their children can be helped, and a great debt of gratitude is owed to the many local self-help groups around the country which are run entirely voluntarily, and also such national organisations as the Hyperactive Children's Support Group, Action Against Allergy and The National Association for Research into Allergy, which have pioneered the way in making the whole subject of allergy one to be reckoned with seriously at all levels.

Parents who take their children for medical treatment connected with suspected food allergy generally have a fairly good idea, from their own experiences, of the foods, additives or chemicals that are most likely to be upsetting their children. Accurate tests, when they are available, frequently confirm those suspicions, so GPs should surely be encouraged to take note of the views and feelings of the parents, as after all they are the ones who are living with the patient twenty-four hours a day. It is to be regretted that many GPs, however well-meaning, display obvious feelings of resentment or disbelief when a patient shows some knowledge and understanding of his problem; too many doctors in general practice seem to prefer patients who understand nothing of their symptoms or of the cause of their illness, and who will be open to any suggestion without questioning it. Of course there are many patients who expect their doctor to cure any ailment with a swift stroke of the pen on a prescription form, and after many years of this attitude of ignorance prevailing, perhaps we have finally got the sort of doctors we deserve.

Tartrazine – a case history

A case history would illustrate the above point well, that of my own son, James. When about eighteen months old, James had a bad bout of tonsillitis, for which he was prescribed a course of a penicillin derivative. This was not successful in treating the condition and his fever continued unabated for several days and nights, putting great strain on his system and ultimately causing a

A Balanced View of Food Additives

heart murmur, which needed to be monitored for at least five years thereafter. Some years later, James was now a teenager and perhaps fortunate to live in a family where we had all learned to understand something about food sensitivities, and as a result he was usually very careful when selecting foods, especially if on his own. On one occasion, however, he was out with friends and, showing normal social considerations, accepted a can of soft drink from one of them. Later that evening when at home he developed severe pains in his chest, for which the doctor was called, and he diagnosed that the heart murmur had recurred. The symptoms subsided after a day or so, but when we reflected over what might have been the cause, we realised that the particular drink that James had chosen contained tartrazine, something he had always taken care to avoid. The doctor had recommended that he see a specialist just to confirm that there were no lasting effects of the murmur, so on presenting themselves at the hospital James and his mother mentioned to the specialist that they were fairly certain that the cause of the attack was the tartrazine in the drink, although they would appreciate James' heart being checked to make sure that everything was now normal. This examination was duly done, but the specialist made it quite clear that he did not believe tartrazine to have anything to do with it. However he suggested that, if our hypothesis was to be put to the test, James should come into hospital for two days, on the first of which he would be given a diet entirely free of tartrazine, while on the second day his food would contain controlled amounts of the colour: it would then become apparent if this was indeed the cause. The realisation that the hospital was prepared to subject James to a course of treatment of this sort, which might well result in yet more suffering, was enough to make his mother very determined that, come what may, her son was not going to be treated as a human guinea pig. She and James left the hospital forthwith, and on a diet free of tartrazine the symptoms have not recurred over a number of years.

Now, while this is no proof in itself that tartrazine was the cause, the circumstantial evidence certainly suggests it and is strong enough for our family to support the avoidance of that particular additive. Why was this reaction forthcoming from the specialist concerned? Was he not prepared to recognise that those involved knew something of the problem from their experience? In retrospect, it

34   *The Last Straw*

also becomes apparent that the penicillin preparation administered to James when a toddler almost certainly contained tartrazine, and that maybe his body, under great stress at the time, responded to tartrazine the way it did because it was just 'the last straw'.

However the current view of many manufacturers of both foods and food colours seems to be that the storm about artificial colourings is just about over, and that there is plenty of room for both natural and artificial colours and other additives, as long as the customer is given some choice in the matter. From the point of view of conformity it makes sense for many food manufacturers, especially those who do a lot of exporting, to use colours and other additives which have more or less world-wide acceptance so that a standard product can be made without the need to change recipes for different countries. This is probably the reasoning behind the fact that packets of a children's favourite chocolate-based sweet now contain a blue-coloured variety for the first time. This colour, Brilliant Blue FCF, has not been permitted in food in the U.K. until relatively recently, so now that the opportunity has arisen to use it here, it has been grasped immediately because it will be no longer necessary to produce a special product just for the U.K.; we are now getting the same as all the rest of the EEC and, probably, the rest of the world.

I would like to digress just for a moment to record that when I was responsible for my own food company, the most successful product that we ever introduced (with the cooperation of a very sympathetic and willing manufacturer) was an alternative to the confectionery mentioned above, but produced without any milk or wheat, and using only colouring matter that could be correctly labelled 'natural'. Over the several years that this product has been available, I have never heard a report of any consumer having sensitivity problems with it, and every customer of the company is on a special diet for one reason or another. One allergy clinic has even used the product to demonstrate how safe the product is for genuinely hyperactive children!

For anyone intimately concerned, as I am, with the food sensitivity problem, it is gratifying to note that the use of tartrazine, the colour that has had the worst press for whatever reason, is still on the decrease, both in foods and in medicines; this surely must be to some extent a reflection of public concern getting through to the

A Balanced View of Food Additives

manufacturers. But there is really no point in anyone getting worked up overmuch about the subject of artificial food additives; these substances are so widely used throughout the world, quite legally (and many of them for good reason), that it would be completely impracticable to consider banning them *in toto*.

Are natural foods and ingredients any safer?

Most of the controversy about additives stems from the realisation that they are 'artificial' and 'synthetic' substances manufactured in chemical factories; but perhaps it is only fair to ask: are 'natural' foods and ingredients any safer? In general, people like to believe that something 'natural' is preferable to something 'synthetic' or 'refined', and while this is a perfectly understandable attitude to adopt, is it necessarily a valid one? Have you never found a stone in your breakfast muesli, or a caterpillar in your vegetables? Minimally processed foods are bound to suffer with problems of this sort. I well remember seeing a film some years ago produced by Rentokil, which showed the gathering and processing of sugar cane. After the cane was cut, the stems were scooped up mechanically onto a vehicle and transported to the factory; there they were offloaded onto a conveyor belt and hence transferred into the production area where the cane juice was squeezed out. It did not take much imagination (and the commentator played on our natural fears) to realise that among the debris included with the stems may have been stones, earth, diseased plant debris, insects and small animals along with their droppings. Although this is necessarily an oversimplification and perhaps exaggerates the hazards, doesn't it make you consider whether you might prefer pure refined white sugar to molasses?

Apart from the question of contamination by foreign matter, many natural products can be toxic to some degree, as was discussed in Chapter 2. If the same tests that are now applied to food additives had been applied in the past to such staple foods as sugar and potatoes, we would probably be permitted to eat them only in carefully regulated doses! And what about the naturally-derived colours that are being used increasingly in our food as more acceptable alternatives to the artificial colours? It has been suggested recently[6] that 'the present trend being in the direction of increasing consumption of natural colour usage could lead us to a situation where these

36 *The Last Straw*

higher levels of ingestion may bring us into an area of uncertainty regarding their safety in use.' In simple terms, what the writer is trying to say is that we don't really know enough about the safety of these natural colours when consumed in ever-increasing amounts. The case of the naturally derived yellow pigment annatto, used in much of our margarine and cheese supply, has already been mentioned, and now at the time of writing there is talk of banning both annatto and crocin (another yellow pigment derived from gardenias or saffron); I understand that this is largely because of insufficient evidence that they are safe.

So do consumers really need, or want, any colours added to their food? Some years ago, a well-known and respected food retailer decided to market several products without added colours in the belief that its customers wanted to see only the genuine colour contained in the food in question. However, without added colour the canned peas were greyish, the canned strawberries became straw-coloured, and the jams turned brown on storage. Customers were not impressed, sales levels fell dramatically and then took two years to recover. It seems as if consumers do not want the natural colour, they want what they *believe* should be the natural colour; there is quite a difference.

The threat of food poisoning

However, there is a darker aspect to the controversy about food additives; some workers in the field of environmental health are understandably concerned that, with the emphasis on decreasing the amounts of preservatives in our food, a vast outbreak of food poisoning is inevitable in due course. They may well be right; a recent statement by the Ministry of Agriculture, Fisheries and Food has expressed concern at the increasing levels of food poisoning and food spoilage detected throughout the U.K. (the information being culled from reports submitted by local Environmental Health Officers), and possible links with the removal of preservatives are being examined. While there were just 9,000 food poisoning cases reported in the UK in 1970, this figure had risen to 25,000 by 1986, and these were just the cases *reported*. The occurrence of *Salmonella enteritidis* in eggs has recently become a highly contentious issue, and even the organism *Listeria monocytogenes*, which has probably always been present in some chilled foods,

A Balanced View of Food Additives

made the headlines when it was widely reported that it was quite capable of surviving at refrigerator temperatures and possibly contaminating products such as pâtés and soft cheeses. Food poisoning outbreaks, either from well-known organisms which have had an opportunity to thrive only due to poor 'housekeeping', or from others about which we know very little, constitute a new potential health hazard that the food manufacturers and supermarket chains are taking very seriously.

Dr V. Wheelock recently expressed the views of many of those concerned professionally with the public food supply when he said[9] that 'food-borne disease is a time bomb', and blamed sensationalism on the part of the media for diverting attention away from bacteriological hazards and focusing them instead on the 'food additives' issue. In support of this view he quotes from a MAFF survey which reported that food-borne disease was not considered as being of concern to most respondents whereas over 50% of them agreed with the statement that artificial additives are harmful. He also blamed those in the food industry who 'have promoted individual products with claims such as 'no preservatives' and 'no artificial additives' . . . The presence of these claims can only serve to reinforce any incipient fears that consumers may have about the safety of additives.' He quite rightly supports more and not less money being made available for research in this field, and recommends a massive public education campaign starting in the schools.

While it is now widely acknowledged that sensitivities to food additives are not as unusual as used to be thought, it is surely unbalanced to ignore the even greater dangers of widespread food poisoning, which according to an assessment made some years ago was about 100,000 times more common!

It would be very unbalanced if we were to take either of the extreme views, as some have done, that (a) food additives are responsible for all our ailments, or (b) that they are not responsible for any of them. The extra stress on the body generated by consuming food that the body considers in any way toxic is very real and significant, yet it is only one contributory factor to be taken into consideration along with many others that are described in this book. At the same time, we are bound to acknowledge that there is no way in which individual members of the public can 'beat

The Last Straw

the system' and effect a ban on something that they consider harmful. However, through properly constituted channels that are available to them it is possible to make significant, though slow, progress provided that the evidence needed for scientific proof is indeed available: that is often the stumbling block, as scientific bodies will reject, quite rightly, evidence which does not stand up to close examination.

If we are aware that certain additives, or foods, affect the health of our family, then let us make a conscious selection of acceptable alternatives, which are now becoming more widely available both through health food stores and supermarkets (see Chapter 2). Only we should remember that healthy eating is not cheap eating: successive governmental policies promoting supplies of cheap food have led the majority of the electorate to expect that by right their food should be both good and inexpensive, obviously a contradiction in terms. Have you noticed that in times of difficulty when spending money is tight, the first thing that families look to for a saving is their food bill (they may be able to save several pounds a week by buying cheaper alternatives)? At the same time spending on cigarettes, alcohol and cosmetics seldom suffers, as the public appear to need these things as 'crutches' in times of real or imagined hardship.

In recent years the amount spent on food in the U.K., expressed as a proportion of total consumers' expenditure, has actually fallen from 18.3% in 1976 to 13.0% in 1988. This is particularly noticeable since about 1980, when an increase in disposable incomes began, but it is thought that changes in dietary practice are also involved; our daily intake of calories has certainly declined in recent years. However, absence of additives and a low calorific content are not necessarily reliable yardsticks of food quality, as becomes apparent immediately one pays a visit to a country such as France or Italy; there they enjoy their food and are prepared to pay for it. Are we that afraid of becoming part of the European Community? Its influence on food and diet could well be beneficial for the health of all of us in this country.

REFERENCES

1. *Food*, Vol. 10, No. 7, p. 50.
2. *Food* Processing, April 1986, p. 4.
3. *Food*, Vol. 8, No. 7, p. 25.
4. *Not All in the Mind*, Mackarness, Dr. R., Pan Books (1976), p. 37.

A Balanced View of Food Additives 39

5. Faelton, S., *The Allergy Self-Help Book*, Pan Books (1987), p. 5.
6. Mikkelson, M. et al., 'Hypersensitivity reactions to food colours with special reference to the natural colour annatto extract', *Arch. Toxicol. Suppl.* 1:141 (1978).
7. Stenius, B.S.M. & Semola, M.: 'Hypersensitivity to acetylsalicylic acid and tartrazine in patients with asthma', *Clin. Allergy* 6:119 (1976).
8. Hill, A.: 'Food Additives, Allergy & Cancer', *Journal of the I.F.S.T.*, March 1982.
9. Wheelock, Dr. V., 'The Food Time Bomb', *Food*, February 1989, pp. 33, 35, 37.

Chapter 4
Our Water Supplies

Out of all the commodities that we tend to take for granted in this life, maybe water is near the top of the list! After all, over 70% of the planet's surface is covered by it, so surely we could never run out? Of course there is in fact a finite amount of water in existence, which due to the natural water cycle is evaporated from the oceans, carried along as clouds and deposited over the land, from whence it runs into the rivers, and thus arrives back at the ocean again. It is what it does on its way round the cycle that is so important, making it possible for crops to grow and for us to indulge in our insatiable appetite for wasting it, especially in industry. To make one motor car needs the recycling of over 50,000 gallons of water, while another three gallons are needed to process every gallon of petrol put in its tank. In the U.K. the average household uses about 100 gallons daily, whereas in the U.S.A. the figure is 75 (US) gallons *per person*.

Will we always have enough?

Awake! magazine[1] suggests a way of visualising the tremendous volume of water around us; it says: 'Imagine, for example, a pit one mile long, one mile wide, and one mile deep – one cubic mile. To fill this cube with water would require over a million million (1,000,000,000,000) gallons (US). Now multiply this volume by 326 million such cubic miles, and you approximate the amount of water on the earth.' But these figures are really still too large for us to appreciate fully!

Will there always be enough water to go round and will it always be in the right place at the right time? Or will there be surfeits in one region and droughts in another as we have experienced in recent years? A conference of meteorologists in Canada in 1988

Our Water Supplies

predicted that in the future the weather patterns look set to change, with a global increase in temperature resulting from our cutting down of the rain forests, the increase in carbon dioxide in the atmosphere due to the burning of fossil fuels, the damage to the ozone layer and other factors. From the evidence collected over the past twenty years it seems as though in future the countries nearer the equator will have less rainfall (thus making their drought problems even more severe) whilst the more temperate zones can expect more.

The unique properties of water

Despite its abundance, water is really a unique and surprising substance. A theoretical chemist, trying to predict the properties of dihydrogen oxide (H_2O) from his knowledge of other known chemical compounds of similar constitution would be likely to assume that it would turn out to be an evil-smelling gas (similar to hydrogen sulphide (H_2S), the toxic gas that smells of rotten eggs). Yet as we all know from practice, water is a colourless odourless liquid, which when unadulterated is not only refreshing to drink but is vital to life. (Actually it is not quite true that water is colourless; when in large quantities it is seen to be blue.)

Water has other unexpected properties too; it has the greatest solvent power of any known liquid, which coupled with its complete safety makes it ideal for carrying nutrients to plant life in the soil. It is also the main constituent of the blood that similarly carries life-giving nourishment to our body cells. It remains liquid over a wide range of temperatures, too; if it evaporated more quickly the rain would not stay in the ground long enough to dissolve the minerals necessary for the vegetation, and plants would lose their moisture so quickly that the deserts would expand even more quickly than they do today.

But there is yet another unusual property of water! Most substances contract when cooled, like mercury in a thermometer, and so does water down to 4°C (39°F). Then, as it is cooled further, it expands down to its freezing point of 0°C (32°F). In practice, this means that ice (being less dense) floats on the surface of unfrozen water, ensuring that lakes and ponds never freeze solid, permitting fish and other aquatic life to subsist even in very low temperatures without coming to any harm. This property of expansion at low

42 *The Last Straw*

temperatures has another purpose; as water runs into cracks in the rocks and then freezes, it expands, breaks down the rocks further, and thus starts off the process of soil formation. This unique property results from the spatial and electrical configurations of the water molecule which cause it to attach itself easily (by what is known as hydrogen bonding) to other similar molecules forming helical chains, and even today much research is still being carried out to try and understand the properties of this unique fluid still better.

Could water have any harmful properties?

Is there any way in which water itself could be harmful to the living organism? In particular Dr Cyril Smith, along with Dr J. Munro and Dr R. Choy, has been investigating an unusual sensitivity to water shown by multiallergic patients; many of these have been found to have an extreme sensitivity to electric and magnetic fields. Dr Smith reports as follows[2]. 'Drinking water is also a problem for these patients. Some can only tolerate bottled spring water, triple distilled water or water as fruit juice. In some cases the bottled spring water (in glass bottles, plastics are not tolerated) must even be buried in the garden for a few days before it is tolerated . . . Biological systems have sensors which are almost single quantum sensitive. To amplify a signal from such a sensor to the level at which it can trigger a nerve impulse requires a gain of the order of 10^9 or 10^{10}. The characteristics of such high gain amplifiers depend only upon the feedback arrangements, if the feedback path goes open circuit for any reason then the smallest signal above threshold will produce a 'panic reaction' which is exactly what seems to be happening to these multiple-allergy patients.'

I personally have met through my work several individuals who are unable to drink water as such, no matter how pure it is. This could be because the spatial configuration of the water molecule is such that it appears to be able to absorb and retain minute electromagnetic field patterns.

Water pollution

The *Awake!* magazine quoted earlier goes on to say that of all the water on the planet, only 3% is fresh water, and that more than three quarters of this 3% is locked solid in glaciers and polar ice

Our Water Supplies 43

caps, while another 14% (of the 3%) is underground water too far down to be made available. The amount that remains is just 0.027% of the total, and more and more of this is being contaminated in many lands as demand rises and water tables lower. The *U.S. News and World Report* of March 1985 stated of the water supply situation: 'America's most precious resource is in peril.' The *New York Times* reported: 'There is wide agreement, however, that the contamination of ground water is by far the most serious and difficult problem affecting the quality of drinking water and now constitutes a subterranean time bomb'. The Worldwatch Institute has reported that a third of the water in China's rivers is polluted beyond safe limits for human consumption. Seventy per cent of India's drinking water is polluted and is the cause of much of the country's illness. Misconceived religious views have to be held responsible in some cases, as the following true story will illustrate: a village well, to be used only by members of a certain caste, was visited and used by a man of a lower caste, whereupon the villagers, believing the water now to be contaminated, threw handfuls of cow dung down the well (the cow being considered sacred) in order to 'purify' the water!

Much water pollution arises from the creation and widespread use of new chemical compounds, developed initially in an effort to make our lives easier. In 1980 there were over 60,000 such compounds on the market, of which 35,000 were classified as either deadly or hazardous to health. *Awake!* comments that 'from these chemical cocktails have come equally dangerous and highly toxic wastes that are disposed of by dumping them into the earth, rivers and streams, with little thought of the consequences it would have on people or environment.' As an example the magazine then reports: 'For years farmers in California's San Joaquin Valley sprayed their grapes, fruit and tomatoes with the pesticide DBCP, only to discover in recent years that it can cause cancer and sterility in humans. Although the spraying has stopped, the poison hasn't stopped percolating through the layers of the earth and into the underground water system.' Modern chemistry has a lot to answer for: detergents, solvents, dry-cleaning fluids, petrol, septic tank cleaners, to name but a few – all these eventually find their way into the water supply. The American Environmental Protection Agency estimates that in the U.S. alone one and a quarter

44 *The Last Straw*

trillion gallons of hazardous waste leak into the underground system each year, but that country is not alone in experiencing these problems. In various parts of the industrial Midlands of the U.K. rivers have long been used as open ditches for factories to discharge their waste, until they are now devoid of life; the local water companies, rightly concerned about this horrendous state of affairs, appear to have been almost powerless to compel the offending companies to comply with the law. Disastrous mistakes can occur too, even on the water company's own property; we have all been made aware by the media of the incident in Cornwall during 1988 in which large quantities of an acid aluminium sulphate solution were discharged into the wrong tank and resulted in the poisoning of the public water supply used by thousands of residents.

There is hope however, as at last both authorities and public alike are showing a renewed and practical concern for public water supplies; the cleaning up of the Thames and other rivers over the years is a case in point. However we cannot expect to undo in a short time all the damage that has been done over a hundred years and more.

Drinking water quality

The quality of drinking water is very much on people's minds. In November 1986, *Which?* Magazine published the results of its survey into drinking water, and was able to give an indication of the parts of the country most at risk from certain pollutants. Some idea of the degree of dissatisfaction with what comes from our taps is reflected in the amount of money that is spent in the U.K. on bottled waters – £115 million in 1987, far more than we spend on the fashionable vitamin and mineral supplements which are claimed to sustain our health! The privatized water companies have a lot of hard work to do to convince the public that their product is safe, especially in the face of the escalating charges that may be levied for the service. Dr C.W. Wilson reported in 1982[3] that as many as 40% of patients sensitive to foods are also sensitive to tap water; the true figure may well be much higher. What can the water companies do about this, if anything? And exactly what impurities are there in water which could be responsible for this large-scale sensitivity?

Our Water Supplies

Impurities in our water supply

Hardness

This is largely due to the presence of calcium and magnesium salts, primarily the bicarbonates and sulphates; these are derived naturally from the rock strata through which the water has percolated, so in a chalky or limestone area the water will contain appreciable amounts of these substances. When the water is boiled, the bicarbonates (generally referred to as 'temporary hardness') break down to form carbonates which are insoluble, and these then form the scale or 'fur' on kettles and pipes. However the other compounds present (referred to as the 'permanent hardness') are not decomposed in this way, and remain dissolved in the water.

It is generally considered by the medical profession that these salts are beneficial to health and may retard the incidence of heart disease and osteoporosis in later life. If they are removed in some way (e.g. by using a water filter) then it is advisable to supplement the diet with tablets containing them.

Chlorine

Traditionally, many accusing fingers have been pointed at chlorine, which is added at the water works to kill off any bacteria present and to protect the water from contamination on its journey to the consumer. In a society such as ours we can all see the common sense of this practice to an extent, after all it is one of the responsibilities of a supplier of public potable water that the product is not contaminated and hence a danger to public health; yet when we reflect that chlorine was used as a poison gas very effectively during the 1914–1918 war, there must be some question over its effects on humans in small but regular quantities. By preventing one kind of disease, we may perhaps be encouraging another: this is perhaps the most common medical dilemma of our age. Dr J. Price, a researcher at Saginaw General Hospital, Michigan, has charged that chlorine 'is the greatest crippler and killer of modern times' and has noted that 'two decades after the start of chlorinating our drinking water in 1904, the present epidemic of heart trouble and cancer began.' After experiments involving adding chlorinated water to the diet of chickens, he reported that 'every chicken treated with chlorine showed evidence of either atherosclerosis (degeneration) of the heart artery, or obstructions of the circulatory system.'

46   *The Last Straw*

Apart from the obviously unpleasant taste and smell, chlorine reacts with organic impurities in the water to form by-products called chloroorganics. These impurities are derived from such things as leaves, tree roots, aquatic plants, herbicide and pesticide residues and sewage treatment plant effluent. If you have ever brewed a cup of tea that then tastes of disinfectant, and wondered what could be causing the unpleasant odour and flavour, chloroorganics are to blame. As the water is heated, the chlorine combines with the organic impurities to form chlorophenols; as the common antiseptic known as TCP comes into this category it is not surprising really when your tea tastes rather like it. But of even more concern is the ability of these chloroorganics to be potentially carcinogenic, such as in the case of THMS (trihalomethanes); there appears to be increased evidence for an association between rectal, colon and bladder cancer and the consumption of chlorinated drinking water.

Are there any viable alternatives to using chlorine? In France they tend to use ozone but its effect is not as prolonged as that of chlorine. Irradiation with ultra-violet light is another possibility, but most water companies in this country seem to be relatively satisfied with continuing the use of chlorine. However as we will see later it is relatively easy to remove it again if we should so wish.

Fluoride

The addition of fluoride to drinking water was a contentious issue twenty five years ago and still remains so today. The pros and cons of the subject from a medical point of view have been well covered in many publications, but in most people's minds the real issue is whether mass medication of the water supply is an infringement of the liberty of the individual. At the same time the wide availability of toothpastes containing various forms of fluoride, and tablets containing measured doses of it, mean that there could be a real danger of overuse. Even fluoridated milk for young children was produced in the South of England on a limited commercial scale. A further hazard of fluoride arises when fluoridated water is used in combination with aluminium cooking vessels (see Chapter 7).

Certainly the dental profession are encouraged to see that the problem of dental care, particularly in children, is not as great as in previous generations, and they attribute this to the popular use of

Our Water Supplies 47

fluoride-containing toothpastes rather than to medication in the water supply. Should we not be allowed to choose for ourselves what precautions we take to safeguard our health? And in any case is not the real culprit our sugar-rich diet? How many of us are strong-willed enough to reduce on a permanent basis the amount of sugar we consume? It is not as easy as it might seem because, like smoking, addiction is often involved.

One recent incident concerning the addition of fluoride is worth a mention. In one area where there was a group of parents with hyperactive children who were dedicated to improving their condition by diet as far as was possible, the local water authority started to fluoridate the supply; children whose behaviour and general health pattern had been stabilised over a period of time due to careful management began to exhibit their old symptoms again almost immediately.

Nitrates
There can be no doubt from the accumulated evidence that the content of nitrates in water supplies has risen in recent years, this rise being quite dramatic in some areas. It is ironic that only about half of the inorganic nitrogenous fertilisers applied can be taken up by the plants for which they are intended, the remainder leaching into rivers or through underlying rock formations into underground water sources. In the latter case it can take up to twenty years for the increase in drinking water to become apparent, and since fertiliser use has increased about eightfold in the last two decades there is genuine reason for concern.

The World Health Organisation's *Guidelines for Drinking Water Quality* states that 'Nitrate is toxic when present in excessive amounts in drinking water.' Bacteria in the mouth and stomach can reduce nitrates to nitrites, which are even more toxic. Nitrites compete with oxygen in combining with blood haemoglobin, and can cause the potentially fatal condition known as Methaemoglobinaemia (Blue Baby Syndrome), especially in infants under three months of age. Nitrites will also combine with specific aminocompounds in the body to form nitrosamines which are considered to be potential carcinogens. (Incidentally, you increase your intake of nitrates and nitrites by eating any cured meat products such as ham, bacon, corned beef etc., due to the widespread (and quite

48 *The Last Straw*

legal) use of these additives; they have two main purposes, firstly for 'curing' i.e. retaining the pink colour of the meat during processing, and secondly for ensuring that canned and presumably vacuum-packed products remain free of the dangerous food poisoning organism *Clostridium botulinum.*)

Aluminium

Another intentional additive to some water supplies is aluminium sulphate, used for clarification and the removal of particulate matter from potable water supplies; there is great concern about the possible link between aluminium intake and the gradual deterioration of the brain in the elderly (see Chapter 7).

The whole of the U.K. learned via the media of the tragic mistake in North Cornwall in 1988 when a tanker-load of the treatment chemical (an 8% solution of aluminium sulphate) was discharged into the wrong tank, thereby contaminating all the water supplies in a wide area. How many people will be affected on a long-term basis no-one really can tell at present. There is also grave concern in parts of Scotland due to the action of acid rain on the soil, which is leaching the natural aluminium out of the soil and into ground water, thus making it impossible for local water companies to meet the EEC standards for aluminium content (50 ppm) even before they use any further treatments.

Heavy metals

Contaminants in this category include lead, copper, iron etc., and their presence in drinking water generally results from the fact that pipes are made of one of these metals, usually copper in modern times. A blue stain around the basin where the tap drips indicates copper, and a brown one iron. Because the compounds of lead are almost without exception insoluble in water, any lead contamination has traditionally been largely in the form of very fine insoluble particles such as lead sulphate which can form particularly when the water is soft; these are usually invisible to the naked eye although easily removed by a filter. However with the increase in nitrate levels the nature of the contamination could be on the change, as chemical interaction between acids, lead compounds and nitrates could produce lead nitrate, the only commonly occurring soluble form of the metal. The dangers of lead, a powerful brain and nerve poison, are only now being recognised for what

Our Water Supplies

they really are, after generations of children (and adults) have been affected. Lead water pipes have not been used for many years, however copper pipes are sometimes soldered with a lead-based solder which can then react electrochemically with the copper, releasing lead into the water!

Metals such as chromium and nickel can sometimes be found in water that has been boiled in kettles and stainless steel vessels. These metals, used for electroplating the elements in kettles, will be gradually dissolved away due to reaction with the impurities in the tap water, and if you inspect your kettle you may well find that, apart from the scale that has formed on the element due to the 'hardness' in the water, the bright metal plating has been completely eaten away; and you, of course, have drunk the water! To my knowledge, only one domestic kettle manufacturer has had the foresight to place the heating element *under* the water container so that it never comes into contact with the water itself during the heating process.

Even stainless steel saucepans, long thought to be amongst the best materials for cooking because of their inertness, may not be quite as inert as we think. They are usually manufactured from a special type of steel called 18:8, which has been used traditionally in shipbuilding for its anti-corrosion properties; apart from iron it contains chromium and nickel, but when scoured, the inert surface film is destroyed. According to one writer[4]: 'Tests in the U.S.A. have discovered small amounts of chromium and nickel in meals cooked in a well-scoured stainless steel pan.'

Organic and other contaminants

These can be many and varied, and occur for all manner of reasons, from pesticide and herbicide residues to the specific variety of trees that grow on the banks of the reservoir. In some areas of peat moorland the water will be quite brown in colour and also acidic, and the problem can be so severe, apart from the unpleasant appearance, that pipes, tanks and kitchen equipment can be corroded.

But such contaminants are not necessarily from natural sources. *Fitness* magazine reported[5] that 'arguably we are responsible for some of the contaminants in the water supply. Our high intake of drugs such as antibiotics, valium and contraceptive pills are being

50
The Last Straw

passed into the drinking water. An alarming 75% of most active drugs are excreted by the body and when you consider that in London, a third of the tap water is treated sewage effluent, the problem doesn't bear thinking about, much less drinking. . . . Female hormones from the contraceptive pill are the biggest problem, because of their high stability. They can survive in purified water almost indefinitely.' In 1987 there was concern in one area of Surrey when small amounts of radioactive Iodine 125, originating from a local hospital, were found in the drinking water. Perhaps we should all think twice before flushing unwanted drugs down the toilet as we have often been advised to do.

Microbiological quality

The issue of microbiological quality has traditionally been one area where we in this country, thanks to the use of chlorine and other chemicals, ultra-violet treatment etc, have not needed to be too concerned provided we are on a mains supply. However a recent occurrence of illness in the Swindon area was traced to the parasite cryptosporidia, so *nothing* in this world can be assumed to be safe, it seems. Many bacteria will survive in water, even in bottled spring water according to recent reports, but cannot multiply unless sufficient nutrients are present.

Cleaning up our water

We are of course entitled to clean up our domestic water supplies in any way we choose by removing from it bacteria, chlorine or any other constituent that we consider as unnecessary or undesirable. In fact any individual is entitled to approach the local water company and ask to see a typical analysis for the water in his area. If a particular problem is suspected, then arrangements will be made for samples to be taken locally for analysis; this may be done entirely free, although a charge will perhaps be levied in some areas. There is no harm in enquiring what services are available, so do make use of the local water company if you have a genuine concern with the quality of your water. They, more than anyone else, should have the technical resources and the local expertise to advise you. Also ask if, in their report, they will relate the figures quoted in the analysis you receive to the maximum levels recommended by the E.E.C.[6] If you still have difficulty understanding

Our Water Supplies 51

this, there are consultants available who will be able to assist you with analyses and other relevant information. Once you know the nature of the problem, you are then in a much better position to choose a purifying system best suited to your needs.

Water filters

The most common problem is the chlorine content. While we can well understand the safety reasons why the water company puts it in, this does not mean that we cannot remove it again on our premises if we choose to do so. Activated carbon filters do an excellent job of removing chlorine, and also organic residues, particulate matter, and colour, flavour and odour taints. Many people begin with a jug filter, in which water from the tap passes through a small activated charcoal filter (sometimes containing added silver compounds to arrest possible bacterial growth) into a storage jug beneath; the water is then used from this jug. These filters also contain ion exchange resins which remove some of the natural hardness of the water (see the section on hardness earlier), replacing the calcium and magnesium with sodium; for this reason it is not a good idea to give this water to babies or indeed any person whose sodium intake should be carefully controlled. The charcoal used in these filters may be from one of a variety of sources including bones, anthracite and coconut, so those people with a great degree of sensitivity should check first that they are unlikely to be affected by the carbon used in the filter.

When using one of these filters, you will notice that in the advertising literature they are claimed to last up to a month, and are designed to purify some 60–100 litres (approximately 15–20 gallons) of water. However, from my experiences I would strongly recommend that the filter is renewed after a maximum period of ten days, and preferably every week. The reason is that these filters were originally produced for people living in hard water areas and who preferred their tea without the 'scum' caused by the hardness; also the filtered water was crystal clear and preferable to tap water for drinking. But there are now a large number of consumers who use their jug filters to purify *all* the water that they use in the kitchen, for drinking, washing and cooking vegetables, meat etc., so there is no way that the filter refills can be effective for a month under those conditions. It is strongly recommended that for the

52 *The Last Straw*

first few days of use, you measure the exact amount of water that passes through the filter; you will be surprised at how short a time it is before you have used the 15–20 gallons recommended (the lesser quantity would apply to areas of very hard water). It usually works out that the filter should be replaced after about a week, and of course if you omit to do this it means that every time you use the filter thereafter you are flushing out the impurities that you thought you had eliminated and ingesting them. Do check on the claims made by the manufacturer of the filters as they do differ substantially.

For convenience and also because of the regular expenditure involved in replacing filters, many people have chosen to purchase a carbon filter of a more 'heavy-duty' nature. These generally do not include the ion exchange resins so they do not soften the water at all, but they still remove the same contaminants. They can be either fitted to the tap or plumbed in under the sink, and in this case the preferable models will have a by-pass arrangement so that you can still obtain unpurified water from the tap for the washing machine or watering the garden (although you may well feel that your plants deserve the same quality of water that you do).

Some people who are so sensitive to chlorine that they come out in a skin rash after taking a bath have found great relief from installing a carbon filter just downstream of the stopcock on the rising main. In this way *all* the water entering the house is purified and baths and showers are therefore no longer a problem. In such a case a second filter should also be installed under the sink as a precaution, in order to remove any contamination picked up during the water's journey along the pipes.

Chlorinated water can exhibit unexpected addictive properties. *Here's Health* magazine[3] published a shortened version of a research paper by Dr C.W.M. Wilson, a consultant psychiatrist at the Law Hospital in Lanarkshire in which she found that 'patients with water allergies often bathe daily, while the average for the rest of us is once a week. The water-sensitive patient, stimulated by the contaminants in water, becomes addicted to it. The patient bathes daily in a very hot bath and tops it up with more very hot water. The heat increases absorption of the water antigens. He or she lies dreamily in the bath and may not have the energy to wash. However, a hyperactive child, or one with eczema, may actively

Our Water Supplies 53

struggle against being put in the bath, in unconscious self-defence. He will fight until the water antigens are absorbed and depress the brain. The child quietens down and even forgets the stinging skin, which is caused by the allergic reaction to the water. Getting out of the water restimulates the tissues. A child may become hyperactive again, and an adult may be dizzy and irritable. Sleep is later disturbed by dreams and nightmares caused by the antigenic stimulation of the brain.' These findings can explain to some extent the differing attitudes of people towards bathing, but a water filter can make it possible for most people to enjoy an occasional bath or shower in perfect safety.

When you go away on holiday you may decide to take your jug filter with you, but if not it is advisable to dispose of the cartridge and replace it with a fresh one on your return. If you have a plumbed-in filter system, you should flush it through on your return with five to ten gallons of water to remove any possible bacterial contamination before you consider drinking water from it.

For those whose requirements for drinking water are even more stringent, there are other alternatives. A few have tried stills, which produce relatively pure water on the first distillation, but they are expensive to purchase, tend to be made of glass which is easily broken and then expensive to replace, and consume prodigious amounts of electricity. If you own a still you may expect a visit from your local Customs and Excise Officer who will want to make sure that you are not using it for producing illegal alcohol!

A more sensible approach is to use the technique called reverse osmosis (R.O.), which has been used for some time in the U.S.A. (where they are even more conscious of water quality) and is now finding its way onto the U.K. market. As usual you tend to get what you pay for; the more expensive units costing several hundred pounds will be installed under the sink, with a storage chamber for the purified water which is then fed by pressure to a separate tap at the sink. At the other end of the scale are small portable units which you affix to the mains supply and then collect the purified water in containers. It has to be mentioned that some companies selling water purification equipment may do so without having sufficient technical expertise, and are possibly more interested in your money than your health.

54 *The Last Straw*

How does reverse osmosis work, and what are its advantages? The principle of operation is that water under mains pressure (which should normally be at least 40 psi) is forced through a specially-produced cellulose acetate membrane; in theory only water molecules can pass through this membrane because of the nature of its construction, while all the impurities are flushed away without passing through. In practice this is not achieved, but the membrane does a satisfactory job in removing very nearly all contaminants (over 90% of most), and providing water at a relatively cheap cost whose quality is acceptable to almost everyone. Its main practical disadvantage is the slow flow rate, necessitating a collecting vessel from which the water must be used, but with the more expensive systems this drawback is overcome by having an undersink storage tank as described in the previous paragraph.

If you are away from the house for any length of time, it is advisable to leave a R.O. unit running, albeit very slowly; the flow of water continuously flushes the membrane surface and prevents any build-up of bacteria which would otherwise occur in static conditions. The expense of following this practice is negligible.

What is best?

The method you choose for purifying your water supply is of course a personal decision dictated to by the needs of the family, and taken after due consideration of (a) the general quality of the water supplied, (b) what you need to remove, and (c) how much you can afford to pay. Do you prefer a small but regular outlay, or a larger but very infrequent one? Obviously the jug filters work out the most expensive to use, but many people prefer them and cannot afford the initial expense for a plumbed-in filter of any sort. A consultant or a knowledgeable retailer in the water trade should be able to give you impartial advice. At least we can be grateful that there is now plenty of choice when it comes to selecting a suitable water purification system, but how sad that what should be a natural resource available to everyone at minimal cost should have become so expensive and controversial.

REFERENCES
1. *Awake!* 22 November 1986, p. 4.
2. Smith, Dr. C., 'Water – Friend or Foe?', *Laboratory Practice*, October 1985.

Our Water Supplies   55

3. Wilson, Dr. C.W.M., *Here's Health*, September 1982, pp. 37–38.
4. Petersen, V., *The Natural Food Catalogue*, Macdonald & Co., 1984, p. 140.
5. Young, L., 'On the Water Front', *Fitness* October 1986, pp. 25–28.
6. Council of the European Communities Directive, 15 July 1980.

Chapter 5
Stresses From Our Social Way of Life

Some of us might confess that even the act of getting up in the morning generates enough stress to be going on with! But some stress can be beneficial, provided that it is not too prolonged; otherwise why would anyone be prepared to make any effort to do anything worthwhile? And in particular, why would athletes take the trouble to train so that they can push themselves to the limits of their endurance when the big race comes? But our 'civilised' way of life can generate much chronic stress that we have to try to live with the best way we can. Some of it occurs because we try to do too much in the time available, and some because of difficulties with inter-personal relationships either at home or at work. Perhaps each of us expects everyone else to be perfect, so it is not really surprising that life can often disappoint us!

A true experience from when I was a boy makes a comment that is still relevant some thirty five years later. The Assistant Chaplain of our school was well known and popular for his unique and refreshing approach to the problems of everyday life, due partly to a droll sense of humour which made itself known in the chapel as well as in the classroom. One summer afternoon he had invited a small number of senior pupils to take afternoon tea with him in his rooms, at which the treat of the day was strawberries and cream. In typical schoolboy fashion the bowls were emptied in double-quick time, after which one observant lad noticed that his host had not touched his strawberries at all, but was sitting quite still just looking at them. When asked why he hadn't 'tucked in' he turned to the boy, paused in a meaningful way and made the following pronouncement, pausing between words for maximum theatrical effect: 'The anticipation of the pleasure is almost as great as the pleasure itself.' Applying that principle to life today, don't we

Stresses From Our Social Way of Life

often find that the anticipation of something pleasurable is often *better* than the thing or event itself when it is realised? For example, we may look forward to a meal with friends in a restaurant, but are we always entirely satisfied with the quality and quantity of the food we are paying for? And if we are on a special diet which the restaurant promises to accommodate (such as milk- or wheat-free) can we really be sure that our needs will literally be catered for?

Spending money

We all like spending money, and when you take delivery of the new car which you have been looking forward to so much, don't you have to admit that maybe you could have managed just as well with your previous one? It is very true that with additional possessions come additional responsibilities, so it is not really surprising that many people stand by the expression 'better the devil you know'.

Getting into debt

Even when a surprise is on the surface very pleasant and desirable, like winning a million pounds on the football pools, the upset and heartbreak that can follow has made the recipient wish in many cases that his circumstances were still as they were before. Look at the way we are encouraged by advertising to spend, spend, spend on things we don't even want, let alone actually need; the psychology of selling is very deep, and advertising must be successful overall, otherwise why should there be so much money spent on it? Yet Henry Ford was once reported as saying 'Half my advertising budget is wasted; the problem is that I don't know *which* half.' Because of the desires generated by advertising and a materialistic approach to life, many fall into the trap of owing more than they can afford to pay back, with resulting heartache and perhaps even lasting damage to the family. When debt becomes an apparently insoluble problem, some even take their lives; a few years ago a United Press International dispatch from Tokyo reported: 'A businessman and his son, anguished over millions in debts, strangled seven members of their family and set themselves on fire in a three-generation murder-suicide pact.' Fortunately most of us would never dream of going that far, as such extreme action solves nothing in reality and only creates even more problems for those left behind.

58 *The Last Straw*

Yet most of us use credit cards, and if not controlled these can be an open invitation to get deeply into debt. Both a shortage or an excess of money can affect us deeply; the television news frequently makes us appreciate that. But people get into debt all over the world in different ways: they do not have to be rich to be materialistic. Gambling is one of the most common, whether on a lottery, doing the football pools, at the racetrack or in the casino; it is not really the open door to a satisfying life, as we all know deep down, but we all fool ourselves into reasoning that this time it must be our turn to win. Perhaps all we are really doing is to line the pockets of the promoters, which is why they are in business in the first place. Maybe some philanthropist should rent a few billboards and, misappropriating a famous slogan, have it declared to the nation that 'Gambling is dangerous to your health'!

The spirit of competition

Another source of stress can be the spirit of competition encouraged by both parents and schools from a very early ago. No one would argue that it is beneficial for a child to pay attention, to learn as much as possible, and to try to do well in examinations. But children soon learn that a lot is expected of them if they are to be fully acceptable to parents, teachers and peers (the latter often being the hardest taskmasters of all), and they are taught to understand that if they can succeed where others have failed, the future is theirs to choose. But in practice only one pupil can receive the Form Prize, and by no means all will attain the high entry standards required by the universities. Surely children should not be made to feel that they are failures just because they are not the very best at a particular subject or sport? There are far more important attributes, as every good parent knows. Would you not rather have children who were honest, moral, amusing, caring and industrious?

If you left school thirty years ago with good 'A' Level results, and then studied for a few years at university, you could expect to find a good job after you qualified, and embark upon a career for life if that was what you wanted. But that is not the way it is any more: having a degree is no longer the open door that it used to be, and many young people have been greatly disillusioned. Getting ahead isn't necessarily desirable any longer, and we see much of

Stresses From Our Social Way of Life 59

the young generation's talent being wasted by a system that has very little of value to offer them any more. Doctors in West Germany blame most of that country's stress on the *Leistungs-gesellschaft* or 'performance society'; this concept dates back to the 'economic miracle' of the thirties, which featured as important the pursuit of achievement in a material way. Surely it would do us good to recognise that whether we are rich or poor we will never be satisfied if we look to money, fame or achievement for our happiness. Two years before he died, the millionaire Paul Getty said 'Money doesn't necessarily have any connection with happiness; maybe with unhappiness.' A recent study reported in the *Boston Globe* concluded that 'depression seems to be the price of civilisation.'

Making decisions

Decisions, decisions! Life is full of the need to make them; yet some people find it extremely difficult and stressful to make a decision about almost anything. Sometimes they just are not prepared to think objectively about the subject at that time (maybe because of other preoccupations) so when asked for their opinion can only manage the well-known phrase 'I don't really know.' But often the problem is that a conflict is involved which the individual finds it impossible to resolve in his mind. T.M. Higham summed the process up in this way[1]:

> You can train a pig to open a box with its snout by the simple expedient of putting some food inside it. If you then present a well-trained pig with two boxes – one with food in, and one wired up to give an electric shock (a mild one) to anyone touching it, you present the pig with a conflict. It soon learns that one box contains food, the other gives it a shock; but which is which? In the end the pig has a 'nervous breakdown'. It shows . . . signs of stress . . . and it reaches a state of porcine indecision when it can do nothing at all.

Most of us at some time must have found ourselves in that sort of situation. Suppose you have an important appointment involving a number of people, and your partner or child is suddenly taken sick, what do you do? And what is the first priority? Life is full of these situations and it is hardly surprising that stress can be generated very rapidly by them!

60   *The Last Straw*

Naturally we are concerned with the outcome of our decisions, be they at home or at work, but we cannot always be expected to make the right decision. If we think we can, or should, then are we not introducing even more stress into the picture? As Dr Higham says: 'We can reduce stress if we admit to ourselves that we cannot be a success by every standard, or always be right, or never suffer a setback. A lot of stress stems from people trying to act the role of superman. A well balanced man of high ability thinks little of admitting his failures – and thus he is able to conserve his strength.'

Stress at work

Stress at work can take many forms. Many spend all day in an environment that is permanently noisy due to machinery, women may run the risk of being harassed sexually, or someone may persist in having the radio on all day when you are trying to concentrate on some complex mental task; researchers have noted that having to listen to music which is not to your taste does cause symptoms of stress. Studies have shown that any noise to which we have to try and adapt will do this, so let us be grateful if we do not live or work in a building that is directly under the approach to Heathrow! I had to do just that for three months when I worked for a company in Hounslow, and well remember that all conversations and telephone calls had to be 'frozen' every few minutes as the next big jet made its approach, not the most productive way to spend each working day.

Commuting is not everyone's idea of bliss either. Many spend several hours each working day travelling in overcrowded conditions, and are prepared to put up with the inconvenience for the job that awaits them. Others work from home and find that they have a lot more time available.

Workplace stress is said to affect mainly blood pressure, heart and lungs; it is said that in the City you are not considered successful until you have an ulcer! At work, often the problem is that we cannot react to stress in the natural way programmed into our bodies, using the 'fight or flight' mechanism; we just have to stay where we are and get on with the job. But even people on the move during their working day are not immune; according to a recent television report, one in three London bus drivers are

Stresses From Our Social Way of Life 61

affected by stress, and the most stressful occupations in the National Health Service are claimed to be in the ambulance service.

This country also has an unusual attitude to employment. Many young and intelligent people with a lifetime of useful work before them find themselves in jobs that are so stressful that they are 'burned out' by the time they are in their mid-thirties. Indeed most advertisements for employment vacancies make it quite clear that anyone over forty, or forty five at the most, is 'over the hill' and need not apply. What utter nonsense this is! A quality that middle-aged people can bring to their work is one that youngsters cannot, and that is experience, and the balanced judgements that come with it. In Europe, age (and the experience that ensues) is an attribute that employers appreciate; why not here? In the U.S.A. they have a different approach; instead of keeping to a career progression all their working lives, many Americans take a break after every ten years or so, stop and reflect, and then set out on a completely different tack. In this way they acquire a more balanced overall view of life as they grow older. Unfortunately, our system in the U.K. makes it very difficult to do this, as many prospective employers look askance if your CV is not exactly as they would expect. The mid-life crisis that we are all bound to go through sooner or later need not be the traumatic period that some people find it to be, but you need to be convinced that you will stand by whatever decisions you make at the time, believing them to be the right ones, whether they turn out in retrospect to be so or not. During such a time there is no substitute for a truly supportive family.

However, at work there are many other more subtle pressures that may be brought to bear. For example, do you seldom have the opportunity to finish one task before you are compelled to become involved in several more? Psychological research has shown that a task left unfinished sets up stress in that we are unable to completely stop thinking about it until it is completed. Have you ever wondered how waiters or shop assistants can be on duty for long periods and yet keep running totals of each customer's expenditure including your own? Yet if you were to approach them later in the day for the details you would find that they would not be able to remember anything of them; subconsciously they were

62 · *The Last Straw*

erased from their memory just as soon as you had paid up, as their attention was immediately diverted to new customers. It has been shown that at work, breakages, high accident rates, absenteeism and prolonged tea-breaks are often symptoms of stress caused by the frustration of simple human needs and desires.

A chain of stress is formed when the 'boss' appears to be insensitive to the needs of his staff; one member may be spoken to sharply, feels unjustly treated and immediately takes it out on his assistant; and so it goes on down the chain until the office junior goes home in a thoroughly bad mood and kicks the cat. This makes him (or her) feel better, but not the cat, who has no one else to take it out on even if it could understand the reason for the mal-treatment! It is essential for a relatively peaceful and productive working environment that people learn to recognise these situations as they develop and try to short-circuit them in some way. After all, verbal explosions are not necessarily aimed at us personally, so we must try to realise that at the time and not let it get through to us. Can we laugh the matter off, dismiss it from our mind, and get on with the job? If we can, then we will save both ourselves and our colleagues from further stress. If we have a difficult 'boss', often we can bring out his better qualities if we go out of our way to do our work for him conscientiously.

Another source of stress at work is the faulty design of equipment, which could include such examples as the chair and desk at which you operate a computer, a factory machine which requires the operator to be in at least two places at once in order to manage it effectively, or even your motor car. As you continue using the computer, operating the machine or driving the car, your general movements will, after a period of time, become gradually less co-ordinated as you begin to feel fatigued; while ergonomic design has achieved much in recent years to alleviate such symptoms they are still extremely common.

Fatigue, and the stress which causes it, has been the subject of many experiments, but one of the most interesting was carried out during the last war at Cambridge, where fatigue in R.A.F. pilots was being investigated using a flight simulator. The research was reported by N.H. Mackworth[2], but was commented upon in another article of the same year already referred to[1] from which the following extracts are taken. 'When a pilot was fresh, he could

Stresses From Our Social Way of Life 63

glance at the main dials or signals in the cockpit and interpret the whole panel of instruments . . . When he was tired he could no longer do that. Instead of reacting to the panel as a whole, he responded to isolated dials, and his controlling movements split up in the same way. With these changes came a deeper awareness of physical discomfort, a growing irritability and a tendency to give less and less reliable accounts of what was happening. Stress was taking its toll.' But when a clock was provided for the pilot, so that he could check for himself how he was doing, the results were very different; 'If the check was used, the pilot could keep up a good performance for a long time. . . . The reason was that *he knew how he was getting on.*'

So the lesson for us is surely that if people at work are enabled to check out in some way whether their work is effective and achieving a purpose, their performance, whether it be over the day, month or year, will be maintained over a longer period of time without their feeling stressed. This is of great importance today, especially in the case of larger business organisations, whose offices can seem very impersonal places to work. A friendly comment, a word of appreciation or simply a 'Thank you' from someone costs nothing and can certainly help to keep up morale and efficiency. Companies who run regular 'assessment and appraisal' sessions with their staff find that there is much to be gained for everyone involved.

Life's most stressful situations

Of course stress problems at work are just one of the areas that have been well researched. On a broader basis, two American doctors, Dr T. Holmes and Dr R.H. Rahne, while preparing a book entitled *Modern Maturity* some years ago, interviewed a large number of people to ascertain what were generally considered as 'life's most stressful situations'. It turned out that the top fifteen were as follows:

1. Death of spouse.
2. Divorce.
3. Marital separation.
4. Jail term.
5. Death of close family member.
6. Personal injury or illness.

64　　　　　　　　　　　*The Last Straw*

7. Marriage.
8. Fired at work.
9. Marital reconciliation.
10. Retirement.
11. Change in health of family member.
12. Pregnancy.
13. Sex difficulties.
14. Gain of new family member.
15. Business readjustment.

When lecturing on this subject I have frequently asked those in the audience to raise a hand if they have experienced at least one of those situations in the past few years. On every occasion at least two thirds of those present have done so, showing that most of us know what it is like to be under severe stress. A further question inviting the members of the audience to respond if they have experienced any stress on that particular day usually invokes much laughter and raising of hands! In this country it might be apposite to add somewhere near the top of the list the experience of buying and selling a house, which for many is surely one of the most harassing experiences to undergo. And my son, when small, had his own 'top of the list': 'going back to school'!

Our fears

Children in particular understandably fear the unknown. Back in the 1930s a psychologist interviewed a number of children of primary school age to establish just what were the most common things that they feared. As one might have expected, they included animals, strangers, dark rooms and high places. However the same researcher was able to repeat the exercise only a few years ago (nearly fifty years later) when it came to light that children's most common fears now were divorce of parents, cancer, drugs and war. How things have changed in fifty years.

I suppose that we have all had very real fears at some time or other, and not only when we were still of school age. Even as adults we all harbour fears, sometimes rational, sometimes not, ranging from spiders through polluted water to the threat of nuclear war. But it would be unbalanced if we were to allow such unproductive and negative thoughts to be uppermost in our minds for much of the time; it is better for our state of health if we can

Stresses From Our Social Way of Life 65

make conscious decisions not to contribute unnecessarily towards worsening any existing situation if we are in a position to do so; for example, if we are worried about pollution, at least we can play our part by choosing not to drop litter, not to use certain aerosol cans, not to use chemicals in the garden, not to use leaded petrol, and so on. How we can reduce the threat of nuclear war is a much harder one to crack! But there can be no doubt that, collectively, ordinary people can achieve much in the course of time, and we have seen outworkings of this sort in recent years. Things are certainly very different now from the early sixties; I well remember the confrontation of the U.S.A. with Cuba, and most of us were very worried indeed for a time.

Some people love flying, some hate it. Of course, as the comedian Spike Milligan once rightly said, 'flying is absolutely safe – it's crashing that's dangerous!' But if we are on a business or holiday trip, isn't it honest to admit that we are concerned at the possibility of hijacking or a bomb scare? On a more down to earth level, there can be hidden dangers lurking in the night-time streets of our towns and cities, and when we arrive home after an evening out, could we find that it has been our turn to be burgled? Some people seem to be able to dismiss such thoughts entirely from their minds, preferring a 'psychological switch-off' as it were, but this will not make the problems go away any more than literally shutting our eyes will make the world disappear. Most psychologists will agree that it is much better to be a realist.

Finally, it is worth emphasising again that our attitudes towards other people can either 'make or break' potentially stressful situations. In a *Reader's Digest* interview, Dr Hans Selye, one of the world's most respected researchers on the subject of stress, remarked: 'The two great emotions that cause the absence or presence of stress are love and hate. The Bible makes this point over and over again. The message is that if we don't somehow modify our built-in selfishness, we arouse fear and hostility in other people – not a very favourable environment in which to exist! Conversely, the more we modify that self-centredness, the more we can persuade people to love us rather than hate us, the safer we are, and the less stress we have to endure.' If only we could learn to put this advice into practice on a worldwide basis!

66 *The Last Straw*

REFERENCES

1. Higham T.M., 'Industrial Stress', *Journal of the Society of Dairy Technology*, Vol. 10, No. 4, October 1957, pp. 222–228.
2. *Researches on the Measurement of Human Performance*, 1957, M.R.C. Special Report 268, London; H.M.S.O.

Chapter 6
Stresses of a Biochemical or Medical Nature

When a person is unwell, he is faced with the difficult decision of whether to pay a visit to the doctor (which is free), attend an alternative medicine clinic (which is not), or do nothing except apply common sense and hope that whatever it is takes its course without any lasting effects. It has been the unfortunate experience of some patients who choose to visit their G.P. or a specialist that he has treated them as if they have no right to know anything about their condition; this attitude has already been discussed in Chapter 3, but is probably related to the continual pressure under which doctors have to work (doctoring can be a very stressful occupation), but even so your G.P. should have reason to be pleased, rather than upset, if you should choose an alternative method of treatment, as it will relieve the pressure on his time.

Incidentally, have you noticed how, when you go into the surgery, he generally asks you 'How are you today, then?' The instinctive reaction of course is to say 'Very well, thank you', but if you were feeling all right you would not be in his surgery anyway!

What really is 'allergy'?

One of the major effects of prolonged stress is to deplete the resources of the immune system, but this may become apparent only when allergies or other types of sensitivity begin to show themselves. Many people are aware of adverse reactions when they consume certain foods such as shellfish, strawberries or tomatoes, but often these are difficult to define as they may be mental, physical or both; sometimes however, the effects of ingesting a particular food may be a lot more serious, even life-threatening. Because of the variety of responses reported it has been very difficult to define exactly what is meant by 'allergy', as

68   *The Last Straw*

the terms used by immunologists may not be understood in the same way by the general public.

An Information Sheet issued by the Ministry of Agriculture, Fisheries and Food on 2nd October 1987 said

> True allergic reactions occur when the body's immune system reacts with unpleasant effects to a small amount of a substance to which the individual has previously been exposed. However, these allergic reactions account for only some of the adverse reactions to foods that may be encountered. In a Joint Report of the Royal College of Physicians and the British Nutrition Foundation, published in 1984, adverse reactions to foods were divided into the two main categories of *food intolerance* and *food aversion*. *Food intolerance* was defined as a reproduceable, unpleasant reaction to food which is not psychologically based, and *food aversion* was defined as an unpleasant reaction caused by emotion associated with the food rather than by the food itself.

The First Food Allergy Workshop, held in Oxford in 1980, attempted to clarify and define the various terms used[1], and these, along with the views of other workers in the field, were summarised by Dr K. Miller[2]. For example, she comments that the term *food intolerance* is normally used to describe all abnormal reactions, including truly allergic and also non-allergic responses, and is recommended in cases where the underlying mechanism is not known for sure. *Food idiosyncrasy* would cover non-allergic responses (such as lactase deficiency). *Allergy* should only be used where there is proof that immunological responses are involved. Dr Miller then goes on to discuss four subclassifications of *allergy* as follows:

> Type I reactions, often termed anaphylactic hypersensitivity, are produced by the release of histamine. . . . The effects . . . can be seen either locally, in for example swollen lips . . . or skin rashes. The most common cutaneous symptoms are urticaria and angioedema. Type II hypersensitivity reactions occur when antibodies react with either a cell surface or with antigen bound to the cell surface of host tissues . . . This type of hypersensitivity can be seen in response to certain drugs, for example penicillin, but it is not generally associated with food. However, small traces of penicillin, sometimes found in the milk of penicillin-treated cows, may produce allergic reactions in individuals previously sensitized to this antibiotic by skin contact or drug therapy. Type III hypersensitivity reactions . . . typically (occur) several hours

Stresses of a Biochemical or Medical Nature 69

after eating the food and specific IgG antibodies are generally present ... Clinical symptoms may include asthma, rhinitis, pallor, headache, vomiting and diarrhoea. Delayed-type hypersensitivity (Type IV) is so termed because of the relatively longer period of onset, generally 24–48 hr, although the onset of symptoms may occur 6–24 hr after ingestion of food. . . . Low molecular-weight substances in food, including some food additives ... react with tissue proteins before exerting their effects.

While many of us realise that if a food is going to upset us it may be almost straight away or it may be quite a long time after we have eaten it, a classification of this sort is very helpful to both the public and the medical profession as it helps them to understand the many different mechanisms involved in reactions to food, drugs and chemicals. Most people continue to use the term 'allergy' to describe any individual reaction to foods, chemicals etc., and as a result this term is perhaps in far wider use today than it should be in a clinical sense, but at least we all know more or less what we are talking about.

As to the extent of the incidence of food allergy, wildly differing proposals have been put forward, suggesting, for example, that anything between 0.3 and 20% of children may be affected. However, a figure estimated in 1982 by the European Community's Scientific Committee for Food was only 0.03 to 0.15% of the population. These figures may be compared in general terms with those quoted by Dr Mackarness (Chapter 3).

Depression

Depression can be one of the many ways in which allergies show themselves, especially if the individual's brain is vulnerable to chemical stimuli. It is not really surprising that so many people suffer from bouts of depression in this troubled world of ours, but the nature of the depression itself, and its causes, are different for each individual.

It is common for persons who have apparently 'failed' to live up to the expectations of society to feel a sense of hopelessness and desperation. An overwhelming feeling of loneliness, the feeling of guilt that results from a bad conscience, the break-up of a love affair, the result of an unpleasant experience such as sexual abuse, the realisation that one's general health is never likely to improve,

The Last Straw

all these and more can contribute. Some see suicide as the only way out of their dilemma, but this is obviously beneficial for no one and is really a very selfish attitude to adopt when one considers the additional problems caused for those left behind; in fact some psychologists consider that suicide attempts are endeavours to attract attention or to influence others to do what the person wants. A young girl who had considered suicide but held back from going through with it later commented as follows: 'Pain, sorrow and guilt are what suicides leave behind – a lot more devastating and lasting than the problems that seemed unbearable to them.'

Some, though, are surprised to discover that their depressive moods may originate with the consumption of a particular food or beverage; chocolate, coffee, tea, wheat and other common items of diet can be responsible. So if a person is suffering a bout of depression, it is well worth investigating the cause really thoroughly. In such cases of food-related depression the problems are compounded if the patient is prescribed valium or some other tranquilliser or anti-depressant, as the drug can work in opposition to the food and it can then become increasingly difficult to stop taking either of them because of the addictive effects.

But whatever the cause, psychologists generally are agreed that the best advice is not to keep your feelings and fears bottled up as so many tend to do, but to confide in others who can be really trusted. Another young girl, three of whose friends had committed suicide, said 'How could we have known? . . . How could we have been there when they needed us if we never knew how they felt?'

Pain

Whilst allergy and depression are really the *results* of stress, how about some of the *causes*? Pain is something that we have all suffered; while it can act as a protection, as when you instinctively withdraw your hand from a hot stove, chronic pain in particular, such as in certain types of cancer, arthritis, headache, earache, toothache, urinary infection or backache, can be extremely wearing and hence stressful. Medical scientists have tried many times to define pain, but it has not proved easy by any means.

Dr P.J.D. Dyke, Professor of Neurology at Mayo Medical School, has said: 'We do not pretend to know how pain works.' It

Stresses of a Biochemical or Medical Nature 71

has usually been assumed to be a sensation, like sight, hearing and touch, which is felt by nerve endings on the skin, and transmitted via nerve fibres to the brain. But in fact it is almost certainly far more complex than this. Doctors at the University of Saskatchewan examined a woman who could feel no pain, yet her nervous system was found to be in perfect order throughout, as was her brain. They said: 'According to all existing knowledge and theory, this girl should have felt pain normally, yet she couldn't even feel tickling.' Yet others feel pain at the slightest provocation, and some can feel pain in a limb that has been severed. Sometimes pain in a particular area is 'referred' from quite another site on the body. Yet everyone agrees that prolonged pain, whatever its cause, is unpleasant and generates stress.

When undergoing an operation in a western land, the patient is usually given a chemical anaesthetic to make him unconscious so that he cannot feel the pain inflicted (the effects of the anaesthetic itself can remain in the bloodstream for some considerable time afterwards and cause stress to the system). But acupuncture, as used in lands such as China, has thrown new light on the nature of pain; there even open heart surgery is performed with only acupuncture anaesthesia, and patients are said to remain awake, alert and relaxed! In 1975–6 scientists found that humans produce their own pain-killing drugs, called enkephalins and endorphins. Dr A. Goldstein of Stanford University in California says: 'The endorphins are probably not constantly secreted; they are held in reserve for extreme situations.' Dr B. Pomeranz of Toronto University believes that the existence of endorphins can explain why acupuncture kills pain so effectively, and suggests that the acupuncture needles stimulate nerves that then cause certain body cells to release endorphins. Some individuals may naturally possess higher levels of these natural pain-killers in their brain or bloodstream, and this could explain why some are far more sensitive to pain than others.

How much stress pain causes us depends on a number of factors. Dr J. Bonica explained that it is 'influenced by early learning, ethnic background, personality, susceptibility to suggestion, concentration, mood and other factors. Fear and anxiety cause an exaggerated response.' So the feeling of pain, or its apparent absence, could to some extent be a conditioned reflex, such as

72 *The Last Straw*

when a fakir lies on a bed of nails, a sportsman breaks a world endurance record or a soldier is severely wounded but carries on till he has finished his assignment.

Postural problems

Many people go through life without becoming uncomfortably aware of any chronic aches and pains, and yet it is quite likely that at some time they have caused minor or even major disturbance to their skeletal structure, particularly their back. I once heard tell of a man who bent over to pick up a ten pence piece and put his back out, with very painful consequences. Well, of course it was not just the act of picking up the coin that was responsible for his acute attack, this was the result of the sudden aggravating of an already existing condition of which he was not aware, (another example of 'the last straw'). Postural condition can remain disturbed but undetected over many years after the initial event that caused the problem, and yet most people are not likely to visit a specialist chiropractor, osteopath or manipulator unless they experience symptoms of discomfort that are sufficiently acute to warn them that something must be wrong.

Just one maladjustment in posture will cause muscles and body parts other than that initially affected to accommodate the new circumstances as best they can to try and restore balance to the system, but this means that the entire frame of the body, and maybe vital organs too, will be put under stress. Really, a periodic check-up of our posture is really just as important to us as a six-thousand-mile service is to our car, yet most of us never think of having one, never mind actually paying for it! The advantages are that many potential health defects can be prevented from developing into anything serious.

Perhaps the most useful way of identifying postural problems and stress on bodily organs is to use the technique of kinesiology, which is able to assess imbalances in the system, a sure sign that all is not what it should be. There is further discussion of kinesiology in Chapter 10, but many chiropractors now use this technique.

Infection by bacteria

Many cases of pain are the result of severe inflammation of some sort, often the result of an overgrowth of pathogenic (disease-

Stresses of a Biochemical or Medical Nature 73

causing) microorganisms, an effect known since the time of Pasteur. Although in harmony with his views of well over a century ago, we tend to consider such microorganisms to be the *cause* of disease, there are now some indications that it might be more correct to consider them as the *product;* this is significant as being the view of Pasteur's compatriot Béchamp, and it is said that on his deathbed Pasteur is said to have acknowledged this possibility himself. If this is the correct viewpoint, then it must be the imbalances in our systems which cause disease when they become so great that they permit organisms which occur naturally in controlled numbers to multiply out of control (just as the yeast Candida may do). As antibiotics tend to destroy beneficial organisms as well as those involved in disease, the use of probiotics, which encourage the growth of healthy internal flora, open up a new approach to treat some types of illness in a positive and preventative way.

We have all been alerted during recent years to the potential hazards of Legionnaires' Disease, propagated by bacteria which thrive under certain conditions in moist environments such as in air-conditioning systems; also to parasitic infections in mains water derived from reservoirs. There have also been recent food poisoning scares and outbreaks due to *Salmonella enteritidis* in poultry and eggs and to *Listeria monocytogenes*, which survives in many foods such as cold meats, soft cheeses etc. stored at refrigerator temperatures of above 5°C. If our general state of health is good, we are unlikely to be affected seriously, but those with impaired immune systems due to stress, the very young and the very old are always most at risk, which in itself tends to support Béchamp's view.

Many other bacteria in our food and water supplies have been known for a long time to be potentially harmful to man when in large quantities; these include Coliforms (especially *Escherichia coli*, found in raw meat and milk, salads and water), *Brucella abortus* (associated with undulant fever in man and present in some untreated cows' milk), *Vibrio cholerae* (from fish, shellfish and water, causing cholera), *Shigella spp.* (associated with raw vegetables after contamination with sewage, causing dysentery), *Clostridium botulinum* (occurring in much vegetation and producing the most potent toxin known to man which causes botulism),

74   *The Last Straw*

Bacillus cereus (from fried and boiled rice, other reconstituted cereal products, and milk stored at ambient temperatures), *Campylobacter jejuni* (thought to be the most common cause of food poisoning, particularly from raw milk, water, poultry and carcass meat), *Yersinia enterocolitica* (from raw milk, water and even tofu), *Staphylococcus aureus* (from meat and poultry, cheese and egg dishes etc., particularly by cross-contamination from infected humans) and so on.

Other food- and water-borne hazards would include toxins from fish and shellfish, Hepatitis B virus, and some mycotoxins (fungal poisons, which have been found in such foods as peanuts and figs). All through 1989 there was great concern at all levels about the potential hazards of food poisoning outbreaks, as was discussed in Chapter 3.

Blood transfusion

A common medical practice which has recently attracted much controversy is the surgical use of blood. Most of us are brought up to believe that donating blood constitutes a sacrifice that we give willingly on behalf of our fellow man in trouble, a very personal kind of help, and it is possible that many lives may have been saved by its use. It is thought that the practice of transfusing blood was known by the ancient Egyptians, but the first recorded transfusion was given to a Pope in the Middle Ages, and cost the lives of two young boys. Medical fashions concerning blood can change; it was not that long ago when leeches were used to suck or 'let' blood out of a patient who was ill, but now in the twentieth century we tend to pump it in instead.

Blood is administered mainly to augment the volume of fluid circulating in the patient, who may have suffered great loss. The British Journal *Anaesthesia*[4] stated that 'even if an adequate supply of whole blood is available, however, it is doubtful if it is the fluid of choice for the initial treatment for the rapid transfusion of grossly hypovolaemic patients' (those who have lost a lot of blood). But even small transfusions of one unit (one pint) are regularly given, which does not really make much sense when one considers that a blood donor gives a pint of blood and then after a few minutes' rest gets up and carries on with the day's activities. What about the effect of a massive injection of blood into the body

Stresses of a Biochemical or Medical Nature 75

just when the system is at its lowest ebb? It takes quite some time for the body's immune system to decide whether to accept or reject the fluid, which it initially recognises as foreign, so during the very critical time when it should be getting on with the natural process of healing itself it has to divert many of its already depleted resources to coping with yet another crisis. So this is one of the main reasons why it is necessary to consider the issue of blood transfusion so carefully.

You may at this point be still somewhat sceptical that such an obviously beneficial practice could be harmful, or cause additional stress to the patient. However, consider the comments made by three professional sources. Dr D.L.J. Freed of the Manchester University Medical School has expressed the opinion[5] that 'blood transfusions are dangerous medicine, as medical students are taught already.' Professor M.M. Wintrobe has gone on record[6] as saying: 'A frank appraisal of the facts proves that blood transfusion must honestly be regarded as a procedure involving considerable danger and even as potentially lethal.' And a United States Government publication warned[7] that 'donating blood can be compared to sending a loaded gun to an unsuspecting or unprepared person.' According to a 1976 report it was estimated that anything up to 30,000 Americans died each year as a direct result of being given a blood transfusion, and since then the situation has become far more serious with the advent of AIDS. The Toronto Star has reported that as many as 40% of Soviet AIDS victims have contracted the virus through contaminated blood.

In Western countries the record is really no different. The *Medical Post* of Canada reported the view of Dr T. Peterman, a medical epidemiologist with the AIDS branch of the Centers for Disease Control, who estimated that 12,000 Americans became infected with AIDS virus from contaminated blood transfusions from 1978–1984. Even if these figures should be an overestimate (and regrettably this seldom turns out to be the case in retrospect) then this is another reason for a patient to consider his position most carefully if in need of urgent medical attention. Another threat from transfusing blood is the risk of hepatitis; as an example, researchers believe that between ten and fifteen people die in Australia each year because of hepatitis C contracted from transfusions of contaminated blood. So the whole subject is not quite as clear-cut as it might first appear.

76 *The Last Straw*

One religious group, Jehovah's Witnesses, have been well-known worldwide for many years for their stand against the taking in of blood in any form, especially as transfusions; while their literature indicates clearly that the primary issue on which they base their decisions in such matters is a scriptural rather than a medical one[8], many people who do not share their beliefs prefer to avoid the use of blood purely for reasons of personal concern. As was discussed earlier, the primary use of a transfusion is to provide extra fluid volume, but this was shown to be perhaps a doubtful reason for carrying on the practice as the body is unable to benefit immediately from it in any case. As an editorial in the magazine *Anaesthesia* said[9]: 'It is worth remembering that the haemoglobin of stored, citrated red cells is not fully available for the transfer of oxygen to the tissues for some 24 hours after transfusion . . . rapid blood transfusion must therefore be regarded primarily as a mere volume expander in the initial stages.' In practice other non-blood fluids are readily available for this purpose and carry none of the hazards of blood; these include saline solution, Ringer's lactate, dextran solution, Haemaccel and hydroxyethyl starch solutions. It is a recognised fact, and accepted by medical experts, that patients who have had non-blood expanders rather than blood transfusions tend to recover more quickly and with fewer complications. Many open-heart operations in the U.S.A. are now carried out successfully without the use of blood.

Candidiasis

Whilst the use of blood can constitute a severe shock to the system, there are other more insidious causes of stress such as Candidiasis. There are now several excellent books that discuss this subject in detail[10, 11] and anyone concerned would be recommended to turn to them for more detailed information on the causes, effects and treatments.

Candidiasis results primarily from our diet and our way of life; in the West we have tended since the last war to eat increasing amounts of sugar, and at the same time the use of antibiotics has proliferated and there is a good case for arguing that they are prescribed far too freely. The gut naturally contains a combination of beneficial bacteria such as various species of Lactobacilli, which aid in digesting our food effectively, but also present is a yeast organism

Stresses of a Biochemical or Medical Nature

known as *Candida albicans*. Sugar or any simple carbohydrate is of course a prime food for yeasts, and an abundant supply encourages its growth. At the same time a course of an antibiotic effectively kills off not just the organisms concerned with our illness but the natural beneficial ones as well. The effects of antibiotics in disturbing the balance in the gut has been known for some time, and this is why people are encouraged to eat cheese or live yogurt after a course of antibiotics, but in reality it is unlikely that any of the organisms will survive passing through the stomach, and even if some of them do, it is doubtful if they would be able to begin repopulating the gut. Some products such as BA yogurt, cultured with the organisms *Lactobacillus acidophilus* and *Bifidobacterium bifidum* instead of the more usual Streptococcus thermophilus and Lactobacillus bulgaricus, could be marginally beneficial as these organisms can better survive the acid conditions in the stomach. However several preparations are now available which contain millions of beneficial bacteria in a freeze-dried form, and are sold with the claim that each dose will result in at least a small percentage of viable organisms surviving into the gut, where they can begin to repopulate it. Laboratory tests have revealed that most of these preparations contain bacteria which are already dead and can therefore do no good at all; however in one or two brands the organisms are still viable and therefore able to exert the effect claimed.

If a person is blissfully unaware of what is going on in his digestive tract, the candida yeast cells will continue to multiply without any opposition, often the first visible signs of the imbalance being diarrhoea, 'athlete's foot', vaginal discharge or a white coating on the tongue. As the blood acidity lowers, the yeast develops a mycelial form which then penetrates the wall of the gut and grows right through it, perforating it in the process; the candida yeasts can then exist in the bloodstream, which is slightly alkaline and thus provides ideal conditions for it to prosper, and this is when one can really start to feel unwell with candidiasis. The damage caused by the perforation of the gut wall can be long-lasting, and is a prime cause of multiple allergies, as partly digested food molecules can leak through into the bloodstream, where they are immediately identified as 'foreign' to the system. A wide variety of symptoms can arise, mimicking any one of a number of other known conditions, and as the human body naturally contains candida yeasts it is not easy to

78   *The Last Straw*

identify the cause of the condition by scientific tests. Some of the more severe symptoms reported are: chronic ear infection (many children who have a minor operation to place grommets in the ears may have candidiasis), multiple allergies to foods, drugs, chemicals etc., depression, a sensation of losing one's sanity with many unpleasant 'spaced-out' mental sensations, and so on.

In my own case of candidiasis (as it turned out to be), the main symptom was that of a severe urinary tract infection; over many years I underwent several IVP X-rays for possible kidney stones, gall-bladder X-rays and internal examinations for the prostate. Also, with each attack I was given a course of antibiotics, just in case there was an infection; it used to puzzle me that these never seemed to be at all effective. I can remember sitting at home for days and nights on end in severe pain, unable to relax or sleep, and at one stage I was on the point of submitting to an exploratory operation in hospital. Finally the penny dropped: the pathology lab. had never found any urinary infection, only red blood cells. Therefore if there was no build-up of pathogenic bacteria, the symptoms had to be due to something else, and I kicked myself for not thinking much earlier that it might be *Candida albicans*. Over a period of about six months of applying sound dietary and nutritional principles I made gradual improvement, and was able to relax the diet a little after that time. Since then I have had no recurrence of the symptoms, for which I am forever grateful! I only mention this episode just in case it may be relevant to what many others are suffering.

The man responsible for highlighting this modern-day scourge of candidiasis was the American specialist Dr Orion Truss, who had to be quite a detective in order to fathom out the complex story behind the epidemic. It is now thought by at least one immunologist, Alan Levin of the University of California at San Francisco, to affect one in three Americans; presumably the U.K. is not more than a few years behind. Many physicians are now investigating the possible connection between candidiasis and other even more serious conditions such as autism and AIDS, and Levin is reported[12] as saying that

Candida is an opportunistic organism, and AIDS patients develop candidiasis because their immune systems are so bad. I treated several

Stresses of a Biochemical or Medical Nature 79

patients at high risk for AIDS whose T-cell helper/suppressor ratios looked as though the patients would develop the disease. After Candida treatment, and life-style changes, the ratio normalized. So although a virus causes AIDS, I think there's a chance you might be able to reverse the onset of the disease by getting rid of the Candida early on.

This approach is also being worked on currently in the U.K., and there also seems to be a definite link between Candidiasis and myalgic encephalomyelitis (M.E.) as well; certainly all three conditions tend to respond to similar treatments involving diet, supplementation etc.

On a day-to-day basis, what can one do to help keep this yeast infection at bay? Dietary control is essential, as foods high in carbohydrates encourage it and seem to make worse any existing physical and mental problems. The birth control pill alters the body's hormonal balance and stimulates yeast growth. It is best to avoid mouldy environments and also any foods containing moulds or yeasts such as cheese or bread. But above all cut down on sugar and also refined foods which the body can turn rapidly into food for the Candida. Many clinics can provide sound practical help, and various specialized recipe books are available which provide a wide variety of alternative meal suggestions.

Hypoglycaemia

Blood sugar levels are also critical in the discussion of other common conditions. As Martin Budd says in the introduction to his book *Hypoglycaemia*[13]: 'Why is low blood sugar a common problem when many people eat far too much sugar? Why do sufferers from high blood sugar (hyperglycaemia) and low blood sugar (hypoglycaemia) have to follow similar diets when their problems seem to be opposite?'

He then remarks that 'The medical establishment insists that hypoglycaemia is an extremely rare condition and that the functional hypoglycaemia due to faulty diet is a trendy condition invented by health-food faddists. Some nutritionists and scientists claim that the hypoglycaemia is a temporary, easily-rectified imbalance; others see it as the basis of many serious diseases, a contributing factor to cancer, heart disease, diabetes, asthma and arthritis etc.'

The problem with hypoglycaemia is that the symptoms are so varied that it can be mistaken for many other conditions, and many

80   *The Last Straw*

other conditions can be mistaken for it. *Awake!* magazine says[14]: 'The victim may feel weak and may experience higher blood pressure and an increased heartbeat. He may be more nervous, apprehensive, and may break out in a sweat for no apparent reason. There may also be headaches, dizziness, numbness, a lack of co-ordination, 'thickened' speech, trembling and hunger.' But of course these symptoms can be due to other causes, and tests of blood sugar levels may suggest that this is the case.

After a meal sugar levels rise in the blood as the carbohydrates consumed are gradually converted into glucose; to counteract this, the pancreas releases insulin. Functional hypoglycaemia (as opposed to organic hypoglycaemia, which is caused by a physical abnormality, such as a tumour in the pancreas) results when the pancreas has become overly sensitive to carbohydrates and produces too much insulin, thereby lowering the level of blood sugar too far. If these conditions prevail over a long period of time, the pancreas will remain chronically stressed and gradually will produce less and less insulin until it is unable to provide enough to deal with the blood glucose, causing the condition known as *hyper*-glycaemia, in which the blood sugar level remains consistently too high; the onset of diabetes is then not far away unless checked.

So what can cause this situation to develop in the first place? *Awake!* continues 'Some persons are born with a predisposition to hypoglycaemia. A second factor is the total environment a person finds himself in, which includes the daily stress and emotional pressure that he is under. Too much stress and emotional anguish can cause a deterioration in the body's ability to withstand illness. As a reaction to this, the symptoms of hypoglycaemia can occur during periods of high or prolonged stress or emotional upset.'

Because of the nature of the condition, some people could be too quick to put a 'label' on their symptoms, and there is also the possibility that medical specialists could do likewise; but common sense dictates that we should all consider eating a diet with more of the unrefined carbohydrates, unburden ourselves of as many stressful and emotional situations as we are able, and obtain good medical advice and attention.

Nonetheless, some are finally diagnosed as diabetics. Type II diabetes (Non-Insulin Dependent Diabetes Mellitus) tends to occur more in older persons, when the pancreas just cannot make

Stresses of a Biochemical or Medical Nature   81

enough insulin. It is often controllable by diet alone, but some-times injections may be given, or pills prescribed to encourage the pancreas to produce more insulin; this can be compared to 'flog-ging a dead horse'. Nutritional supplements are a kinder and gen-tler alternative and can be extremely effective in restoring some balance to the system; in particular, chromium, zinc, and man-ganese are beneficial along with pancreatic enzymes, Vitamin E and high-quality soluble fibre such as pectin or oat fibre. Type I diabetes is less common though more serious, and the normal procedure is for insulin to be administered on a regular basis, generally by the patient himself; the techniques are rapidly becom-ing more acceptable and many such diabetics, by strictly following a prescribed diet in addition to receiving the insulin, can lead a relatively normal existence for many years.

But it is as well to remember that as even the emotions can alter blood sugar levels, it is extremely counterproductive to become unduly worried about the problem.

Cancer and AIDS

This chapter could not end without reference to cancer and AIDS, undoubtedly two of the major scourges of our century caused by defects in or a total breakdown of the immune system. It is good to see that many types of cancer can now be treated with a good chance of success, and there is no doubt that diet plays a large part. There are also encouraging signs from the U.S.A. that AIDS suf-ferers are living longer as a result of treatment based on diet and supplementations, particularly with certain trace elements; this treatment is now available in the U.K. also.

The evidence for the necessity of a correct diet is growing. As an example, Dr. T. Hirayama of the National Cancer Research In-stitute in Tokyo analysed over 100,000 cancer deaths over a sixteen year period ending in 1981, and found amongst other things that eating vegetables regularly dramatically lowered the chances of getting cancer. For example, cabbage is said to be particularly beneficial for preventing cancer of the stomach or colon.

It is also good to see signs, again in the U.S.A., that attitudes towards smoking are really changing; according to the American Cancer Society, three out of four Americans now feel that smokers should not smoke in the presence of others. And more positive

82 *The Last Straw*

health warnings are beginning to appear on cigarette packets, such as 'SURGEON GENERAL'S WARNING: Quitting Smoking Now Greatly Reduces Serious Risks to your Health.' According to the World Health Organisation, one million people were expected to die in 1986 from smoking-induced cancer.

But the battle is not over by a long way, and there will doubtless be many more cancer victims yet as people's immune systems are put under increasing pressure. There can surely be little doubt that stress is a major causative factor in many sorts of ill-health, so it is not really surprising that it has also been linked to cancer. Dr V.T. Riley, working at the Pacific North West Research Foundation in Seattle, found this from experiments with animals. He concluded: 'Stress does not cause cancer in animals, stress permits it to take place', and observed that maybe steps to reduce tension could be a means towards preventing cancer in humans. The last three chapters of this book are intended to show how a reduction of stress levels can be achieved: stress doesn't *have* to make you ill.

REFERENCES
1. *The Proceedings of the First Allergy Food Workshop*, Medical Education Services Ltd, Oxford, 1980.
2. *Food and Chemical Toxicity*, Miller, Dr. K., Vol. 21, No. 1, pp. 113–120, 1983.
3. Wheelock, Dr. V., *The Food Time Bomb, Food*, February 1989, pp. 33, 35, 37.
4. *Anaesthesia*, July 1968, pp. 395–396.
5. Personal communication.
6. *Clinical Hematology*, 1974, p. 474.
7. *Oasis,* February 1976, pp. 23–24.
8. *Jehovah's Witnesses and the Question of Blood*, Watchtower Bible and Tract Society of New York Inc., 1977.
9. *Anaesthesia*, March 1975, p. 150.
10. Crook, Dr. W.G., *The Yeast Connection*, (3rd Edition), Professional Books, Tennessee.
11. Chaitow, L., *Candida Albicans*, Thorsons, 1985.
12. *Omni*, Vol. 7, No. 6, p. 122.
13. Budd, M., *Low Blood Sugar (Hypoglycaemia)*, Thorsons, 1984.
14. *Awake!* 22 July 1978, p. 6.

Chapter 7
Chemical Stresses From the Environment

Until the last century, the progress of man did not involve great changes to the environment as far as chemicals were concerned. Then the railways were built and man began to travel faster and further than ever before, puffing out large amounts of coal by-products into the air as he went; this was an early example of chemical pollution. Also, increasing amounts of the by-products of industry, which relied almost entirely on coal for sources of power and chemicals, were produced. Chemical research became fruitful and a large number of new and useful materials became available, some of which were crude copies of natural substances, but many of which were synthesised in an attempt to 'improve' on nature. These advances in chemistry have continued at an increasing rate down on through the twentieth century, and we undoubtedly benefit in many ways from the advances made; however the long-term implications of chemical research and manufacture, and the subsequent disposal of the resulting waste products have not been considered nearly enough in the past; in recent years we have become only too familiar with the tragedy of Bhopal, acid rain, the greenhouse effect, depletion of the ozone layer, and the Chernobyl disaster, to mention just a few. The stress on the environment, and on us as individuals, is continuing to grow.

These effects were well publicised in 1989, which was in a sense the first 'green' year because of the attention that both politicians and the media rightly accorded to them. But what about other less publicised sources of chemical stress? In a special interview with Dr Theron Randolph, one of the pioneers of allergy treatment in the USA, *Awake!* magazine quoted him as saying that

After treating over 20,000 patients over a period of 30 years for various allergic reactions, I think that the chemical problem is rapidly becoming –

84 *The Last Straw*

if it is not already – the number one offender. The lead exposure from the environment and our industrialised diet is rapidly increasing. These chemical sensitivities don't hit everybody immediately, but it hurts most those who are subjected to the chemicals with any degree of persistence . . . But really, *individual susceptibility* is the crux of the problem . . . Individual susceptibility is tremendously important. One out of five persons who work with asbestos will die of lung cancer. Why not the other four? But this is true in many, many things.

As *Awake!* commented, 'The state of your health, heredity, mental outlook and stresses are all factors.'

Exposure in industry

As an example, the dangers of asbestos have received much publicity. It is thought that about 10,000 persons previously exposed to asbestos in their working environment may die each year from now until the end of the century from its effects; workers in the building and automotive industries are still particularly at risk.

Exposure limits have been set by law for many industrial chemicals, and employers in industry must by law provide adequate protective clothing, equipment and facilities, so there is little excuse for an individual to be overly exposed to any toxic chemical, whether organic, inorganic or radioactive. Those working with such chemicals will generally take a shower and make a complete change of clothes before returning home, which may help to protect the whole family. Full instructions for use are available for all chemicals with which workers are likely to come into close contact and should be followed closely as, after all, they have been designed for the benefit of the user. It should go without saying that the same principle should apply to the use of chemicals in the home environment.

Dr K. Anger of the National Institute of Occupational Safety and Health believes that nearly 20 million workers in the U.S.A. are exposed to at least one of the thirty or so workplace chemicals (other than drugs) which can affect the nervous system. Worldwide it is considered that 10% of workers are exposed to carcinogenic substances of one sort or another.

Exposure in the office

Even the office environment is not exempt from chemical

Chemical Stresses From the Environment 85

contamination. For example, many types of electrical equipment such as photocopiers can produce substantial amounts of ozone, which can be detected by its unusual odour. While ozone would be beneficial in the right place (in the upper atmosphere) it is not good for humans; the old wives' tale of ozone at the seaside being good for you refers in reality just to the distinctive smell of seaweed! The *Sunday Times* carried an article a few years ago[1] blaming tiredness at the office on copy paper. Modern carbonless copy paper is coated with chemicals and also tiny microcapsules containing yet more chemicals. When the paper is struck by a typewriter key or computer printer the capsules are crushed and release the chemicals they contain, which react with those in the coating to form permanent dyes. The *Sunday Times* went on to say that 'people working in a confined office, where automatic machines are using a great deal of paper, often have dry eyes and throats and experience abnormal tiredness. In some modern offices, the condition is aggravated by overheating and lack of ventilation, causing what Scandinavian doctors call 'indoor climate syndrome' or, more specifically, 'paper sickness'.

In recent times it has been found that certain modern office buildings which were designed to create ideal working conditions for the staff have in fact had the opposite effect, giving rise to what is now termed 'sick building syndrome', in which many workers in a specific building are known to suffer regularly from headaches, eye strain, dry eyes, sore throats, tiredness, aching limbs and other flu-like symptoms. Whereas it was initially thought, in view of recent outbreaks of legionnaires' disease, that the symptoms would likely be associated with air conditioning systems, this has proved not to be the case. From detailed surveys that have been carried out, which have covered not only air conditioning but many other aspects such as computers, office chemicals, carpeting, temperature levels, carbon dioxide levels and fluorescent lighting, tentative conclusions have now been reached as to the cause of 'sick building syndrome'; it seems that it is the total toxic load from all these sources which, when combined in a work environment over a period of time, can cause certain individuals who are particularly sensitive for one reason or another to be affected (c.f. the illustration of the barrel in Chapter 11). If the work itself is stressful for other reasons this will of course increase the chances of an individual being affected.

Lead

Other chemical contamination with long-term effects originates from metal-based compounds, such as those of lead, mercury and aluminium. Most paint is now lead-free but tetraethyl lead, used as an anti-knock additive in petrol, is a major pollutant. There is also concern about lead in the solder used in some tin cans. After lengthy campaigns in the U.K. by doctors and ecologists, and some recent financial encouragement for the public from the Chancellor of the Exchequer, we are at last seeing lead-free petrol becoming more widely available. A study in the U.S.A. revealed that the average amount of lead in the blood of U.S. residents fell by more than one third between 1976 and 1980. The *New England Journal of Medicine*, which published the study, reported: 'The most likely explanation for the fall in blood lead levels is a reduction in the lead content of gasoline during this period.' While the level of lead in U.K. petrol supplies was cut in 1986 from 0.4g/litre to 0.15g/litre, the volume of traffic has increased since then, so levels which are measured, for example, on the M25 motorway and in inner city areas have not really improved very much. How much irrevocable damage has already been done to children, adults and the environment itself is almost impossible to estimate; while adults will absorb up to 10% of the lead they consume, the corresponding figure for children, who can also absorb through inhaling, is nearer 50%.

Mercury

For over a hundred and fifty years mercury has been used widely for scientific purposes and especially in amalgams with other metals for fillings in dentistry; until recently it was thought to be quite innocuous because it was so tightly locked up in the amalgam compound. But in the 1960s this view of mercury began to change as laboratory workers and others thought to be at risk were advised to use goggles and gloves when handling the metal. Later, fears began to be voiced about its long-term safety even in amalgams, until now it is not that uncommon to hear of individuals having all their fillings replaced with one of the new compound materials. One U.S. dentist is reported as saying that the effect of mercury is such that many in his profession for over about ten years are no longer able to draw a straight line on a piece of paper.

Chemical Stresses From the Environment 87

The variety of conditions thought to be caused by mercury are of a neurological, cardiovascular and respiratory nature, but its toxicity has in fact been known for a long time, since even before Lewis Carroll's *Alice in Wonderland* was written; workers in the hat-making industry came into contact with mercury compounds during processing and it was not uncommon for the brain to be seriously affected as a result of prolonged exposure – hence 'The Mad Hatter'.

Dr K. Mumby, in his book *The Allergy Handbook*[2] says that 'sensitivity to electrical fields can be made worse by metal in the mouth' (this frequently being mercury), and quotes the American Space Agency NASA as having 'a ruling that those working in strong electric fields must not have metal in their mouths.'

Some chemists now consider that mercury is one of the most toxic substances known, so anyone with symptoms that leads them to believe that mercury could be implicated should consider a series of visits to the dentist as worthwhile. Because of the electrical properties of the amalgam it is desirable to have the fillings removed in a specific order (that of descending levels of electrical potential), so that any side effects of the treatment are minimised.

Aluminium

Aluminium, although not one of the 'heavy' metals which are commonly thought of as toxic, has also been in the news recently for several reasons. Its effects in water supplies were discussed in Chapter 4, but some of its other properties are included here. *Science News* magazine first reported in 1980 that two scientists, using scanning electron microscopy and X-ray spectrometry, had detected 'a lot of aluminium in neurones containing neurofibrillary tangles' in brains of the aged. Also minute deposits of aluminosilicate material have been found at the centres of areas of brain damage now termed 'senile plaques'. It is estimated that about half a million people in the U.K. suffer from senile dementia, two thirds of which have the characteristics of Alzheimer's Disease.

In elderly people and those with kidney failure, softening of the bones can occur as aluminium replaces calcium. It was shown in the 1970s that chronic kidney disease often showed side effects such as soft bones, anaemia and dementia; these most commonly showed up in cases where patients had been exposed to large

88 *The Last Straw*

volumes of water from dialysis treatments, and particularly when they had also been taking antacid preparations based on aluminium.

Even those at the other end of the age scale, young babies, can be adversely affected by aluminium; soya-based milk powders have recently been found to contain 100 times more aluminium than does human milk. Although some are concerned about soya itself, the natural levels found are normally very small indeed, only about ten parts per million, and it is more likely that aluminium vessels used in processing or for storage are the source.

Of course one can ingest the metal from many sources other than water, such as baking powder, antacid tablets and foil wrapping; tea also contains considerable amounts of it, and regular tea drinking is probably a major reason for one of the commonest mineral deficiencies, that of zinc, as the aluminium in the tea prevents zinc being absorbed into the system. Aluminium cookware will also contribute a small amount of the metal to one's diet; aluminium is an unusual metal in that although a dull film of the oxide quickly forms on its surface, this readily dissolves in both acids and alkalis. An inspection of aluminium saucepans can be quite revealing, a bright surface indicating attack by acids, a grey pitted surface by alkali. When fluoride has been added to the drinking water, a chemical reaction with aluminium causes a dramatic increase in uptake of the metal from cooking vessels, especially if acidic foods such as cabbage or tomatoes are being prepared.

Domestic chemicals

There are many other domestic sources of chemicals too. John Seymour and Herbert Girardet reported in their book *Blueprint for a Green Planet*[3] that each year the average family gets through enough chemical cleaners to fill a bath. Often these are toxic or pollutant, and frequently one of the main selling points for a product is its 'power'. So the relatively clean water that enters our homes may be a great deal more polluted when it leaves; as an example the use of an enzyme-active washing powder is not recommended if there is septic tank drainage on the property. When a particular automatic washing powder was introduced in the U.K. a few years ago, not only did the public complain (over 7,000 of

Chemical Stresses From the Environment 89

them) but so did many of the workers in the plant; although the product, made under more carefully controlled conditions, is still available for those who appear to be unaffected by it, the 'original' product was reintroduced and still sells side by side with the new one. Nevertheless washing powders and liquids remain one of the prime sources of chemical allergy in the home. In addition, one only has to look in the cupboard under the sink and in the garage to realize how dependent we have become on the chemical industry.

Gas

A US Environment Protection Agency Study showed that many products used without question in millions of households cause 'indoor pollution', and cited as examples plastics, foam rubber, insulation products, paints, moth crystals, deodorants, adhesives, fixers and propellants, the fumes from which can cause people to inhale higher levels of dangerous gases indoors than outdoors. A study showed that the two main causes of 'indoor pollution' were smoking and gas fires, and that many people were breathing air in their own homes of a quality which would have been illegal in a public place. In the case of gas fires, the problem frequently stems from the lack of regular servicing of appliances, resulting in the incomplete burning of the gas (methane) and the subsequent formation of some highly poisonous carbon monoxide along with the relatively harmless carbon dioxide. With the traditional 'coal gas' the smell was so obvious that it soon became apparent if there was a leak or incomplete combustion. But methane is virtually odourless, and so chemical markers are added (the main component being tertiary butyl mercaptan) so that gas leaks can be detected. To give an indication of the strength of these markers, after an accidental spillage at a site in South Dorset early in 1989 complaints of gas leaks were reported in the Isle of Wight, some 35–40 miles to the east! While most of us do not seem to be affected noticeably by methane itself, which is a very common and naturally-occurring gas in biological systems, it does seem that some are sensitive to these chemical markers, which have therefore to be considered on balance as yet one more necessary evil to be endured.

Both propane or butane gas, sold in canisters under various trade names, do not have strong odours, and do not have chemical

90   *The Last Straw*

markers added, so it is not so easy to detect a leak. But they do not appear to cause many sensitivity problems provided that adequate ventilation is available.

Smoking

The American study referred to earlier cited both gas and smoking as major sources of indoor pollution. The risks of smoking, both to those who smoke and to passive smokers, have been widely publicised and accepted by many. Dr N. Wood of Surrey University found in a study of new-born babies that those born to 'passive smokers' weighed significantly less than those born to non-smokers, in fact even less than those born to mothers who themselves smoked. Other recent research has indicated that smoking genetically alters white blood cells, and that regular smokers have a 50% greater risk of contracting leukaemia than non-smokers. Dr W.G. Cahan of the Memorial Sloan-Kettering Cancer Centre (U.S.) has concluded from his studies that smoking whilst pregnant or in the presence of young children may be 'the most pervasive form of child abuse'.

However, outspoken reactions against the smoking habit are by no means new. It was Samuel Johnson who said: 'It is a shocking thing, blowing smoke out of our mouths into other people's mouths, eyes and noses, and having the same thing done to us.' Sherridan Stock reported[4] that 'about 75% of non-smokers find it annoying to be in the presence of a cigarette smoker, while at least 50% of non-smokers say they suffer definite ill-effects from passive smoking.' He then quoted the work of Dr F. Speer of the Children's Mercy Hospital, Kansas City, which showed that even non-allergic passive smokers suffered eye irritation, nose itching, sneezing, coughing, sore throat, hoarseness and wheezing, whilst the effects were aggravated in those who knew already that they had an allergic disposition. Those with asthma, emphysema, or chronic bronchial, heart or lung disease are especially vulnerable, as is the unborn child. Stock commented that, apart from the carcinogenic chemicals such as benzpyrene and nitrosamines given off in cigarette smoke, 'a cigarette generates up to about 70 mg of carbon monoxide, some 50 mg of which is released in side-stream smoke; the concentration compares with that in vehicle exhausts.' He then quoted from the US Surgeon General's Report on Smoking and

Chemical Stresses From the Environment 91

Health, which concluded '. . . it is possible to demonstrate changes in psychomotor function (the ability to perceive and react to stimuli like light and sound) at levels of carbon monoxide found in passive smoking conditions' and made the strong comment that 'drivers who smoke may thus create risks for others'.

There is a further danger from drivers of motor vehicles who smoke, and it is not unreasonable to ask how long it will be before legislation is passed to prohibit the driver of a motor vehicle from smoking. Research reported in the Italian newspaper *La Provincia* of Cremona, showing that about five percent of all traffic accidents in Europe were from this cause, has prompted the Italian Government seriously to consider making smoking whilst driving a criminal offence. This surely is a desirable development as it cannot be considered safe for an individual to be in charge of a motor vehicle (a potentially lethal weapon) whilst holding a burning object in his hand or mouth; if the driver was to be distracted, the possible outcome in terms of loss of life and property is quite alarming.

The smoking habit is, of course, an addictive one, which is why it is so much easier to carry on than to stop; Dr Mackarness's book *A Little of What You Fancy*[5] describes the techniques he is using successfully in Australia to rehabilitate smokers and drug users, based on his own proven methods for treating allergy sufferers.

Bonfires

Turning now to smoke of another kind, what about the effects of that most common of gardening pursuits, the bonfire? And what about the big municipal incineration plants, are they not the most sensible way of disposing of the enormous amounts of rubbish our society produces, rather than it ending up on yet another tip? Sadly, nothing is that simple. The common plastic material PVC, as used in most clingfilms for example, produces when burned small amounts of one of the most feared pollutants of all, dioxin. And what about the foamed polystyrene containers used for fast food? Their incineration may well contribute to the further destruction of the ozone layer by releasing more CFCs. Many manufacturers are now taking great pains however to point out that they have ceased to use CFCs in the production of plastic packaging materials (or aerosols). All burning of chemical waste is bound to contribute in some way to acid rain and the greenhouse effect.

The Last Straw

Even if we do not add any household waste to our bonfires, they are at best unsociable, and at worst positively dangerous both to our health and that of our neighbours (c.f. passive smoking). Professor Pybus, a cancer specialist working at Durham University, found that the concentration of benzpyrene (a carcinogen of major significance) in a typical bonfire smoke could be as much as 140 times higher than in tobacco smoke. Other pollutants include carbon monoxide, organic acids, nitrogen oxides and formaldehyde, not to mention enormous amounts of carbon dioxide to contribute even further to the greenhouse effect. If we have used chemical preparations in our garden, such as wood preservatives or herbicides, then burning the resulting rubbish could release arsenic, copper or dioxins. Once we add our unwanted household rubbish too, then we liberate hydrogen chloride, complex hydrocarbons, formaldehyde, hydrogen cyanide and ammonia and Sherridan Stock[6] has coined the term *pyromania suburbium* for the pandemic of bonfire burning, and rightly points out that, although we 'might think pollution from bonfire smoke to be minimal because of rapid dilution in air, this is not necessarily so. Being a low-level pollutant it becomes trapped in the wakes of buildings. Adverse weather conditions can also prevent dispersal, particularly thermal inversions.' He claims that 'repeated exposure to bonfire smoke could predispose to lung disease in healthy persons. Smoke from any source is likely to acutely discomfort those already suffering from respiratory disorders such as asthma, bronchitis and emphysema.' The solutions are either to take garden waste to an approved tipping site, or, if you can, to use it for composting, which is one of the basics of organic gardening techniques (see Chapter 2).

Pesticides & herbicides

Many agricultural chemicals in the pesticide and herbicide class have been found to exert far longer-reaching effects on the environment than was originally thought. *Awake!* commented[6]:

> Much of the world's food is lost each year to pests. One estimate says over 40%! Thus, in 1979 alone 6.4 billion pounds (2.9 billion tonnes) of pesticides were produced – well over a pound for every person on earth! Many of these chemicals – some of which do not easily break down – cling to our vegetables or fruits or enter the food chain where they are

Chemical Stresses From the Environment 93

stored in the meat we eat. Pesticides banned in the United States because they cause birth defects and cancer in laboratory animals are still produced and sold to other countries, and the United States gets these back in many of its imported food. So virtually everyone on earth has in his body a small amount of these pollutants. Just how hazardous this is – especially in the long term – no one can say with certainty.

The dangers of using DDT were recognised several decades ago and its use is no longer allowed. Does that mean that we can afford to forget about it altogether? Regrettably not, for being fat- and not water-soluble, DDT remains in the tissues of the organism ingesting it; so insects are eaten by small birds and mammals, they in turn are eaten by larger bird and mammal predators, and so on up the food chain. Many other agricultural chemicals are also oil-soluble and resistant to degradation. Is it surprising then that in a survey in France some years ago, the level of DDT in human milk was found to.be four times that considered to be tolerable? This is because, being stored in the fatty tissues, it appears to be released only when breastfeeding or when slimming, when amounts of body fat are eliminated; could this be why some people feel so ill when trying to lose weight?

Evey a fly-repellent strip hung up in the kitchen can affect more than just flies; it may well contain organophosphorus compounds which, apart from being a lethal nerve poison to flies, can begin to affect the respiratory symptoms of susceptible humans within a matter of minutes. Even traditional mothballs contain naphthalene, a polycyclic hydrocarbon that may be carcinogenic, and the more recent replacement paradichlorobenzene, is likely to be no safer. In the garden, maybe we should all give more thought to how friendly an environment we are making for plants, insects, animals, and ultimately ourselves. For example, the weedkiller paraquat is widely used, but lung specialist Edward Block has stated: 'Paraquat is probably the most effective herbicide that exists right now on Earth. But it is also one of the world's worst poisons.' It accumulates in the lungs, making them brittle, and there is no effective antidote for those who come into intimate contact with it.

Other sources of chemical stress

When buildings are treated for woodworm and dry rot control, the

94 *The Last Straw*

chemicals commonly employed were until recently made up as solutions dissolved in an oil base, which caused the smell of the treatment to linger for many months; nowadays most treatments are provided as dispersions in water with the result that there is far less of an objectionable smell. However, considering the length of the guarantees given for the work (normally a minimum of twenty years) the chemicals must presumably to known to remain active for at least this length of time.

It is widely known that formaldehyde, potentially an extremely toxic substance, is released from the chemicals used for cavity wall insulation, but the amount can be minimised if the proportions of chemicals used are measured correctly and accurately; however it is safer to use alternative methods if at all possible. But help is at hand from the common 'Spider Plant' Chlorophytum, which was found by NASA a few years ago to have the capacity to absorb formaldehyde; it is recommended that plants are placed some 2.5 metres (7 ft 9 in) apart for maximum effect.

Even the act of insulating the roof of your home with fibreglass can make the inhabitants more vulnerable to the radioactive gas radon (see Chapter 8), which does not *just* come from the rocks around us, but also from the building materials used for your house (which themselves originated in the earth!) Unless insulated buildings are properly ventilated, it is possible for the gas to be inhaled in minute quantities into our lungs, where it decays into lead, giving off cell-damaging alpha-particles in the process.

No wonder we feel better when we have the opportunity to breathe fresh air in an unpolluted environment. But how much longer will we have the opportunity to do this without being charged for the privilege?

REFERENCES
1. *Sunday Times*, 19 December 1982.
2. Mumby, Dr K., *The Allergy Handbook*, Thorsons 1988.
3. Seymour, J., & Girardet, H., *Blueprint for a Green Planet*, Dorling-Kindersley, 1987.
4. *New Scientist*, 2 October 1980, pp. 9–13.
5. Mackarness, Dr R., *A Little of What You Fancy*, Fontana Books, 1985.
6. *Here's Health*, November 1982, pp. 108–112.
7. *Awake!*, 8 June 1983, p. 5.

Chapter 8
Electromagnetic Stresses from the Environment

Electromagnetic fields, microwaves, radioactivity, ionising and non-ionising radiation – all these terms and more are frequently used in discussions about the environment, yet until recently relatively little effort was made to establish the interaction of these sources of energy with living creatures, at least in a way that the general public could begin to understand. Despite all the undoubted benefits that the application of electricity and magnetism has brought to the human race, the evidence which is now being put forward as the result of serious research is sufficient in the view of many to identify electromagnetic stresses as possibly the most insidious known to mankind. However, it now seems as if some of these effects are not due solely to our technological advances in the twentieth century but may have a far older significance.

'Noah's flood'
If the oldest book that we possess, the Bible, is to be believed, then stress from electromagnetic radiation is not peculiar to this twentieth century, but has been having its effect on us for several thousand years. You will have to forgive me if I now take some time to explain what I mean.

Although the views of individual professors, theologians and laymen as to the authenticity of this book may differ substantially, recent palaeontological and archaeological evidence suggests that it is quite possible for Noah's Flood to have occurred just as the Bible says, with a consequent dramatic change in the earth's climate and exposure to radiation. Also many national groups have tales of folk-history passed down through the generations which all talk of floods and survivors, indicating the likelihood of a common history for early man. Interestingly, there have been claims put forward from

96 *The Last Straw*

archaeologists in recent years that the remains of the Ark itself have been identified some 15,000 feet up on Mount Ararat, and that samples of wood have been retrieved and dated as genuine in laboratory tests. It is perhaps unfortunate for the archaeologists that the area is virtually inaccessible at present as this mountain range is in eastern Turkey, near to the borders with Iran and the U.S.S.R., and thus in an area of severe political instability.

'Noah's Flood' has intrigued researchers for a long time. What has puzzled many scientists is why so many carcasses and skeletons of dead animals not normally found in the same areas should be found piled together in huge dumps and caves. The *Sunday Evening Post* reported[1]:

> Many of these animals were perfectly fresh, whole and undamaged, and still either standing or at least kneeling upright. . . . Here is a really shocking – to our previous way of thinking – picture. Vast herds of enormous well-fed beasts not specifically designed for extreme cold, placidly feeding in sunny pastures. . . . Suddenly they were all killed without any visible sign of violence and before they could so much as swallow a last mouthful of food, and then were quick-frozen so rapidly that every cell of their bodies is perfectly preserved.

And why should a mammoth be found in Siberia with vegetation still in its mouth and stomach and with flesh well-preserved enough still to be edible? With further evidence such as the remains of palm trees and other tropical vegetation being found in what we today call the polar regions, does this not indicate that at one time the earth must have had a climate very different from what we know today, with equable conditions spread over the entire surface of the planet?

Supposing then that a world-wide flood did in fact occur some thousands of years ago; it would have caused extremely rapid and dramatic changes to the climate of our planet. As to where all the water could have come from, it is perhaps relevant that both scientific and Biblical evidence indicates that there used to be a thick band of hot water vapour, the 'thermosphere', at a high altitude surrounding the earth, and that it could have been this that collapsed onto the earth. The climate would have been suddenly cooled, resulting in the tragedies to man and animal life that are so well documented. Incidentally, it may be significant that the history of

Electromagnetic Stresses from the Environment 97

astronomical observations goes back only to about 2000 B.C., so with the thermosphere in place the sun, moon and stars may not have been as readily visible as they are today.

But there would have been other unseen yet significant changes in levels of radiation from the sun which would also have occurred simultaneously. After all, one of the functions of this 'thermosphere' would have been the protection of life on earth from the potentially harmful portion of the sun's rays reaching the earth's surface. Once this protection had gone there would have been a sudden increase in the numbers and varieties of emissions from the sun reaching the earth, with far-reaching results for the future, particularly with regard to the longevity of man. Interestingly, the Bible record reveals a sudden decrease in average life-span; e.g. Noah lived to 950 but Moses only to 120.

Physicist R. Brown of Andrews University claimed in 1976 that the radiocarbon dating method for archaeological specimens was highly inaccurate; after a ten year study, he concluded that there was virtually no radioactive carbon in the atmosphere before about 2000 B.C. and that objects from before that time could not be accurately dated. Later the same year two scientists, Dr R. Burleigh and Dr A. Hewson, working at the British Museum's Research Laboratory discovered when investigating the accuracy of radiocarbon dating that the method could be seriously in error. As *The Times* for 9 July that year stated[2]:

> The method . . . depends on the assumption that the amount of radio-carbon (carbon-14) in atmospheric carbon dioxide has been constant (or only slowly varying) for several thousand years. Dr R. Burleigh and Dr A. Hewson . . . have evidence that *rapid changes over a period of only a few years or less occurred several thousand years ago* [my italics]. The amount of radio-carbon in the atmosphere must have altered extremely rapidly . . . perhaps because some sudden increase or reduction in the flow of charged particles, such as protons from the sun, caused an equivalent change in the amount of atmospheric carbon-14. (Carbon-14 is formed when cosmic ray particles, among them those from the sun, interact with atoms in the atmosphere).

More evidence to support the Biblical flood?

Geopathic stress

However it is not only the hazards of electromagnetic radiation

98 *The Last Straw*

from the sun that can affect us; there are many sources of radiation that emanate naturally from the earth itself. The United States Department of Health has evidence that there are relationships between the incidence of cancer worldwide and localized variations in the intensity of the earth's magnetic field. While there is as yet no scientific proof that these disturbances are actually the main cause of various types of cancer as well as other degenerative conditions such as arthritis and multiple sclerosis, it has been shown in Germany[3] that the incidence of these conditions is often confined to a particular geographical area. But even if not the prime cause, it is perhaps reasonable to suspect that these variations constitute an additional stress on our already overstressed bodies, so that if we are predisposed to such a condition it will be more likely to develop.

In Germany after the last war it was noticed that there were concentrations of cancer victims in certain areas, and it was subsequently found that these cases corresponded to areas of land under which were flowing rivers or streams, causing what has been termed, for want of a better name, 'water stress'. This can best be explained as follows: it is a principle of physics that a moving fluid containing dissolved electrolyte will produce an electromagnetic field. So while pure water is a very poor conductor of electricity, an added pinch of salt stirred in and dissolved will greatly increase the conductivity, an experiment that many young science students will be familiar with. Underground streams and rivers frequently contain large quantities of dissolved minerals originating in the rocks through which the water has percolated, so the water becomes a conductor of electricity, and as it moves it sets up electromagnetic fields which interfere with the natural field of the earth in that particular vicinity. In Germany great care is taken to this day in determining the suitability or otherwise of new sites for houses, and many people are aware of the existence and importance of what they term 'water arteries'. In China, where these and other similar effects have been known for many centuries, even greater precautions are taken to ensure that a house is built on a stress-free and hence healthy site. Short-term remedies for coping with water stress will be mentioned in Chapter 9, but living with it longer-term is not to be recommended.

There are also other types of naturally induced stress factors;

Electromagnetic Stresses from the Environment 99

while 'water stress' causes what is known as a discharging field, a geological fault or 'ley line' will cause a charging field, which has entirely different effects on the sensitive human body. These discharging and charging fields appear to correspond in general terms with what the Chinese call 'yin' and 'yang'. Such naturally occurring stresses are generally referred to as geopathic, and the term 'geopathic stress' has been defined by Scott-Morley[4] as 'a geomagnetic disturbance which is geographically localised and which disrupts the homoeostatic mechanisms of the sensitive patient.' It is considered by some experts that prolonged exposure to discharging fields may eventually result in degenerative symptoms such as lethargy, depression and cancer, whereas those exposed to charging fields could develop hyperactivity, hypertension and heart disease.

Natural radioactivity

Yet another commonly occurring stress factor is the natural radioactivity from rocks, granite being the example usually cited, although many other minerals are radioactive. Apart from the radioactivity itself, which comprises largely alpha particles (the nuclei of helium atoms), the gas radon is a product of this spontaneously occurring radioactive decay cycle, and much concern has been voiced in recent years over the concentration of radon which may become trapped in modern draught-proof houses built in such areas. It is also believed that certain deposits such as oil can behave similarly. A 1989 report indicated that homes in some areas such as Gloucestershire and Somerset may have higher concentrations of radon than is considered safe (in Somerset up to six times higher than the national average). Also granite areas such as Devon and Cornwall may be affected. However this does not mean that these areas should be considered as unsafe to live in, just that houses in such areas should be built with or provided with effective means for ventilation (which is best for your health anyway for lots of other reasons).

Smoke alarms

Radioactivity has long been used in industry and even in small ways for domestic purposes, such as luminous watch faces, but in recent years a prominent use has been in smoke alarms, which

100 *The Last Straw*

have been widely advertised as making your home a safer place to be in, due to the audible warning that is emitted by the device if it should detect smoke. Despite the fact that there is nothing printed either on the product leaflet or on the box to the effect that this device contains radioactive material, it does in fact do so; it is only when it has been purchased and opened up for the battery to be connected that the compartment with a 'radioactive hazard' label on it will be found, indicating that it contains the isotope Americium 241. Although various scientific papers have been written in the U.S.A. purporting to show the safety in use of this material because of its low activity (0.9 microcuries), it is quite possible for sensitive persons to be affected as I myself can attest. If you are wondering if you may be sensitive to this type of radiation, try standing in a shop in front of a display of these smoke alarms and wait a few minutes before assessing how you feel. Although smoke alarms do have undoubted uses in promoting safety in the home, in caravans and at work, there is in general so much concern about radioactivity that it is less than honest not to warn the general public fully about the nature of what they are buying. At one stage a bill was introduced in the United States Congress that would prohibit the sale of smoke detectors containing Americium 241; evidence was put forward that they could cause physical harm, including cancer, and that, if damaged, radioactive leakage would be possible. However the products are still on sale everywhere.

Power lines

An extremely controversial subject in the context of electromagnetic stress is the development of the electrical power supply industry during the past century, and the effects that artificially-induced electromagnetic fields are purported to exert. Electricity is always promoted as a 'clean' source of energy, but in view of the accumulating evidence many are now querying the 'cleanness' aspect and are beginning to refer to the polluting effect of electromagnetic radiation as 'electric smog'. *Awake!* recently carried an article on this subject[5], in which it stated:

Numerous studies have shown that growth rates of rats and mice have been affected by these electromagnetic fields. In one study, under high-voltage transmission lines, bees had problems in honey production,

Electromagnetic Stresses from the Environment   101

became aggressive and had a very low survival rate in winter. In some cases they even sealed off their hives. It has been demonstrated that artificial electromagnetic fields can interfere with the way our internal clocks are synchronised. Consequently, our normal biological rhythms tend to adapt to the artificial pulse of electric smog rather than the natural magnetic field of the earth. The result is stress on the human body, bringing with it a breakdown of our general resistance to various diseases.

Naturally, the most significant electromagnetic disturbances emanate from the places where power is generated and from the systems used to transmit this power to where it is needed. In practice not many people live right by a power station, although there may well be a transformer substation not far away from your home, or a transformer on a pole if you live in a rural area; but there are thousands of people (thought to be about 70,000 in the U.K. alone) who have overhead high-voltage power lines nearby, and the continuing practice of building new property immediately in the vicinity of (or in some cases directly underneath) power lines has come in for some sharp criticism recently. The predictable reaction of the authorities is that there is no proven harm in it, yet many countries such as the USA and Sweden have banned the practice. What no member of the public can know is whether there are any *underground* high voltage lines in the immediate locality. It is becoming a more common practice in the USA to bury the lines for aesthetic reasons as much as anything, but they can still be harmful. One British G.P. has reported in a television interview that after obtaining details from the local Electricity Board of the routes taken by underground cables he has been able to correlate their paths with groupings of patients developing cancer.

Simon Best, in an article in the *Guardian*[6], reported on his visit to a village in Dorset where the local people have claimed for many years that the power lines running through their village have been making them ill, causing a wide range of symptoms such as epilepsy, depression, headaches etc. In an interview with Dr Jean Munro (who with Dr Ray Choy and Dr Cyril Smith of Salford University has been pioneering research in this field) she is reported as saying: 'I know it sounds amazing, and it is. The effects (of exposure to strong electromagnetic fields) are so swift that the basic bodily response must be an electrical reaction.' (Although

102 *The Last Straw*

she was referring at this point to the reactions of a volunteer to being exposed in this way, many researchers have come to the conclusion that an electrical reaction could be at the basis of many reactions that would normally be classified as 'allergic'.)

An article in the *Lancet*[7], after acknowledging that leukaemia and cataracts might be occupational hazards of working on high voltage power lines carrying 550,000–750,000 volts, reported that

> as the culmination of more than four years of drafting, redrafting and discussion a World Health Organisation/International Radiological Protection Association working group has now reviewed, as part of the United Nations Environment Programme, the impact on man of extremely low frequency fields. The emphasis is on 50 or 60 Hz alternating currents in overhead cables and on electric fields, though domestic mains have the same frequency and electric fields engender magnetic ones . . .

National standards vary but most countries do recognise the need for caution when the transmission of electricity generates electric fields above 10Kv per centimetre. Such fields may be experienced within the corridors of high-voltage lines but 1000 metres (well over half a mile) away exposure will be back to natural background (around 0.1 millivolts per centimetre). It is now a matter of waiting to see if any recommendations are implemented, but it could be a long time. Those seriously concerned about this subject could do no better than to obtain the book *Electromagnetic Man* by Cyril Smith and Simon Best[8]: although very technical in parts, it would appear to be the most comprehensive work ever produced on this subject.

Microwaves and radar

Cynthia Kee, in an article in the *Observer*[9], quoted Dr Munro as saying that 'electromagnetic waves can alter people's minds.' She then continued to discuss the case of the American Embassy in Moscow, which had been bombarded by the Russians with microwave energy for nearly thirty years after President Nixon's visit in 1959. Eventually, two out of four ambassadors died of cancer and a third developed a rare blood disease. The deliberate exposing of unsuspecting subjects to radiation is known in the USA as 'zapping', and for a detailed discussion of this ominous subject

Electromagnetic Stresses from the Environment 103

recommended reading must include *The Zapping of America* by Paul Brodeur[10]. However 'zapping' is by no means confined to America: Ms Kee reported that women in the Greenham Common peace camp have claimed that they were being 'zapped' since 1984. She says:

> Greenham women are inured to conditions of physical and mental hardship. But the effects of zapping are so different and disturbing that they find them intolerable. Women who have been exposed to it describe stepping in and out of specific areas at specific times where they feel sensations of terror, sickness, disorientation, inability to move or think. The mental feelings are accompanied or followed by such symptoms as severe headaches, bleeding from gums and nose, palpitations, menstrual irregularities – including bleeding in post menopausal women, winter and night-time sunburn, acute sensitivity to fluorescent lighting and radio noise.

Dr M.M. Zaret of New York University has said: 'Some population groupings . . . appear to have been placed in jeopardy' (by zapping). He then referred to an area in Finland close to the Russian border, where there is a high-powered microwave radar early-warning system against possible intercontinental missile attack. Apparently the death rate from sudden heart attack in this area is among the highest in the world, and cancer rates are significantly higher than would be expected. Bob DeMatteo, in his book concerning the safety of computer installations[11], reports the results of research by Dr M. Swicord, a researcher with the American Food and Drugs Administration, who discovered that

> DNA (deoxyribonucleic acid) absorbed 400 times more microwave energy than the surrounding salt solutions, thus demonstrating for the first time a direct interaction of DNA with microwave radiation. In effect, microwaves cause the double-stranded DNA to vibrate like the strings on a violin. Such vibrations can cause transformations in the DNA which could have potential genetic effects.

So it is not surprising that the microwaves used in radar installations cause some concern in medical circles. Dr F.G. Sulman of Hadassah University Medical Centre in Jerusalem has concluded: 'We must now accept the fact that radar is detrimental to the human body. The following organs seem to be specially sensitive: the central nervous system, the endocrine system including the

104   *The Last Straw*

gonads (the reproductive organs), the blood system, the eye, the ear and the genes.'

Radar has for a long time been a very controversial subject. Some 25 years ago, the US researcher Allan Frey noted that people in the immediate vicinity of radar beams could actually hear the radar. This claim seemed unlikely and was challenged as it could not be explained adequately by current scientific theories. The human ear is designed to detect mechanical energy (sound waves consist of moving particles of air) in the range of 20–16,000 Hz (1 Hz = 1 cycle per second), but here were people who were claiming to hear electromagnetic energy in the gigahertz range (1 gigahertz = 10^9 cycles per second). But as Gordon Atherley reported in 1983 in a paper presented to the British Columbian Federation of Labour[12], an explanation was not long in coming. He says:

> The part of the ear in which the sensitive cells reside consists of three compartments each full of fluid, where the fluids differ in chemical composition. And the differences in chemical composition make them into batteries . . . which produce (small) voltage differences between the compartments. . . . This voltage difference creates something like a transistor which acts an electrical detector capable of turning radar beams into a signal which the ear cells could respond to . . . the process is rectification. . . . What is important . . . is the evidence which it gives us that microwaves produce effects on living cells other than the heating effect.

Incidentally, this heating effect of microwave radiation was first noticed during the last war, when birds that had been flying close to radar stations were later found dead on the ground, partially cooked; but these other effects are a lot more subtle.

Further research in Canada compared the effects on animals of both continuous and pulsed emissions. It was found that pulsed emissions (such as microwaves) were the more biologically active, and that under some circumstances could induce electrical voltages across cell walls which were enough, not just to stimulate chemical activity in the cell, but to prick a hole in the cell wall, inducing the contents to leak. No one knows at present whether human cells can be affected in this way, or if they are, what the effects might be. And one of the more alarming facets of this subject as studied in the West is that results are played down as being insignificant, or

Electromagnetic Stresses from the Environment 105

even irrelevant; Bob DeMatteo's book *Terminal Shock*[11] gives the facts as they are known and understood as present. Eastern Bloc countries set exposure limits many times lower and seem to consider the safety of their workers as more important than the making of money – perhaps we have more to learn in the west than we realize.

Rosalie Bertell summed it all up very succinctly by stating in the foreword to the above book: 'Unfortunately, technologically-induced illnesses are denied in the late 20th century with the same vehement resistance which met the theories of invisible germs and viruses in earlier decades . . . Health effects are almost always discovered by workers or the general public and not by the experts.'

Two examples may here be mentioned to make the point that none of us are immune from these problems, the first one being a personal experience. I remember that on one occasion I had to cut short a caravanning weekend in North Devon because the emissions from the airways radar station sited close by began to affect me, particularly by giving me an unpleasant headache and a tightness in the chest. In the early 1980s, when the BBC proposed to erect a powerful transmitting station on a partially disused airfield in Somerset, there was great concern amongst those living in the area when the likely effects of the station were outlined by a local resident, whose work for a government department happened to make him well qualified professionally to speak out on behalf of his neighbours. He showed that in an area measuring about four miles by eight with the airfield at its centre, there would be severe effects with blocking of radios, audio and digital equipment becoming virtually unusable, deaf aids and TV reception seriously impaired. It was also considered that chronic effects would be felt up to twenty or more miles away. A BBC spokesman confirmed at the time that the Corporation had no liability for interference testing or its cure, nor did it or the Post Office have any responsibility for the cost of any remedial work where this would be feasible; under the legislation in force all such costs would fall on the owner of the equipment suffering from interference. Note that the concern was for the most part for electrical equipment, and not people; there can be no doubt in view of what has been discussed earlier that, had the project gone ahead, the health of over 100,000 people would have been put at risk.

Microwave ovens

Microwave ovens were introduced into the U.K. particularly for catering use about twenty five years ago, but it was only in the mid-seventies that domestic microwave ovens became more commonplace; they have now become almost as ubiquitous as the fridge-freezer and the television. It should be mentioned here that although the microwave oven works on a similar principle to radar, the wavelengths utilised are very different; whereas radar transmitters operate on frequencies of 10 gigahertz, microwave ovens operate on about 2.5 gigahertz. Microwave ovens should be treated with caution at all times, as despite the care manufacturers take to check the ovens for microwave leakage, it is possible that leakage could begin to occur after a while, especially if the door seal becomes faulty due to mishandling. For peace of mind it is best to have your oven checked annually (local Councils will possibly do this for you at a nominal charge). U.K. legislation permits a leakage of up to 5 mW/sq. cm. when measured 5 cm from the oven surface, but this would very quickly be noticed in practice by anyone standing close by.

Microwaves must not be confused with X-rays, a form of ionising radiation which strips electrons off atoms and hence produces positively charged ions that can harm tissue. Microwaves do not possess that much energy, but because they have a wavelength of about 12 cm at a very high frequency, they are the most powerful type of non-ionising radiation. The most obvious and useful property of microwaves is the heating effect; food cooks very rapidly as the energy input causes molecules, especially those of water, to vibrate more rapidly, thus generating frictional heat.

Despite the very low levels of leakage to be expected, the effects of microwave ovens have been measured at substantial distances away from the source; a scientist from Jodrell Bank recently said in a television interview that about ten years ago they noticed a lot of interference with their radio telescopes at the Observatory, and this was finally traced (and checked with appropriate equipment) to domestic microwave ovens at anything up to about five miles distant. Although the amount of power leaked was in theory infinitesimally small (about a millionth of a millionth of a watt) nevertheless it was transmitted over this distance and its effects could be

Electromagnetic Stresses from the Environment 107

disastrous to sensitive research projects; such is the potential hazard of microwave radiation. On a more localized scale, it has been known for microwave leakages from an oven to 'wipe' all the information stored on computer discs.

I well remember my first encounter with microwave ovens. In 1978, when they were still relatively novel, I was working for a food manufacturing company and was lent one for product development studies; one weekend I borrowed it to see how it performed in our kitchen at home. However within a short time of leaving it in the kitchen my wife asked me to remove it as it was 'making her head feel funny'. At the time this seemed a ludicrous and pointless suggestion as it was not even switched on, but being a dutiful husband I complied with her request, and the feeling in her head gradually subsided. Some years later this phenomenon has now been recognised as a possibility in scientific terms, for two possible reasons.

Firstly, the device called a magnetron, which produces the microwaves when the power is switched on, depends for its effective operation on its own intrinsic magnetic field; its permanent magnets emit a strong magnetic field even when the appliance is standing idle, and this can affect individuals sensitive to such fields. Secondly, humans emit brain waves (see Chapter 11), and Dr Cyril Smith of Salford University explains[13] that 'sensitive persons may have their reactions triggered by the proximity of an electromagnetic resonator (magnetron); this must mean that the electrical energy is self-generated.' So the strange sensations noticed were perhaps not that ludicrous after all! I also had contact with another lady who had recently purchased a new microwave oven, but it had made her head feel very 'strange'. She concluded that it was so pointless having an oven that had to be kept out in the garage well out of the way that she decided to take the matter up with the retailers; although at first they were reluctant to take any action as they had never heard of a case like it, they eventually agreed to take it back and replace it with another make, which proved less troublesome. So while these ovens may be extremely convenient, they are not necessarily good for your health. This is particularly relevant advice as in 1989 an estimated 38% of homes in the U.K. had a microwave oven, with the figure expected to jump to 50% by 1992 (the corresponding figures in the USA are 65% and 100%). A

108 *The Last Straw*

textbook on microwave servicing[14] warns engineers that their watches could be affected, and that if they wear pacemakers they should seek medical advice before servicing such ovens. So caution both when purchasing and using one of these ovens is desirable.

There was a further scare in 1989 when it was widely reported by the media that the Ministry of Agriculture, Fisheries and Food had had tests done to establish the effectiveness of microwave ovens in cooking food to a temperature high enough to destroy all harmful bacteria; apparently the tests indicated that this was not in fact happening, resulting in further doubts about the safety in use of these ovens. However it now seems as if many of the tests may have been invalid as apparently the manufacturers' instructions were not followed closely enough; I am reliably informed that, instead of a third of the ovens tested being inadequate as was widely reported, in fact only one oven should have been classified as such.

Domestic electrical equipment

Other effects worth considering in some detail may be caused by the wide range of equipment with which we tend to fill our high-tech homes and offices; this all depends for its operation upon AC current (50 Hz in the UK) although the voltage (normally at 240v.) is fairly low. Whereas even the most elementary bar fire or even a simple light bulb works only when a current flows in a loop of wire (therefore producing an electromagnetic field), most available evidence indicates that concern about the effects on health of these relatively simple types of device would be largely unjustified. However I have known individuals who are affected by the fields from power sockets and light switches.

Nevertheless, even minute electromagnetic fields can disturb other equipment. If you are installing a telephone extension, for example, you will notice that the instructions are very explicit; telephone sockets should always be at least two inches away from mains electrical cabling. Why should this be necessary? Because of possible interference to the telephone signal from the electrical mains. In practice such interference can be detected using a simple field strength meter, a very useful device to own if you are concerned about levels of electromagnetic radiation in your home.

However, the introduction of the silicon chip revolutionised the

Electromagnetic Stresses from the Environment 109

thinking on ways of utilising electricity and now there seems to be no end to the inventions that are offered to industry and public alike which will help us at work, at home or at play. Following is a list, at best a partial one, of different types of powerful electrical equipment that we have either at work or in our homes: computer with visual display terminal, radiotelephone, photocopier, fax machine, electronic till, print-out calculator, word processor, electronic typewriter, microwave oven, hi-fi, television, CD player, electronic keyboard, ultraviolet sunlamp, electric blanket, night storage heater, bell transformer, washing machine, tumble drier, vacuum cleaner, food processor, fan heater, hair drier, fluorescent light, and so on.

While it would not be practical (or indeed desirable) for everyone to renounce the twentieth century completely and return to living in the wild, there is a good enough reason to be cautious with certain appliances if there is enough evidence that this would be prudent; it is better to know rather than remain ignorant. Out of all the common appliances, ultraviolet sunlamps have been cited as possibly having the most injurious effects of all, although hair driers and electric blankets have been singled out too; with a hair drier the user is so much nearer to the motor than with other appliances that its effect must be proportionately greater than that of, say, a fan heater. The type of electric underblanket that is switched off before you get into bed should be harmless enough (even though there are those who are concerned about the bedsprings taking up a permanent magnetic field), but if you have an overblanket that is left switched on all night then this is a different matter altogether. You will be lying for approximately one third of your life-span in an unnatural electromagnetic field caused as the current flows round the loops of wire; as mentioned earlier, small fields of this sort can disturb the body's sensitive time-clock mechanism, so if you have one of these blankets and find that you do not sleep very well, or wake up tired, then maybe you should at least consider that the blanket may be the cause. It is advisable to try sleeping without it for a week or two and see if any improvement is felt. Incidentally, some people seem to sleep better with the head towards the north, so a disturbed sleep pattern can sometimes be improved if the position of the bed is changed, always supposing that there is room to do so.

110 *The Last Straw*

Although there are a number of internationally recognised standards to which electrical appliances must be built, some manufacturers take extra safety precautions, and you will generally find that, even if you are very electrically sensitive, that you will be able to find at least one make of appliance that will suit you. The problem appears to be fairly straightforward in principle, one of adequately screening and earthing all those components which produce electromagnetic emissions, although when this is done by the manufacturer, the reason is generally to eliminate interference with other components of the equipment rather than for any altruistic motive.

A few years ago, when I needed to acquire a photocopier for my business, I arranged for several demonstrations; on one occasion I can remember the salesman asking me if I was all right as I looked so pale, and my telling him to switch the machine off immediately because I felt so ill! At the same time my secretary came out of her office complaining that she had suddenly developed a splitting headache. Needless to say, I did not purchase that particular make of copier. An electronic till gave one of the staff palpitations when first installed, but after the entire inside of the casing was lined with aluminium foil and then earthed, we had no further trouble.

Another source of an unnatural electromagnetic field in the home is a particular sort of damp-proof course of the electro-osmotic type. The principle by which it purports to work is that a wire is laid all round the house just above ground level with electrodes positioned at intervals in the walls, and then a current is made to flow continually around this wire, producing an electro-osmotic effect which inhibits any moisture in the walls from rising above the level of the wire. As the current is minimal and at a voltage of only about 12–15 volts, one would not expect any noticeable effects on the inhabitants, but circumstantial evidence that I have experienced indicates that there could be a longer-term effect on the immune system. I am convinced that living for a large part of one's life in an environment modified by a small but unnatural electromagnetic field can contribute towards the eventual development of a faulty immune system, with poor health and a resulting hypersensitivity to foods, chemicals and electrical equipment. However, this would be almost impossible to prove conclusively.

Computers

A piece of equipment to be found in almost every home and office is the computer. There has been much publicity about computers concerning the possibility that both ionising and non-ionising emissions from them can be harmful, especially to the pregnant mother but also to the eyes of any operator. Ionising emissions comprise cathode rays which are not thought to penetrate very much further than the screen, although it is a good idea to fix a mesh screen (that must then be earthed) to the front of the monitor. Despite a 1988 U.S. study which linked the usage of VDUs with birth defects and miscarriages, the U.K. Health and Safety Executive, in its pamphlet 'Working with VDUs' has dismissed this claim.

There are several different types of non-ionising emissions that emanate from a computer, as can be easily demonstrated in a qualitative way by the use of a simple portable radio. You will probably be aware already that radio reception can be affected by all manner of things, such as the switching on or off of a household appliance. So switch the radio on to Medium Wave or Long Wave, but in such a manner that it is not actually tuned to a specific station (i.e. just a hiss, or 'white noise' will be heard). This can now be used as a simple detector of emissions of various kinds coming from VDUs or indeed any sort of electrical appliance. Just switch on the appliance you want to test, say a computer, TV set or electronic keyboard, and move the radio gradually around the appliance. You will find anything from slight to severe interference of different characteristics. It is said that a rod antenna will pick up the electrical component of the emissions whilst a ferrite rod will respond to the magnetic component. It is not uncommon for a home computer, even if screened, to produce enough interference on long wave to be very obvious some fifteen to twenty yards away i.e. right through a house of average dimensions. In contrast, it is unusual for a television set to do this more than two to three yards away, although early models of colour TV sets were particularly bad in this respect. These are physical effects which can be detected by a field strength meter, and one is bound to raise the question of whether these emissions can affect human beings in some way; while regular VDU operators can experience a number of symptoms which are often attributed purely to sitting posture,

112 *The Last Straw*

chest pains and headaches are frequently an effect of non-ionising emissions. As such emissions are detected mainly to the front and sides of a monitor, it would be courteous to position the computer screen so that it faces *away* from any hypersensitive person who is in the immediate work area.

However there are various aids to reducing computer emissions which have been claimed to be effective. The electrostatic field from a computer monitor results from the discharge from the cathode ray tube; a screen typically builds up a positive electrostatic charge, attracting negative ions from the operator, and the positive ions in the intervening air space are repelled away from the screen onto the operator.

Ioniser: an Ioniser, which generates large amounts of negative ions (generally considered as possessing invigorating properties), will neutralise the excess positive charge and some people find them very beneficial.

Filter Screen: this was mentioned briefly in an earlier paragraph, and will be found to be very effective in reducing ionising emissions. The screen comprises a fine wire mesh in a frame, to which is connected an earthing lead; the frame is attached to the front of the monitor using self-adhesive Velcro. The mesh traps the radiation, and then the earthing wire takes away the resulting electrical charge to the earth pin of the mains supply via a special plug.

Quartz: a decent-sized lump of crystal quartz, (of at least the size that will fill the palm of your hand), will absorb radio frequency emissions provided that it is placed in front of the VDU screen (not necessarily a practical solution!); this is not really as strange an idea as it might at first seem as natural quartz possesses a number of useful piezo-electrical properties which make it invaluable in watches, computers, etcetera; also those of us old enough to remember the 'cat's whisker' radio will acknowledge that a quartz crystal was used to pick up the transmission signal.

Shielding with Aluminium Foil: shielding the casing of the computer with aluminium foil has also been known to improve matters, as it will absorb non-ionising radiation from the sides and back of the computer (however it will not affect the magnetic component of the emissions). A simple way of reducing emissions is to obtain a cardboard box large enough to house the VDU and line that with foil (both inside and out if you wish), ensuring that

Electromagnetic Stresses from the Environment 113

this is then well earthed. The computer can then be slipped into the box, but remember to leave a gap all round of at least two inches (5 cm.) so that there is enough air circulation for the effective cooling of the unit while it is operating. If you have any doubts on carrying out any of these suggestions, it is recommended not to attempt them yourself but to call in a qualified electrician.

'*Cereus Peruvianus*': even plant life has been found to have beneficial effects: the cactus Cereus peruvianus, which was originally discovered on the high mountains in Mexico, is claimed to noticeably improve working conditions in an office containing a computer by absorbing emissions, thus reducing the background levels of artificial radiation to more normal levels. It has been suggested that the fearsome spines of the cactus act as antennae and thus absorb the radiation. Apparently employees at a New York stockbroker's office have been trying out this technique and are pleased with the results. While these cacti are not easy to obtain, there are a few specialist suppliers, including the one mentioned in the Names and Addresses section at the back of the book.

Measuring emissions

There are several instruments on the market which have been specifically developed for measuring non-ionising emissions, and which give an indication of the electrical component (in Volts per metre) and the magnetic component (in nanoTessla) separately. Dr Cyril Smith warns[15]:

> The level of leakage from electrical equipment is a matter for technical as well as environmental concern . . . Apparatus is being developed . . . to measure the spatial distributions of environmental electric and magnetic fields over a range of precisely determined frequencies . . . The theoretical threshold for possible magnetic field effects in man is of the order of 20 nanoTessla (nT). Thus . . . up to distances of the order of a metre from a television there are frequencies which can trigger (and neutralise) allergic responses and signal levels adequate to exceed the triggering threshold.

In general terms computers emit greater signals than television sets but the warning is clear: do not let a child sit immediately in front of the TV screen, and do not sit nearer to the monitor than

114 *The Last Straw*

the distance recommended by the manufacturer, usually about 2 ft (60 cm).

One of the main difficulties with assessing the biological effects of electrical appliances is this: emissions are generally measured with a meter of the type mentioned above, but of course a meter will only measure that which it has been designed to measure. This implies that the meter designer must have had sufficient knowledge about the nature of the effect he was going to try to measure to enable him to produce the meter in the first place! Now emissions of biological significance are not necessarily those which are normally measured in universally recognised scientific units, so this means that in practice the use of a field strength meter may not identify appliances that are potentially harmful to the bioelectrical system of the user. The only method known at present is somewhat subjective, yet it works well enough, and that is kinesiology, which is discussed in detail in Chapter 10. Hopefully before long someone will identify the biologically significant emissions in scientific terms, and then make an instrument to measure them; that will really be a breakthrough.

What of the future?

One of the most famous figures to research the effects of electromagnetism on living creatures is José Delgado. An article in the magazine *Omni*[16] described his work and its implications for us all. We cannot see electromagnetic fields from TV transmitters, power lines etc. because our eyes are designed to pick up only frequencies in the range of 375–775 ångstroms or so. It has been said that if our eyes were more sensitive, astronauts could see the earth shimmering around its perimeter, with the brightest glow at the magnetic poles. Delgado uses tiny fields of as little as one fiftieth the strength of the earth's field; yet if the signal is tuned to a precise frequency with a long wavelength in roughly the same range as power-line waves, the effects on laboratory monkeys were very obvious. Delgado has said: 'All the cells that make up living organisms are packed full of highly charged atoms and molecules that may change their orientation and movement in the presence of certain types of fields. This might in turn have an impact on innumerable chemical processes within the cells.'

Even the earth's magnetic field can play an important role in the

Electromagnetic Stresses from the Environment 115

functioning of living organisms, and research in recent times has shown that many species, including bacteria, salamanders, bees, pigeons, whales and tuna all depend, unknowingly, on field patterns for direction-finding and migration. The West German scientist Peter Semm has shown that the brain's pineal gland, responsible for controlling biological rhythms, is sensitive to magnetic fields of similar strength to that of the earth. In the earlier manned space flights the lack of a normal geomagnetic background was found to disturb the bodily equilibria of the astronauts, and later flights had low-level magnetic generators built in to compensate for this.

But down on earth we continue to make electromagnetic changes to our environment whose ultimate effects are unknown. As an example, the electromagnetic properties of our immediate environment, wherever we are on the surface of the planet, have been altered dramatically since the discovery of radio by the multitude of broadcasting channels. Wherever we go we cannot escape, as the radio will confirm when we switch it on. It seems as if every segment of the wavelength range has been commandeered by some organisation or another, if not by the broadcasting and TV channels, then by the police, aircraft, CB, and so on. And now we are to have yet more satellite television. No wonder that Dr R.O. Becker, formerly of the Veterans Administration Hospital in Syracuse, New York, who has spent much of his working life evaluating the effects of electromagnetic treatments for improving the rates of healing after certain types of accidents and operations, is quoted as saying[17]:

> It should be obvious by now that abnormal fields cause acute physiological stress, a major predisposing factor toward disease. So if we continue to fill the airwaves with endless new frequency broadcast channels, we can look forward to increased incidence of cancer, birth defects, central nervous system abnormalities, and maybe the extinction of life.

We can't have a fairer warning than that!

REFERENCES
1. Sanderson, I.T., 'Riddle of the Frozen Giants', *Saturday Evening Post*, 16 January 1960, pp. 82–83.
2. *Nature 262*, 128, 8 July 1976.
3. 'Erfahrungen einer Rutengangerin', Geobiologische Einflusse, Kathe Bachler.

The Last Straw

4. Scott-Morley, A., 'Geopathic Stress: the Reason why Therapies Fail?' *Journal of Alternative Medicine*, May 1985, pp. 18–21, 27.
5. *Awake!* 22 April 1984, pp. 14–17
6. *Guardian*, 24 October 1984.
7. *Lancet*, 17 November 1984, p. 1169.
8. Smith, Dr. C., & Best, S., *Electromagnetic Man*, J.M. Dent, 1989.
9. *Observer*, 8 March 1987.
10. Brodeur, P., *The Zapping of America*, W.W. Norton Company, New York, 1977.
11. DeMatteo, B., *Terminal Shock*, NC Press, Toronto 1986.
12. 'A Safe-Place Approach to VDTs', Atherley, Dr. G., 23 March 1983.
13. Private communication (1989).
14. Webb, D., *Microwave Oven Servicing*, M.I.S., 1988, p. 17.
15. Smith, Dr C., 'The Measurement of Enviornmental Electromagnetic Fields and the Values Effective in Triggering Responses in Hypersensitive Patients', *6th Annual International Symposium on Man and His Environment in Health and Disease*, 25–28 February 1988.
16. *Omni*, Vol. 7, No. 5, pp. 41–42.
17. *Ibid.*, p. 103.

Chapter 9
Choosing the Right Foods and Remedies

The first, and major, section of this book has discussed the many different sources of stress to which we are all exposed on a more or less day-to-day basis. If you are aware that you do have health problems related to stress, then you will also realise that knowing the scale of the problem is part of the battle, and having read thus far, you are doubtless determined to identify and remove as far as possible the sources of stress that you can do something about; this will give your overloaded immune system an opportunity to recover a bit.

The 'free radical' theory

A recent theory has been put forward in America about the cause of most degenerative diseases and their relationship to stress; this theory claims that the only common factor in all modern degenerative diseases is cell damage due to the overproduction in the body of cell toxins called free radicals. Free radicals are molecules with unusually reactive properties due to an inherent electrical imbalance (i.e. with either too many or too few electrons for stability). We can have excess free radical activity in our body as the result from stress caused by such things as environmental pollution, radiation, excess sunshine, poor nutrition and emotional upheaval; but as the *Sunday Times* reported recently[1] the ingestion of large amounts of polyunsaturated fats (which have been heavily promoted as health-giving in recent years) could put us at increased risk because they alter the chemical structure of cholesterol-rich substances circulating in the blood. The article reported that 'Professor Maurice Brown, who heads the Cambridge team, said polyunsaturates made bigger metabolic demands than other fats, increasing the risk of the free radical

118 *The Last Straw*

production that could turn cholesterol into a killer.' The most healthy oils and fats are now thought to be the monounsaturated ones, such as olive oil, or the recently introduced rice oil (see the section on Cooking Oils later in this Chapter for more details).

Dr Z. Baranowski, in his booklet on this subject[2] says:

> One of the biggest ways in which free radicals pose a threat to our cells is by turning our body lipids (commonly known as fats) rancid . . . Lipid peroxidation . . . is a major factor in ageing and disease because. . . . (when) . . . the cell membrane. . . . is oxidised by free radicals, it is either hardened so that nutrients cannot get into the cell, or it is punctured so that the cell collapses as the cell fluid drains out.

No wonder we acquire wrinkles so easily!

While the body is designed to combat free radical production to a reasonable extent by natural means, it needs extra help if severely overstressed, and a range of antioxidant enzymes is needed (superoxide dismutase and others), working synergistically in a natural food source; fresh grains, fruits and vegetables are rich sources, but special preparations derived from such things as wheat or barley sprouts are now available. Dr Baranowski continues: 'One of the best ways to reduce free radical activity in our bodies is to remove the stress in our lives.' Unfortunately, we all know that it's not a simple task.

Doctors

Apart from any other considerations, it is important to learn how to select foods and remedies that will be most likely to benefit you. Also, even if you favour alternative medicine, do not neglect your doctor entirely. Doctors have undergone long and arduous training and constitute one of the last remaining dedicated professions. The fact that some may not have the manner or attitude which suits *you* is really neither here not there; when you put yourself in their shoes, you can see why, with only a few minutes available to them, they cannot afford to become too involved with each patient unless there is a genuine emergency. Also if the treatment that they recommend does not appeal to you, or would offend you for personal reasons, then you have a perfect right to refuse it, but you have to be prepared to live with any consequences. This applies to the prescribing of drugs, recommending an operation, transfusing

Choosing the Right Foods and Remedies 119

blood or indeed any other procedure, and the patient is entitled to ask for a second opinion. Also, if a parent, you have the right to decide what treatment you will accept for your child.

A Council of Judges in the U.S.A. wrote[3]: If there is a *choice* of procedures – if for example, the doctor recommends a procedure which has an 80% chance of success but which the parents disapprove, and the parents have no objection to a procedure which has only a 40% chance of success – the doctor must take the medically riskier but parentally unobjectionable course.'

More and more qualified medical specialists are realising that it is important to deal with the patient as a 'whole person'. After all, the patient's feelings and beliefs may well influence strongly his response to a treatment. Dr. G.F. Begley wrote[4]: 'When I treat an illness that affects the body, mind and spirit of the person in my care, it is what *he* believes that is important.' Dr. M.A. Casberg urged[5]: 'The perceptive physician must be aware of these separate but interrelated facets of the body, the mind, and the spirit, and appreciate that healing the body in the face of a broken mind or spirit is but a partial victory, or even an ultimate defeat.'

Some doctors have failures because their patients expect them to achieve the impossible. For example many believe that a prescription for a course of tablets will make it possible for a long-standing complaint to disappear almost miraculously; this of course seldom happens. But if you have made repeated visits for the same chronic complaint and have had several courses of treatment that do not seem to help, then you are within your rights to ask for another specialist to be involved; you do not have to accept the 'dead-end' comment that so many patients have heard: 'I'm sorry, there's nothing more that I can do; I'm afraid you'll just have to learn to live with it.' It is in cases like this that another doctor or practitioner, perhaps involved with a branch of clinical ecology, may well be able to offer the hope of relief.

Allergy clinics

Food and environmental sensitivities are not easy to diagnose with certainty. It is a fact of life that we all react differently, not only because of genetic uniqueness but also because we have all undergone very different and individual experiences in life. Often a sensitivity to a food or chemical first makes itself known at a 'weak

120 *The Last Straw*

point', for example, our lungs if we have ever had pneumonia, or our ankle if we have previously broken it. This explains to some extent the bewildering array of symptoms associated with 'allergy'; these can include angina, arthritis, asthma, back pains, colitis, catarrh, coeliac disease, diabetes, depression, diverticulitis, eczema, hyperactivity, hypoglycaemia, migraine, nervous attacks, psoriasis, stomach pains, tiredness and many more. Consequently a treatment that works for one person may not necessarily work for everyone.

Nevertheless, there are so many approaches to the subject that every one of us can be sure of finding some help. However it is important to choose a practitioner most carefully; it is regrettable that there have always been entrepreneurs who are ready to 'jump on a bandwagon' and hence make a large amount of money out of the unsuspecting public, whether it be in health care or any other field. The columnist Christine Doyle wrote[6] that

> past neglect of allergies by mainstream medicine are enabling fringe and 'bogus' clinics to have a field day. . . . The Consumers Association attacked five such clinics in its magazine 'Which?'. The clinics charged up to £80, and failed to spot genuine allergies from strands of hair or dried blood samples sent through the post, but discovered extraordinary non-existent allergies to long lists of food.

The study[7], carried out in conjunction with Guys Hospital, found that in only 13 cases out of 90 were samples of hair or blood diagnosed correctly. On this basis it is obviously worth making detailed enquiries before committing yourself and your cheque book to a particular clinic; but despite the comments recorded above, there are many good and caring clinics well worth your trust. Many are run by clinical ecologists, who, as Dr T. Randolph puts it 'take the holistic view, that is, the body as a whole and the way it responds to the environment. We attempt to treat the causes rather than the effects of the illness.'

Allergy testing techniques

So what are some of the main techniques employed? They include the following:

(a) Challenge Testing: if a particular food is considered likely to be causing a problem, the patient is fed different diets on consecutive days with the suspect food included in a disguised form on one

Choosing the Right Foods and Remedies 121

day without the knowledge of the patient; the responses are then noted. While this can be an effective technique, much time is needed and of course the patient has to expect to endure whatever symptoms develop.

(b) Elimination and 'Stone Age' Dieting: fasting for several days, using spring water only (after which time the patient feels hungry but generally very much better otherwise), followed by a gradual introduction of other foods; this makes it relatively easy to identify the culprit foods. A very effective method but it may entail being an in-patient at a clinic, so be prepared for your life to be disrupted for a while.

(c) Enzyme-Potentiated Desensitization: the patient is injected with a very dilute mixture of commonly encountered food and inhalant extracts with the enzyme beta-glucuronidase (which also occurs naturally in our bodies). The patient's immune system is stimulated over a period of time to produce suppressor T-cells, which enable him to consume at least some of the foods represented in the injection without ill-effect. However, it can be several months before really significant improvements are shown.

(d) Miller's Neutralising Technique: the patient is injected with a few drops of a food extract, and time allowed for any symptoms (or reaction such as a skin weal) to develop. Dilutions of the same food are then injected to ascertain the correct dilution that will 'turn off' the reaction. Specially-prepared drops of this dilution are taken before eating the food, but it is also recommended to keep to a special dietary regime.

(e) Cytotoxic Testing: a sample of the patient's blood, as fresh as possible, is tested with a wide range of food extracts, and the effects of the white blood cells noted under the microscope. The patient is given a print-out indicating which foods are at risk and to what degree; the recommended diet may be over-restrictive to begin with, but this is probably just as well anyway.

(f) Vega Electrical Therapy: there are several similar instruments available although the Vega is probably the best known. The patient holds an electrode, a food (or other) sample is placed in the circuit and a probe touched onto the patient's finger end or toe. Those samples that lower the reading on the instrument dial (and also the acoustic tone emitted) are the ones to which the patient is sensitive. Theories that have been advanced to explain why the

122   *The Last Straw*

instrument should work as well as it does usually recognise the
bioelectrical nature of most sensitivities; one view is that an adverse body response to a certain food causes an immediate increase in the moisture level of the skin which then reduces the
resistance to the flow of electrical current, and it is this that the
machine is measuring.

(g) Kinesiology: many clinics use this technique very effectively,
and ways of using a version of kinesiology at home will be discussed in Chapter 10. Simply speaking, a sample of the food is put
in the mouth or in the hand, and the strength of the arm muscles is
measured. A food which is toxic for the patient causes an immediate loss of muscle strength; the response is so rapid that bioelectrical phenomena almost certainly are involved.

Homoeopathy

Many have found relief not only for allergic symptoms but for all
sorts of health problems through homoeopathy, and many excellent books have been written on the subject. Homoeopathy depends for its success on *extremely* dilute preparations of a chemical
substance. As an example, if you were to give a healthy person a
small dose of arsenic (not enough to be fatal) it would produce
symptoms such as stomach aches, diarrhoea and vomiting. But
'homoeopathic arsenic', as prepared by a qualified practitioner,
can be used for *treating* exactly those symptoms, which might for
example have been brought about by food poisoning. As a leaflet
by the Hahnemann Society (who promote homoeopathy) says:
'This similarity of symptoms, not the smallness of the dose, as is
popularly thought, is the basis of Homoeopathy.' While the mode
of action of homoeopathic remedies is still the subject of much
research, it would appear that the 'smallness of the dose' is in fact
very significant also. Homoeopathic preparations, which in many
cases are so dilute that *none* of the original material can remain,
are claimed to possess an electromagnetic potency derived from
the atomic and molecular structure of the original substance. If this
is the case, then when a dose is taken, the body will be fooled
because of the electromagnetic properties of the medication into
thinking that it has received a dose, for example of arsenic, and as
a result all the natural processes are immediately set in motion to
rid the body of what it senses as being highly toxic. In this way the

Choosing the Right Foods and Remedies 123

food poisoning organisms etcetera are eliminated rapidly before they can build up to possibly dangerous levels.

While there will always be a homoeopathic remedy suitable for any symptom, not only does it have to be identified but also the correct potency has to be established for the maximum effect. So the chance of 'getting it right' first time would be many thousands to one against, although a competent practitioner will reduce those odds so that there is in fact a real chance that the patient is helped immediately; if both the correct remedy and potency are given, then the effect can be quite remarkable. It is very unusual for side-effects to occur, although not unknown; I remember my wife being given a preparation which within half an hour made her feel schizophrenic, in fact she was so disturbed mentally that I was concerned enough to ring the homoeopath on a Sunday; fortunately he didn't mind and said 'Oh, I'm glad it's working so well!' At the time I just wished that he had had the forethought to warn us of this possibility, but when the symptoms subsided my wife felt better than she had for many months! However, such severe side-effects are *very* uncommon indeed. If only the correct potency could be identified in advance, then homoeopathy would be seen to work more reliably and might thus gain a lot more credibility in the eyes of mainstream medical practitioners.

There is no doubt that homoeopathy works, although some individuals seem to benefit more than others from this form of treatment. Those people who know that they are electrically sensitive may also be aware that the potency of a certain remedy that they need to give relief may vary according to their general state of health and also their current environment (e.g. a remedy may not be effective in an area where there is a strong electromagnetic field). So why not give homoeopathy a chance if up till now you have dismissed it? Many conditions will respond and you will have the added knowledge that you are not doing yourself any harm. A principle to bear in mind is that weaker potencies work best on physical symptoms, whereas stronger potencies are more suited for deep-seated mental problems. Even somewhat vaguely described conditions such as S.A.D. (Seasonal Affective Disorder), suffered by many in the winter months when sunlight is scarce, could be alleviated by homoeopathy. Although practitioners usually operate their own clinics, there are several homoeopathic hospitals in

124 *The Last Straw*

the U.K., for example in London and Bristol, to which patients may be referred by a sympathetic G.P.

Know your foods

During the past year or so there have been a number of warnings issued through the media concerning the potential dangers to our food supplies, whether they be from Salmonella in eggs, Listeria in soft cheeses, aluminium in baby food or chemical treatments such as ALAR given to apples. Consumers tend to overreact *en masse*, as they always have (remember the sugar shortage some years ago when women fought over the spilled contents of the last bag of sugar in the supermarket?), and sales of certain products can be far more severely affected than is warranted, as was the case with the recent egg scare. In this modern world, very few foods are quite as nature intended, due to one type or another of adventitious contamination; of course there are those who claim to eat a healthy diet and say 'I never ever eat any of those nasty chemicals!' What they fail to realize is that foods, like everything else in the world around us, are composed of a complex blend of different chemical substances, so in truth we are eating chemicals all the time. For this reason it is always possible that you may be sensitive to one of the chemical substances naturally present in a particular food, so not all sensitivities are due to additives (either intentional or unintentional). For example, it is not uncommon for people to be able to eat certain varieties of apples, potatoes, lettuce, tomatoes etcetera but not others, due to the differences in chemical composition. This fact reveals one of the shortcomings of allergy testing; you can only be checked out on a very limited number of foods, and how are you to know how they relate to what you would normally buy in your local supermarket or health food store? So if you know that you are very sensitive to many foods, you may find it helpful to have some more detailed information about the characteristics of some of the more common foods in our diet.

Sugar: Beet sugar causes more sensitivity problems than cane sugar, probably because of the impurities it contains. Although the two sugars are ostensibly identical i.e. they are both sucrose, in practice they can behave differently under certain conditions, proving that it must be impurities that are responsible. For example, confectioners and soft drink manufacturers prefer to use cane

Choosing the Right Foods and Remedies 125

sugar in their products as beet sugar can cause undesirable amounts of frothing, largely due to chemicals known as betaines. One common brand of sugar is always beet sugar, while others are generally cane sugar; however packets of the latter will always be identified as such, Fructose (fruit sugar, as used by many diabetics) is not obtained directly from fruit in commercial quantities; it is derived from corn in the U.S.A., whereas within the EEC the source material is beet sugar.

Flour and Flour Products: As mentioned in Chapter 2, it is preferable to eat products made with wholemeal flour (especially if stoneground), and there are several proprietary brands of bread, rolls etc, which meet these requirements. If white flour is used, do ensure that it is unbleached. Although the sale of completely unfortified flour is not generally permitted by law in the U.K., I was able to obtain for my company a special dispensation from the M.A.F.F. to sell it to specific customers with known dietary problems, and this remains the only officially approved source.

If you are like me and enjoy indulging in the occasional biscuit, there are some that are made partially or wholly from wholemeal flour, and one famous brand of digestive biscuit, although it contains both wholemeal and white flour, is very widely accepted by many people on special diets, even those with hypoglycaemia. However a recent change in packaging also highlighted what at first sight appeared to be a change in ingredients, as these biscuits (and their chocolate-coated cousins) now claimed to contain 'cultured skimmed milk'. When I first noticed this I was dumbfounded, as for some years I had not only been eating them myself without ill-effect but had also been recommending them to many allergic people as being entirely milk-free. Letters and telephone calls to the manufacturer finally revealed that the milk had *always* been included in the recipe, but that it had been utilized in such a way that a declaration on the ingredients list was not required by law (what is termed in the Food Labelling Regulations a 'compound ingredient'). Apparently, in view of public concern about accurate ingredients listing the company had taken the decision to 'come clean' and declare the milk on the new packaging, but I was told that I was the only member of the public so far to contact them regarding the change in labelling! Despite the widespread sensitivity to milk, for some reason these biscuits remain just as

126 *The Last Straw*

acceptable to those with food sensitivities as they ever did. Other biscuits made by that particular company are all made with unbleached flour, but in general it is only bread wrappers that tell you whether the flour used is unbleached or not. Also it is worth bearing in mind that most biscuits and cakes produced on the Continent are made with unbleached flour.

Pasta, either white or wholemeal, is completely free of additives, because it is made from semolina which is really a halfway stage between wheat grain and flour. Pasta is produced from a type of hard (high-protein) wheat called Durum which is grown specially for the purpose.

Margarine & Butter: Margarine was originally developed as a substitute for butter (actually for Siberian butter which as you might expect had a very hard texture which made it ideal for producing the best puff pastry), and as a concession to the cow it has often been made with skimmed milk or whey, especially for the more modern retail market. However, much commercial margarine used in the manufacture of cakes, biscuits etc. is free of any milk ingredients. In recent years many brands of milk-free margarine have become available, and these seem to suit most milk-sensitive individuals, but you may need to know what oils have been used and these are not always identified on ingredients lists. The reason is that the exact blend used is likely to vary, depending on the relative costs of the individual oils, so when a batch is made the manufacturing company will select the blend most cost-effective at the time which will impart the required properties to the end product. If a margarine has salt in it, as most do, the salt used is normally free of additives (unlike much table salt which contains the free-flow agent sodium hexacyanoferrate II). Milk-free margarines are made with water in place of the skimmed milk or whey, but this will be ordinary mains water.

Some varieties of butter are tolerated much better than others, and although the reasons are not fully understood, it may well be due to the particular process used for manufacture. Traditionally, butter was made by churning cream, and then discarding the resulting buttermilk before the butter granules were well washed with water; using this process the only ingredients of the butter, broadly speaking, were butterfat, water and added salt. But today much butter is produced on continuous butter-making plant and the

Choosing the Right Foods and Remedies 127

buttermilk may be incorporated as part of the liquid content of the butter; if this is so, then the butter could contain measurable amounts of whey proteins, which as we saw in Chapter 2 are possibly the most allergenic fraction of cows' milk. So it would not be surprising if people reacted to butter made in this way. The problem is that apart from enquiring of the manufacturer the general public cannot know which brand is produced by which method. In general terms, I have found that West Country, Irish and Continental butters seem to be the best tolerated. I have recently been informed that some butter manufacturers are actually adding non-fat milk solids to butter to ensure that the level is only just below the legal maximum. In this way the fat content is only just above the legal minimum!

Nuts: There is some evidence that Turkish hazelnuts may still be affected as a result of the Chernobyl disaster, whilst Italian ones are not. It is obviously preferable to buy all varieties of nuts in the shell for as long a season as possible as they will remain at their freshest, but this is only possible for a relatively short season in the U.K. Nuts that when broken look discoloured are no longer fresh and are best disposed of. Out of all the 'nuts', peanuts seem to cause the most sensitivity problems, and contamination by aflatoxin moulds has been known to occur.

Apples and Pears: It is difficult to obtain certain varieties of apples and pears for more than a short season only. Coxes are normally well tolerated. Many imported apples (and pears) may have been dipped in various chemicals to impart a longer shelf life to them in that rotting is inhibited, but sometimes a fruit which looks perfectly all right on the surface will be found to have turned brown around the core.

Citrus Fruit: Most oranges have been treated e.g. with diphenyl (see Chapter 2) . Try Clementines or Satsumas in season and see if you can manage them, although they may be treated with chemicals such as Imazalil. Lemons, grapefruits and limes, provided they are fairly fresh, can brighten up a diet, and being very low in natural sugars can often be allowed in a candida diet regime. However a grapefruit box I acquired recently claims that the fruit had been treated with sodium orthophenylphenol, waxed with thiabendazol and wrapped with diphenyl.

Other Fruits: It is now common to see exotic fruits such as fresh

128 *The Last Straw*

pineapples, kiwi fruit, mangoes, starfruit (carambola) and others in the local supermarket and they normally cause few problems even for sensitive individuals.

Dried Fruits: Most sultanas and some raisins are treated with vegetable oils, normally a cottonseed and soya blend. The use of mineral oil (paraffin) is being discontinued. Many sultanas, apricots, bananas, mixed peel and other dried fruits are treated with sulphur dioxide as a preservative and colour-retaining agent. Beware mueslis, fruit and nut bars et cetera where ingredients listings do not reveal added preservatives. All dried fruits have to be fumigated, and this is normally carried out using the gas methyl bromide which evaporates away almost immediately; no known ill-effects of this treatment have been noted as yet.

Jams, Marmalades etc: These in general terms are now almost free of artificial colourings, and many makes have few ingredients beyond the essential fruit, sugar, pectin and maybe citric acid. 'Sugar-free' jams are also widely available, and are made using either apple juice or grape juice as sweetener, so be careful if you are sensitive to either of those.

Fruit Juices: A few brands of fruit juice claim to be made directly from fresh juice, but these are the exception rather than the rule. Most juices, especially those in sterile block cartons, are actually produced from imported fruit juice concentrates which have then been diluted with water (presumably from the mains) to achieve the correct strength. Look at the labelling on the container and read between the lines.

Fruit Squashes: This is one area in which there have been significant improvements during recent years as gradually the artificial colours have been replaced with natural or nature-identical ones. 'Nature-identical' implies that each colour component used occurs as a natural colouring matter but in this case has been produced synthetically: a typical example is the yellowy-orange pigment beta-carotene. However, it is extremely difficult to produce a fruit squash with a long shelf-life without using preservatives based on either sulphur dioxide or benzoates.

Meat: It is good to see the increasing numbers of outlets for 'organic' meat, in which it is hoped that there will be no residues of the chemicals which are so often added, such as growth-promoting hormones in beef etc. While it is in many ways very

Choosing the Right Foods and Remedies 129

energy inefficient to produce meat, some people may be on such restricted diets that meat is necessary to ensure that a reasonable balance of nutrients is taken in. We would all like to think that commercially-reared animals and birds were all well cared for, and some of us can be so distressed to find out what does go on in some establishments that we may decide to become vegetarians on principle. However, the practice of eating meat is unlikely to cease.

Many pigs are fed on skimmed milk or whey, and very milk-sensitive individuals may have to avoid such meat. There is evidence that much English lamb is still contaminated after Chernobyl, and hence New Zealand lamb may be preferred. Beef is not as popular as it was for various reasons, including price, its association with saturated fats, and now BSE.

Tea and Coffee: According to figures issued by the Tea Council back in 1982, caterers used 20,000 tons of tea leaf and brewed 10,000,000,000 cups of tea in a year, more than four cups per person per day on average! Presumably these figures do not include the tea brewed and consumed in the home. More recent figures from the same source indicate that in the U.K. we drink a full quarter of the world's total output of tea! Coffee drinking has a long way to go in the U.K. before catching up with tea; however in the U.S.A. things are somewhat different. There most tea is drunk iced, and coffee is the drink of habit; it is generally reckoned that provided you drink less than six cups of coffee a day, this cannot be considered addictive!

Tea and coffee contain physiologically active substances known by the generic name of xanthines, which include caffeine, theobromine and theophylline; these can exert either a beneficial or an unpleasant effect depending upon the individual and the status of his immune system. As they are adrenal stimulants, anyone with food allergies, whose adrenal glands are likely to be severely depleted, should not drink tea or coffee as these will have the opposite effect to the one desired.

Tea is a good source of manganese and other minerals, but the polyphenols it contains (often termed 'tannin') combine with iron and zinc, and it has been found that those who drink tea with their meals generally have a relatively poor iron status. Zinc can be absorbed by the aluminium that occurs in tea (probably because it

130 *The Last Straw*

is often grown on aluminium-rich soils), and aluminium itself is of course under suspicion due to its association with Alzheimer's disease.

A definite link has been proved between the excessive drinking of coffee and pancreatic cancer, which claims the lives of about 20,000 Americans each year; however the results of the survey showed that tea drinking was not implicated at all! This led the researchers to suspect that it was not caffeine itself that was suspect, and they later discovered that other natural constituents rejoicing in the generic name of atractosyl glycosides were in fact responsible! The coffee bean containing the smallest amounts of these chemicals is the African 'Robusta' variety, while Peruvian beans are fairly low in caffeine itself. But if you prefer to drink decaffeinated coffee, just remember that the concentration of every other constituent, good or bad, has been increased during the decaffeination process. Many consumers are now turning to the several very acceptable alternatives to coffee which are widely available. It is also possible to decaffeinate tea, and this is gradually becoming more popular. The procedures used for decaffeination vary, but in principle a solvent is used to extract the caffeine preferentially; there is now concern about the use of methylene chloride and the residues it may leave, and an alternative is methyl acetate, but without doubt the safest and most effective way (though by no means the cheapest) is to use liquid carbon dioxide under pressure.

Apart from pancreatic cancer, other ailments such as heart disease, ulcers and bladder cancer have been linked with the consumption of coffee and tea, although the whole subject is still somewhat inconclusive. But it is certainly possible to become addicted to either of these beverages; how many people *need* their endless cups of tea or coffee to see them through the working day? So moderation, as in all things, seems to be indicated, and because of the stimulant effects of caffeine, it would not be wise to use such drinks whilst on a course of tranquillizing drugs. Nevertheless, there can be no doubt that for some sections of the population, tea and coffee may not be harmful at all and indeed may be beneficial.

As a final thought on this subject, when you examine the stains that are made by tea on your cup or teapot, spare a thought for what might be happening to your stomach! Also beware teabags,

Choosing the Right Foods and Remedies   131

as the special paper used in making them may be bleached or include formaldehyde or other chemicals which can leach out in hot water.

Vegetables: Although many commercial crops are still treated with a variety of pesticides during the growing season, they must not be harvested immediately after such a treatment; the length of time for which they must be left growing depends upon the nature of the chemicals that have been used. British-grown vegetables should not be treated after harvesting with any chemicals at all, but conveyed whilst still fresh to market. This is not necessarily the case with certain foreign-grown vegetables, and care should be exercised in making your choice of purchase.

Cooking Oils: A lot of emphasis has been placed recently on the importance of consuming large amounts of polyunsaturated fats for a healthy life-style, but in truth maybe the balance has swung too far. The molecules of polyunsaturated fatty acids (such as those contained in sunflower oil for example) contain unstable double bonds which break down when subjected to heat, such as frying temperatures, and are converted to polymeric oxides which cause fumes and sticky deposits on your frying pan. In contrast, monounsaturated fatty acids, found in abundance in such oils as olive, are very much more stable to heat and therefore preferable when frying.

There has been shown to be a definite link between the increased intake of polyunsaturates, heart disease and cancer, as was reported at the beginning of this chapter. In our modern society with all its stresses, our bodies are short of natural antioxidants, hence the unstable polyunsaturates tend to oxidise in our bodies producing free radicals which can damage the immune system, leading to premature ageing or at worst cancer. To counteract this effect we need Vitamin A, beta-carotene, Vitamin E, glycine and cysteine. Monounsaturated fats are not harmful in this way and have actually been shown to be beneficial to the heart. So the Italians and others who have cooked with copious amounts of olive oil for centuries have unknowingly been doing the right thing for their health, and southern Europe enjoys exceptionally low rates of heart disease!

Candidiasis
The above controversy about fats and oils is just one more

132 *The Last Straw*

example of a food 'fad', of which there have been so many in recent years. Surely the answer is that we should all exercise caution and try and eat a *balanced* diet, which is not really quite as difficult as it sounds if we develop a genuine interest in the quality of our food; then we may hope to protect ourselves to a large extent from some of the debilitating conditions such as Candidiasis which are becoming so common.

The increasing incidence of Candidiasis was discussed back in Chapter 6; there are many different ways of tackling it, but the first essential is to weaken the yeast organisms and then get at them with as many lethal 'weapons' as you can in an attempt to kill most of them off. A completely sugar-free diet must be followed (that means avoiding *all* simple carbohydrates such as sucrose, fructose, glucose etc.) and because starchy flours are metabolised rapidly into sugars they too should be avoided, at least in the early stages of treatment. Whole cereals, vegetables, and other foods which naturally contain virtually no sugars are acceptable. Yeast, too, must be avoided, and most people miss their bread to the extent that suggests they were addicted to it! Crispbreads, scones, soda-breads, pancakes and waffles are all acceptable and can be made with many different flours[8]. Excellent breads can be made without yeast, using a different kind of leavening system based on glucono delta lactone.

Olive oil, which is active against Candida, should be used for cooking. If you are desperate for a hint of sweetness, try using the new synthetic sweetener Acesulfame K (also known as Sunett); unlike Aspartame, which is turning up more and more on ingredients declarations and has been the subject of much controversy lately, Acesulfame K seems so far to have no known side effects. Also the occasional drink of lemon juice sweetened in this way should do you no harm, though on a sugar-free diet some people have even learned to take it unsweetened! Other foods such as coconut can be beneficial (some Candidiasis treatments are derived from coconut fatty acids), and taheebo (Pau D'Arco) tea, while having a pleasant taste, contains the chemical substance lapachol which is a natural fungicide. Also take as much garlic as you can, subject to the reactions of your family! It is worth mentioning in passing that a diet of this sort would also be beneficial for hypoglycaemia, M.S. and M.E.

Choosing the Right Foods and Remedies 133

Proper vitamin and mineral supplementation is essential during this time, and specialist suppliers can advise you what you need. Some clinics use the yeast-killing Nystatin but the effects seem to vary very much from individual to individual, so if undergoing treatment do ask the advice of your practitioner. Medical conditions such as these, although they may be very deep-rooted, can be helped a great deal provided that you and your family are patient and do not expect miracles! Good self-help and advice groups to whom you can turn for assistance are increasing in number and expertise as time goes by.

Simple remedies

There are also many simple home remedies to which you can turn, so there should be no real need to resort to the chemist or the doctor for minor health problems, unless you feel that you really need professional help. Many physiologically active foods, herbs, aromatherapy oils, Bach remedies and homoeopathic preparations are easily obtained and should have a place in your cupboard so that you can deal with symptoms as they arise. Particularly important are the homoeopathic 'tissue salts' which are available with an explanatory book[9]; these can be extremely effective as will be confirmed in Chapter 10. The book contains long listings of symptoms and indicates the remedies of choice, as well as giving an insight into many of the causes of malaise.

A selection of other homoeopathic remedies should also be kept to hand, and your local practitioner should be consulted for advice; it is possible for many common chronic complaints to be alleviated using homoeopathy. Of particular significance might be mentioned the potencies of heavy metals, which are really the only way of ridding your body of these toxins; for example, if you are having your mercury amalgam fillings removed, a course of homoeopathic mercury is recommended.

Traditional remedies such as ginger (upset stomach or travel sickness), charcoal tablets (indigestion and flatulence), kaolin (upset stomach, diarrhoea etc.) buchu (cystitis), rutin (high blood pressure), witch hazel (bruising) and sodium or potassium bicarbonates (treatment of allergy symptoms) are often very effective.

Other treatments for alleviating the symptoms of allergy include Nalcrom, which is obtainable on prescription from your G.P.; the

134 *The Last Straw*

chemical name is sodium cromoglycate, and it is non-habit forming. Although intended to be taken *before* a meal, experience has indicated that it can also be very helpful *afterwards* if unexpected symptoms develop.

For non-specific headaches and for pain in general, water-soluble paracetamol is normally preferred to aspirin. There are particular types of headache in which alfalfa tablets (preferably produced with American material), homoeopathic Chlorophyll in low potencies or the Biochemic Calc. Sulph. (calcium sulphate) can be very helpful, for instance, in counteracting the effects of geopathic stress (especially water stress), VDU emissions, or even the headache that some ill persons can transmit to you. (We do emit brainwaves, and we can be either 'on the same wavelength' as someone else, or definitely not, in which case they can literally give you a headache!).

I have noticed that some alfalfa tablets contain whey powder, and these are obviously unsuitable if you are milk-sensitive.

Largish doses of Vitamin A (up to 25,000 i.u.) are good for infections of the chest and head, but such doses should not be taken on a regular basis. Vitamin C (preferably the pure powder) can usually be beneficial at relatively high levels (say up to 5 grams daily); the only likely side-effect is looseness of the bowels.

Aromatherapy has many uses that we may not yet have explored, but we are most familiar with the technique when we rub embrocation on our chests! Essential oils are mixtures of complex organic chemicals, many of which are very active physiologically, and inhalation ensures a rapid absorption of the active principles. It is perhaps worth mentioning that some practitioners have found aromatherapy to be especially useful for patients with fatigue syndromes.

Even water can sometimes be effective as a remedy! The *Journal of Clinical Gastroenterology* reported that in an emergency at a jail involving a prisoner when no resources were available, about a pint of water was successful in helping severe pain from a stomach ulcer to disappear in only eight minutes. After further experimentation, the most successful way of using water for this treatment was found to be to take a glass of water half an hour before eating and another two and a half hours later. After documenting the progress of six hundred patients the doctor noted that the prison pharmacy had almost no demand for antacids towards the end!

Choosing the Right Foods and Remedies 135

These are just a few suggestions, then, which hopefully will be found useful; you may be able to find a lot more remedies of your own, especially using the technique of kinesiology which is discussed in the next chapter.

REFERENCES
1. *Sunday Times*, 3 September 1989.
2. Baranowski, Z. *Free Radicals, Stress, Ageing and Antioxidant Enzymes – A Guide to Cellular Health*
3. *Guides to the Judge in Medical Orders affecting Children, Crime and Delinquency*, April 1968, p. 116.
4. *Texas Medicine*, December 1970, p. 25.
5. *Journal of the American Medical Association*, 23 July 1967, p. 150.
6. *Daily Telegraph*, 16 February 1987.
7. *Which?*, January 1987, pp. 6–8.
8. Campbell, H.J., *Foodwatch Alternative Cookbook* (3rd Edition), Ashgrove Press, 1989.
9. *The Biochemics Handbook*, New Era Laboratories, 1969.

Chapter 10
Kinesiology – A Way to Check Your Sensitivities

There are several similar techniques described under the umbrella term 'kinesiology'; in general they describe the process of testing the strength of muscles to establish whether the subject's body is functioning in a balanced way physically, chemically and electro-magnetically. The American chiropractor Dr G.J. Goodheart is normally credited with discovering the phenomenon in 1965, and the technique, often termed 'Applied Kinesiology', is still used by many in his profession today. Apart from identifying imbalances which can give clues as to the causes of illness, kinesiology is widely used, especially in the U.S.A., to check the muscle tone of athletes and ensure that they are in top condition before their performance; but the possible applications of kinesiology are far wider as we shall see, especially in the field of testing for sensitivities to foods and indeed almost any other object in our environment.

Details of kinesiology can be obtained from the organisation Touch for Health, founded in the U.K. by Brian Butler some years ago and dedicated to spreading the use of the technique through the use of 'workshops' during which potential therapists are given suitable training. Brian Butler, who refers to his methods as 'Systematic Kinesiology', has produced a booklet and a video which many have found helpful. In the introduction to his booklet he says:

> Systematic Kinesiology is the science of testing muscle response to gentle pressure to find where imbalances in function or energy blocks are located in the body, and offers ways to resolve them. It enables investigation without intrusion, access to the body's 'computers', and gives insight to the underlying causes of health problems. Imbalances are gently rectified by touch and acupressure massage, which stimulate circulation and lymph

Kinesiology – A Way to Check Your Sensitivities 137

flow, and with nutritional support. In this way, energy balance is restored to the whole person mentally, physically and chemically. It encourages natural healing to take place and enhances a sense of well being in healthy people.

Can you trust kinesiology?

Kinesiology could be considered as a method of exploiting in a somewhat different way the knowledge that the Chinese have used for centuries concerning acupuncture, acupressure, and the body's energy meridians. After all, Western scientists know very well that our bodies depend for their continuing functions on an enormous range of electrochemical impulses, and when we submit to an medical test for heart function, for example, or brainwave patterns, it is these impulses which are being measured.

The book *Applied Kinesiology*[1] quotes Dr Goodheart as follows: 'Applied Kinesiology is based on the fact that the body language never lies. The opportunity for understanding the body language is enhanced by the ability to use muscles as indicators of body language.'

Nevertheless, when we experience kinesiology for the first time it is only natural that we should be curious as to how and why it works, and it is only to be expected that we should be very sceptical at first. The evidence that a technique is truly scientific in nature depends upon whether it produces consistent and reliable results under widely differing conditions. Many of the great scientists of the past first observed that certain things happened, and only later did they find out the reasons why; they first tested out their hypotheses, and from the results of their experimentation formed theories which themselves had then to be tested to ensure that the results predicted were actually obtained and were reproduceable. It is probably true that most of the world's greatest inventions have been the result of curiosity or trial and error initially.

If we do not understand the workings of something down to the last nut and bolt, this is not a valid reason for dismissing it as 'unscientific'. As an example, how many of us understand how a television set works? Very few, and yet this does not stop us from owning one and accepting it as a scientifically-designed everyday piece of equipment which works in a predictable way when we

138   *The Last Straw*

press a particular button. I am labouring this point here only because considerable scepticism has been cast, even in medical circles, on the validity of tests performed using kinesiology; it has been claimed that they are not reproduceable and reliable, yet I am convinced from my experiences that the reason why this view persists is almost certainly due to the fact that it is quite possible, unless certain checks are carried out on the patient in advance (and sometimes during the period of testing), for incorrect results to be obtained.

Nevertheless Dr G. Lewith and Dr J.N. Kenyon have reported[2] that 'testing using applied kinesiology has been done on a double-blind basis (where neither the subject nor doctor knows the identity of the test substance) and has produced reliable and significant results.' In the U.S.A. there is an Institute for Biokinesiology which is continually researching the whole subject and is convinced of the value of the method as a useful practical tool in establishing food and other sensitivities. Many allergy clinics in the U.K. have reported great success when using the technique (which may vary in detail from clinic to clinic but always uses the same basic principles). Because we are using the natural processes of the body there are seldom any side-effects although hypersensitive individuals may experience feelings of tiredness.

In view of the esoteric nature of much alternative medicine practised today, there is also another very important factor that should be considered before proceeding any further with any discussion on kinesiology. Any discovery of man is morally and ethically neutral in that it has the capability of being used for either good or bad; for example a knife may be manufactured for the express purpose of cutting bread (which is a harmless enough exercise), but not for taking the life of someone distasteful to us. When railways and aircraft were developed we were able to travel more quickly than before, and in a safe and comfortable fashion; yet incidents like the Clapham Junction and Lockerbie disasters in December 1988 remind us that trains and planes can still kill. Orville Wright, in a letter written during World War II to Henry Ford Sr, pioneer of the mass-produced car, observed: 'Wilbur and I thought the plane would hasten world peace. So far it seems to have done the reverse.' When Rutherford first split the atom, who would have foretold the immense power for destruction that was

Kinesiology – A Way to Check Your Sensitivities 139

made possible? And so we must be aware that it could be possible for kinesiology, like many other techniques, to be practised by those who do not have altruistic motives at heart. Some of the advertisements in the 'Health' press may make exaggerated promises of certain cures, but common sense tells us that no cures can be guaranteed!

It may help to consider a couple of simple analogies so that we can understand better how our body functions using electrochemistry and electromagnetism. From physics lessons at school, we learned that if an electric current is passed through a wire an associated electromagnetic field is set up, and that a simple electromagnet can be made using a battery, a coil of wire and a nail. We also learned that, whereas *pure* water would not conduct electricity, a current could be made to flow by dissolving in it an electrolyte such as common salt. If we then caused this conductive solution to flow in a tube, it produced its own electromagnetic field. Now our bodies contain a conductive fluid, blood, with a number of different dissolved substances in it including common salt and other minerals such as iron, and as we know this fluid is continually flowing around our bodies fulfilling a number of vital functions including the delivery of oxygen to wherever it is needed. But as it flows, it sets up its own electromagnetic field, and this can be demonstrated using a special type of high-energy photography known as Kirlian. If the field patterns shown up in this way are analysed, they provide scientific confirmation that the energy pathways or meridians known to the Chinese do actually exist, and this has caused many open-minded medical research workers to examine such fields as biochemistry, physiology and anatomy from a refreshingly different viewpoint; one practical outcome is that acupuncture is now accepted and practised by many doctors.

Dr Cyril Smith of Salford University, in an article on the electrical and other properties of water said[3]:

> Classically, allergy used to be considered only in terms of skin and respiratory conditions. Now the allergic responses of all the body systems are considered and the total body load of allergens is the critical quantity. In any given person it is the result of a dynamic balance between the rate of intake and the rate of elimination of allergens. Not only may an allergen provoke a skin or a respiratory reaction, *but for example it may instead provoke muscle rigidity or conversely loss of*

140 *The Last Straw*

muscle tone, [my italics] even cardiac abnormalities have been provoked. The same general pattern of symptoms is likely to be provoked in a given patient whether the trigger is a chemical or biological allergen or an electric or magnetic field, which makes it possible that it is a feedback control system that is malfunctioning. Reactions in multiple-allergy patients have been provided by chemical, biological or electrical stimuli at frequencies from millihertz to gigahertz, and neutralized by any of these stimuli. The effect of increasing frequency seems to be equivalent to increasing dilution. The responses are extremely rapid, an indication of the effect of the allergen is obtained within 10 seconds and the total effect is mostly complete in under a minute.

Muscle rigidity or loss of muscle tone, as mentioned by Dr Smith, is really what is measured by kinesiology, and pretty well anyone can learn to use this technique with a little practice, as we shall see.

How to use kinesiology

One of the practical problems associated with attending an allergy clinic is that in between your appointments you are very much on your own. Many patients have told me that often they are told all the things that they *cannot* eat but are not given nearly enough positive advice on what they *can* eat; this is usually because of the tremendous and never-ending pressure of work on the successful clinics, which make it impossible for the practitioner to spend nearly as much time with each patient as he would wish. Perhaps this is why so many allergy self-help groups have been established with regular meetings at which knowledge and experiences are shared, to the benefit of all. Those who are desperate for help may feel that they just need someone to talk to, even on the telephone, about their problems, someone who will offer both a sympathetic ear and a genuine understanding of their situation. But provided that you have a spouse or good friend to hand, there is something that you can do to help yourself in a practical way and that is to use kinesiology to monitor your progress. The method I am going on to describe is only one of many that can be used, and perhaps would not be employed in quite the same way by a professional kinesiologist, but it works well enough in practice to be really useful in everyday situations. I and my wife have used it ourselves for the past eight years or so, and are convinced that by so doing

Kinesiology – A Way to Check Your Sensitivities 141

we have been able to prevent any further deterioration in our health, and even make noticeable improvements; for example, we have now lost virtually all our food sensitivities.

So how do you go about doing the tests? Firstly two people must be involved, one to carry out the testing and one to be the subject of the test. The person to be tested stands with his (or her) right arm outstretched horizontally and with the palm facing downwards. The tester then places his (or her) right palm on the subject's right shoulder (for the purpose of steadiness) and then rests two or three fingers of the left hand on the subject's wrist. It is best to remove watches or jewellery at this stage, not only for convenience but because they could interfere with the tests.

The tester first warns the subject that he is going to carry out a 'blank' test and then immediately applies a steady (but not excessive) pressure to the subject's wrist for a second or so. The subject simultaneously attempts to resist the pressure and thus keep his arm horizontal. In a controlled situation like this there should be no problem whatsoever in achieving this. The subject next holds in the palm of his left hand a sample of a food or chemical (wrapped in a non-toxic material if preferred) to which he is aware that he is very definitely sensitive; often a small sample of 'paraquat' weedkiller is used as this is toxic to everyone, but a food that is known to be a problem will generally do just as well. (Tests for foods are best done with a sample of the food placed between the lips or under the tongue, but this is obviously not practical in this case!). Putting the test food in glass, paper or plastic before testing will not affect the validity of the test provided that the subject has been shown previously not to be sensitive to the packaging material itself. When the tester gives the warning and then applies pressure, the subject should find that he is completely unable to resist this pressure and his arm will fall to his side. An alternative to using a toxic chemical is as follows: the subject forms a fist with the left hand, tucking in the thumb and keeping only the index finger protruding. He then finds the solar plexus (in the centre just under the breastbone) with his finger, and then withdraws it about an inch with the finger still pointing directly at it. When his arm is tested it should be found to be weak. It is believed that in some way a bioelectrical 'short-circuit' has been caused which disturbs the function of the brain.

142

The Last Straw

It is important that before proceeding further, both the tester and the subject can reproduce both a 'strong arm' and a 'weak arm' situation that is recognisable to both of them. They are then ready to check out substances of unknown qualities. But do ensure that the tests give the result expected i.e. a *weak* arm with the toxic substance; it is possible under certain circumstances for the body's system to respond in exactly the *opposite* way to that expected, possibly due to a temporary imbalance in the individual's autonomic nervous system, and in such a case any further tests will of course give entirely the wrong result, which can be very confusing.

This phenomenon is sometimes referred to as 'switching', and seems to occur with highly sensitive persons when without prior warning they are subjected to a severe stress of some sort; examples would include cases where the patient has a sudden and unpleasant shock for some reason, is tested with a food or substance which proves extremely toxic for him, or finds it impossible to make a necessary and immediate decision about some important matter (remember the pig in Chapter 5!). Switching can sometimes make you feel bad for no apparent reason, but once you have recognised the phenomenon, you must try to rectify the situation immediately. Techniques which usually work straightaway include asymmetric exercises such as marching on the spot (when done properly, this is known as 'cross-crawling'), slapping each side of the head in turn about ten times, and then rubbing the palms of the hands together and pressing them together at the fingertips. All these procedures are considered as restoring the balance of the body's electrical energy. The phenomenon of 'switching' is discussed in more detail in the book *Applied Kinesiology* referred to in this chapter.

After repeating the procedure several times, both persons involved should now be familiar with the sensations of both a 'strong' arm and a 'weak' arm. But what has happened to make this phenomenon occur? Although we do not yet fully understand the mechanisms involved, they are certainly concerned with the electrochemistry of our autonomic nervous system, and depend on the interaction of this with the natural electromagnetic properties of all the objects in our immediate environment.

Everything around us ultimately is composed of atoms and molecules, which have their own interacting electromagnetic fields

Kinesiology – A Way to Check Your Sensitivities 143

and therefore possess their own overall fields which extend beyond the physical boundary of the object in question. The most obvious example of this is a simple iron magnet, in which the field is exceptionally strong because of the alignment of all the atoms of iron; most of us will recall the experiments at school using a magnet and iron filings to map out the 'lines of force' of the electromagnetic field. But other substances normally considered non-magnetic, such as foods and other chemicals, appear to have similar properties too although to a very much lesser extent.

When the tester announces that pressure is to be applied to the arm of the subject, he (the subject) then makes a conscious decision that he is going to resist this pressure; the brain then sends an electrochemical message through the nervous system to the deltoid muscle at the shoulder, which contracts and causes the arm to lock in position horizontally. However, when the subject has in intimate contact with his body (and hence his electromagnetic field) the substance with which he is being tested, the field of this material interacts with that of his own body in one of three ways. With most substances the effect is a neutral one, the interaction is not noticeable and the arm remains just as strong as before. But if the test substance possesses properties which would render it toxic in some way to the subject, the fields appear to interact in such a way that the message sent by the brain to the shoulder muscle never arrives in its correct form; whether it never leaves the brain, or whether it leaves the brain correctly and then gets 'scrambled' en route we do not know. But the effect is definite and repetitive, even under double-blind conditions.

Occasionally a substance will be encountered that makes the subject's arm feel even stronger than before, and he is able to push his arm noticeably upwards against the pressure being applied by the tester; this is indicative of a synergistic effect of the two fields, and identifies a substance which is of biological benefit to the subject at that time. We will discuss this later when considering ways of choosing remedies.

Food testing

Once you and your partner are confident of your ability to perform the test in a reliable manner, you are not restricted to doing it only at home. It is quite feasible, provided that you do not mind a few

144   *The Last Straw*

odd glances from fellow shoppers, to check foods in your local supermarket or anywhere else, provided that you realize that you cannot achieve 100% accuracy under such conditions.

As mentioned earlier, it is best if you can place a small sample of the test substance (if a food) either between the lips or under the tongue, as it is then actually within the body's system. But as a general guide the subject can grasp the test substance firmly in the palm of the hand, or in the case of a larger sample press the palm or finger tips firmly onto it. If the arm goes weak on testing it is an indication that this substance is likely to cause symptoms in the subject if consumed. Our experiences over many years indicate that a test done in this way is about 80% accurate, and certainly we would recommend that any food causing a 'weak' arm at this stage should not be consumed at this particular time (a comment to be qualified later). It follows, therefore, that even if the arm tests 'strong' there is a 20% chance that the food may still not be really suited to the individual. Why should this be so?

As will be discussed further in Chapter 11, we are all different from one another, both genetically and due to the unique experiences of life that we have undergone. One of us may have broken a leg, another suffered with pneumonia, and yet another undergone a traumatic event such as a bereavement which has left its mark, perhaps a tendency to depression. So it is sensible to accept that something that we eat which disagrees with us in some way will probably go for our weakest point first. The test described previously is simply an 'overall' test and not intended to be one specific for any particular area or organ of the body.

However, if we are aware that our symptoms are usually of a specific kind, and affect us in a particular place, we can go a stage further with the test. Suppose, for example, that a subject knows that certain foods are likely to cause him to develop a migraine. We would first ask him to find the place on his head where the symptoms first show themselves by feeling carefully with the fingers until a tender or potentially tender spot is found, for instance over the left eye. Then with the fingers of his left hand on this spot, the right arm is tested by kinesiology to assess its strength. If he has not in fact suffered for some while with the symptoms it is quite possible for the arm to remain strong, indicating that there is no imbalance of electrical energy at that point. But if there have

Kinesiology – A Way to Check Your Sensitivities   145

been recent symptoms, or if the subject is actually suffering them at the time of the test, then the arm will go weak on testing.

Next, take a sample of any of the foods to be tested and hold it firmly against the point where the symptoms are noticed. Regardless of whether this point formerly tested 'strong' or 'weak', if the food is harmless the point will now test 'strong', but if the food is one which is implicated in causing the symptoms the point will test 'weak'. This is a very important principle which holds true for *any* point on the surface of the body that you may be testing. So if you have a stomach ache, find by examination the point which is most tender and place two fingertips on it (or as a rough guide place the palm of your hand across the sensitive area) and then test in the manner described above the various foods that you may have eaten recently. In this way it is almost certain that you will discover the identity of the 'culprit' food. Experiment for yourself and you will discover the truth about the simplicity of this test.

As kinesiology depends upon the operation of electromagnetic forces, it is not that surprising that the effect can be transmitted from person to person. So to test a young child or bed-ridden person with little muscular strength, the subject holds the food in the left hand, preferably across the stomach, while an intermediate holds the subject's right hand with his left. When the right arm of the intermediate is tested, the correct response of the subject to the food will be obtained.

Assessing remedies

The assessment of remedies represents an even more rewarding use of kinesiology. Let us revert to the example of the migraine sufferer. With this ailment, as with any other, it is possible to establish quite straightforwardly which remedy is most likely to alleviate the symptoms most effectively. Suppose that the testing point over the left eye is currently 'weak'. Place a sample of the proposed remedy close to the body, such as in a pocket, or preferably next to the skin, so that the field of the remedy interacts with that of the subject, and then test the weak point over the left eye again; if it still tests 'weak' then this is not a suitable remedy in this case, but if the point then tests 'strong' it means that if you should take the remedy it will have a beneficial effect. This can then be checked by actually taking a dose of the remedy and noticing that

146   *The Last Straw*

when you now test the point that was 'weak', it has become 'strong'. Although there may be occasions when you do not feel any obvious benefit subsequently, this procedure can be considered in general as an extremely useful guide. When on a course of treatment it is also possible to determine in this way when the next dose is due.

The method works with any form of remedy, including homoeopathic ones; for example, use it with the Biochemic salts and you will find that the claims made for them in the accompanying book are almost always substantiated in practice. Also if you have identified a food recently eaten as causing symptoms, make up a *very weak* dilution of the food (say a drop-sized portion in at least half a glass of water), mix well, and test the result by the method described above. Often you will find that a therapeutic effect is indicated, so then place a couple of drops under the tongue. This is a very rough and ready method; if it was possible to get the dilution just right, then the remedy would be at its most effective.

Using the same technique you can monitor yourself on a regular basis to establish that your body is functioning as it should. For serious devotees of this method it would be best to obtain a copy of a chart showing the acupuncture points and meridians of the body, but for most of us it may well suffice just to find the tender spot and treat it in the way described. A word of caution though: there are some indications that the more you use kinesiology the more sensitive your system can become; it is best to use it only when you have a problem that you need to resolve – do not keep on testing everything within sight!

A further function of kinesiology is to warn you about the possible interactions of foods. Many foodstuffs, such as tea, coffee, chocolate, spices, cheese, citrus fruits, ginger, etcetera, contain biologically active principles which may or may not be harmful and may even be beneficial when consumed individually; however they may cause an undesirable reaction if two or more such foods are eaten at the same time. For example, you will often have heard it said that if you are subject to migraines you should never eat cheese and chocolate at the same meal. Testing foods both singly and in combination can reveal that there is a great deal of truth in many of these recommendations that have been handed on from

Kinesiology – A Way to Check Your Sensitivities   147

one generation to another. In fact many of the traditions concerning foods and herbs can be shown to be based on actual observations that must have been made in times gone past. It is likely that the average person living several hundred years ago knew a lot more about the properties of the various plants growing around him than we do today, though there does seem to be a recognition in recent years that we do need to know more in a practical way, possibly because of the frequent failures of modern drug-based medicine to keep us reasonably healthy.

Household goods, furnishings, clothing etc.

It is not only foods and remedies that can be checked out using kinesiology, the same method can be employed to assess whether you are sensitive to virtually anything in your immediate environment. For example, you can check out cooking utensils, or household materials with which you come into intimate contact, such as washing powder, washing up liquid, toilet paper and toothpaste. It has been found, for example, that in some cases where the patient complains of severe eczema which affects all of the body except the hands and face, the culprit is the washing powder used in that home. And if you feel dizzy or sick when doing the housework, perhaps your floor polish or cleaner is giving off fumes that upset you. Formaldehyde is a powerful irritant, and is present in many household products, even in teabags, and also of course in cavity foam insulation. If you feel queasy in your car, bear in mind before taking medication that many chemicals used in the automotive industry for finishing parts, fabrics, etcetera, and those used for valeting the insides of cars, can give off very powerful chemical vapours. So you can check out the inside of your car just by placing the palm of your hand on the dashboard, seat etc, and having your partner test your muscle strength.

What about clothing, furnishings, carpets and so on? Many hypersensitive people are already aware that certain fabrics do not agree with them, but in this age of man-made materials it is possible that far more people are affected than is generally realized. How often have you felt uncomfortable in a particular outfit and said 'I just can't wait to get these clothes off and change into something more comfortable'? If you were to test the fabrics you would almost certainly find that either one garment was contraindicated, or that the problem was due to a combination of different fabrics. Clothes containing a polyester/cotton blend seem to be especially implicated with some people, and of course even some of the chemical dyes used to colour fabrics can cause allergic reactions, so that some colours of fabrics may affect you whereas others of similar pattern but different colours may not. In general, cotton is safest.

Sometimes the effects are due to the differing electrical properties of various fabrics, and of course some types can store huge amounts of static electricity; next time when you take off a garment and hear crackling noises and see sparks, bear in mind that it takes a potential of about 30,000 volts for a spark to jump just 1 inch (2.5 cm)! Clothing can of course be checked before purchase if you are very sensitive, but some prefer to shop using a mail order catalogue so that they can do their tests thoroughly at home before deciding to keep the garment in question.

If you frequently feel restless or have aching feet and legs, it could be floor coverings that you are sensitive to; all carpets (apart from woollen ones), vinyls etc. are made of synthetic materials and even rubber underlay may be a problem. Any chemically-sensitive person would be advised to select traditional woollen carpets backed with hessian, and these should be laid on a fibre underlay; these too can be checked in the store. Of the synthetic fibre carpets, polypropylene seems to be the best tolerated.

Electrical appliances

You also have the opportunity to check out electrical appliances for compatibility, particularly in view of the potential hazards outlined in Chapter 8. If you are at home, first use a radio as described earlier to establish the location in the equipment which is giving rise to the strongest radiofrequency emissions, such as a transformer or computer board. Then place the palm of your left hand on or near that area and have your partner test your muscle strength; a weak arm means that the emissions are affecting you adversely. For more powerful equipment it is better to stretch out your left arm, and cup your palm towards the equipment, using the palm as a crude (or maybe not so crude) receiving dish, then test as before. In this way you can easily establish which equipment will not affect you and which will. A similar technique can be used in a store before selecting a purchase, provided that you do not mind

Kinesiology – A Way to Check Your Sensitivities   149

performing the test in a public place. As I mentioned in Chapter 8, you will usually find that there will be at least one make of television, video recorder, hi-fi, computer, print-out calculator, photocopier etc. which is suitable for you, and if you pursue the reasons why, it always transpires that the manufacturer has taken great care to screen the equipment thoroughly to prevent undesirable radiofrequency emissions. While there is a British standard intended to promote the protection of other sensitive parts of the appliance and to reduce radiofrequency emissions to a minimum, from a biological point of view some appliances appear to be far safer in this respect than others.

Effective screening can be achieved on some equipment at home (see Chapter 8) provided you understand the principles involved. In essence it is quite simple; you need to find the source of the emissions and use aluminium-faced card (or even aluminium foil in some cases) to shroud that section. Sometimes covering the whole of the inside of the casing of the equipment will do. However the aluminium 'screen' must then have an earthing wire attached to it which is connected to a suitable point on the chassis. A strong word of warning at this juncture, though: please do not attempt to do this on your own unless you know exactly what you are doing, as interfering with electrical equipment can be *extremely dangerous*.

Some appliances can 'switch' you immediately they are turned on ('switching' was discussed earlier in this chapter); immediately they are turned off again the subject becomes 'unswitched'. I have recently purchased a fax machine which has this unpleasant effect on me; I wondered why I felt very odd after working even a short time in the office, and have recently discovered the reason. Fortunately some years ago I discovered, quite by chance, a technique for overcoming this problem, which I have now applied successfully to the fax machine (I had not had to make use of this technique for quite some time as we normally test an appliance before purchasing it). Obtain a simple magnet (horseshoe magnets are the most common) and suspend it by a very thin strand of fibre such as cotton so that it can rotate naturally; as it does so the North Pole of the magnet will gradually settle down pointing to the South Magnetic Pole of the earth, and the South Pole of the magnet to the magnetic North Pole; mark the poles with a felt pen for future

150 *The Last Straw*

reference. To render the appliance harmless, unplug it and hold the three-pin plug with the pins facing towards you. Then touch the neutral pin of the plug with the North Pole of the magnet at the same time as you touch the earth pin with the South Pole; hold the magnet there for two or three seconds. When you plug the appliance in again and turn it on, the 'switching' effect should no longer be in evidence. Exactly why this should be so I have no idea, but it does seem to work in a remarkably high percentage of cases, so maybe it has something to do with the polarity of the appliance when manufactured. Perhaps someone can come up with a sensible explanation?

Geopathic stress

It is also possible to test for geopathic stresses using kinesiology, but doing this except in an emergency is not recommended, as too much testing seems to increase one's sensitivity as has already been mentioned. If you are in a discharging field (such as water stress), the left hemisphere of the brain seems to be affected, so that holding your left palm on the left side of your head will give a 'weak' arm when tested. Correspondingly, if you are in a charging field such as an electromagnetic field from power lines, for example, the right hemisphere is affected. If the house where you live is in such an environment, or has been built on a site which is unsuitable for some reason, then you will need expert help and advice, and it may be that the only solution is to move to somewhere else (a source of further stress in itself!)

Summary

While kinesiology can provide you with an enormous amount of information concerning your food, your clothes and the general world around you, it should never be used indiscriminately; none of us actually want to be so sensitive to our environment that we are aware of every small nuance of change. But if we have suffered with ill-health that has so far defied efforts to find a cause, then here is an inexpensive and effective technique that we all have at our disposal.

REFERENCES
1. Valentine, T. & Valentine, C., *Applied Kinesiology*, Thorsons, 1985.
2. Lewith, Dr G. & Kenyon, Dr J.N., *Clinical Ecology*, Thorsons, 1985.
3. Smith, Dr C., *Water* – 'Friend or Foe?' *Laboratory Practice*, October 1985.

Chapter 11
What else can we do?

In the two previous chapters we have already seen that, despite the many sources of stress in modern life, there are practical ways in which we reduce the impact of it on ourselves and our families.

If you are still wondering about the best way to cope with the pressures of life, the following illustration might be appropriate. Consider the building term 'coping stone', which is used to describe a particular type of stone, often specially shaped and made of a particularly hard material, possibly even concrete; this is placed on top of a wall to cover it and protect it from erosion. We can learn to 'cope' better by learning from our experiences, doing what we can do to improve our situation, and being determined in our own minds that life is not going to get the better of us. This does not mean that we have to learn how to be hard and insensitive like concrete; in fact exactly the opposite is the case. By caring for others and not being so concerned about ourselves, we are better able to 'cope', to cover over and protect the deeper foundations of our lives so that they are not eroded away by stress. If we reach the stage when we can no longer 'cope', then everything will begin to crumble all around us and we have lost the battle, temporarily at least. It is almost always the case that the people who have been ill and get better are just those ones who are the most positive in their approach to fighting ill-health and determined that they will be survivors.

The last straw

We have learned from previous chapters that all of us are under attack from stresses of many different types: whether they are from the environment at large, from our homes and families, from our workplace, or from the polluted foods we eat is not in itself

152 *The Last Straw*

significant. It is the *total* stress situation, the total toxic load to which we are subjected that we must begin to understand and do something about. So often we hear that a person's ill-health begins after a traumatic occurrence of some kind, such as a bereavement, a serious illness, a divorce or redundancy. And as Dr Uhlenhuth, a psychiatrist at the University of Chicago, has said: 'While there are other factors involved in causing illness, it is quite clear that *stress plays a triggering role'* [my italics]. So in general we find ourselves able to cope (some better than others because of their genetic make-up and way of life) until something unexpectedly happens which is 'the last straw' as far as our overstretched immune systems are concerned. After all, we are the only generation that has ever lived which has had to cope with such a multitude of changes to the environment; no one has known in the past just what the longer-term and cumulative effects of scientific progress would be, but now we are beginning to find out. It is not just adults that are affected by stress but also children, new-born babies and maybe even babies still in the womb.

Why is it that very few doctors still are prepared to acknowledge that illness is often caused this way? Try using this simple illustration. Suppose you are driving your car and the engine begins to splutter and cough; you come to a halt and immediately start wondering what is the cause. If you were to ask a number of people for their comments as to the most likely reason, most of them will say that you have probably run out of petrol, or that there must be a blockage in the fuel system. So when *you* start to splutter, cough and grind to a halt, why do you not consider first that it could be something that you are fuelling yourself with on a regular basis (i.e. your food and drink) that is to blame?

The 'barrel' – an illustration to remember

We have reason to be extremely grateful to Dr W. Rea, the American surgeon and allergist, who has suggested another most useful illustration: I hope that he will not mind my embellishing it somewhat in order to drive the point home even more strongly. Dr Rea suggests that we consider a barrel with several holes punched in the bottom, which is being filled with water from a tap above. As the water is able to escape through the holes just as quickly as it pours in from the tap, the system is 'stable'. But suppose that the

What else can we do? 153

tap is now turned up gradually so that the amount of water flowing in is increased; there will come a time when the water is unable to flow away as fast as it is coming in, the barrel will gradually fill, and eventually if the tap is not turned down again it will overflow. The barrel represents our body (maybe appropriate in an obese society!) and the inflow of water represents the many and varied forms of stress that come in on us every day from the different aspects of our lives. The holes in the bottom of the barrel represent the ways that we have available for dissipating stress: going for a walk, digging the garden, listening to music, going to the theatre, having a pleasant evening with friends, having a good sleep, playing golf, helping someone less fortunate than ourselves, all these are things which individuals find practical and therapeutic. So in this way we can cope well enough while our lives are 'stable', but when the pressure is really put on us, for whatever reason, and the tap is being turned on more and more, then it is obvious that there may well come a time when our barrel of stress fills to the top and then begins to overflow. The point of the illustration, then, is this: when our barrel of stress overflows, that is when we begin to feel ill.

This explains why so many people feel a lot better once they identify their food and chemical sensitivities; by avoiding certain foods or other products, suddenly a large proportion of the toxic load on their system is removed, so the 'water' level falls below the top of the barrel and the symptoms disappear. We must not make the mistake, though, of thinking that we are thus completely cured; that would be wishful thinking on our part and can cause us to be careless about our way of life, which in turn can start to bring on the symptoms again. However we will find that we can cope better with the general demands of everyday life.

Choosing our foods wisely

When it comes to food shopping, this in itself can be very stressful! Because of the unknown ingredients that may be in many manufactured foods, it is advisable for people who know they are particularly sensitive not to buy more of them than they have to. We are all busy and frequently need to prepare meals in the shortest possible time, but it could be that a carefully chosen nutritious snack might sometimes do more good (and consequently less

154 *The Last Straw*

harm) than a full meal from a deep-frozen microwaveable carton. So it will pay to be selective when visiting the supermarket. Many of us read the ingredients lists with avid interest, sometimes without understanding them fully (see the 'E Numbers' discussion in Chapter 3), but it would be a mistake to think that absolutely everything that is in the prepacked or manufactured food is mentioned on the ingredients list. The Food Labelling Regulations[1] give plenty of scope for food processors not to have to declare certain ingredients; for example: 'the names of the ingredients of a compound ingredient need not be given in a case where (a) the compound ingredient is identified in the list of ingredients by a generic name . . . (b) the compound ingredient constitutes less than 25% of the finished product.' This means, for example, that if margarine is used in the production of a factory-made cake, it will likely be declared just as 'margarine', giving the purchaser no information on whether the margarine used was milk-free or not (actually, margarine often is milk-free when produced specifically for manufacturing purposes). And the ingredients list of a fruit and nut bar containing dried apricots and sultanas will not reveal whether they contain the preservative sulphur dioxide (which they almost certainly will do).

If you buy a sliced and wrapped white loaf, you may be pleased to note that the flour used is declared as 'unbleached', but the other statutory flour additives are not stated (see Chapter 2). Neither is any mention made of the chemical preparation used for greasing the tin in which the loaf was baked; could this be derived from vegetable oil, or could it perhaps be a silicone derivative? How are we to know? This situation is made possible only because the Food Labelling Regulations[2] provide for some ingredients not to be declared, such as: 'any additive whose presence in the food is due solely to the fact that it was contained in an ingredient of the food, if it serves no significant technological function in the finished product', or 'any additive which is used solely as a processing aid'.

There are other reasons, too, why an ingredients declaration may not be entirely accurate; if one of the ingredients is temporarily unavailable and a substitution is made, or if a recipe is 'improved', who is to say whether new labels are scrupulously applied to every packet containing the altered recipe? Would you

What else can we do? 155

not be tempted to use up old labels or packaging if you still had 50,000 of them still in stock, all paid for?

While it is sensible for all of us to broaden our diet, it is particularly important for children, who otherwise can reach adulthood with only a very small range of foods that they are prepared to consume. However, many of us are becoming more adventurous with our choice of food, and this probably reflects to some extent the amount of travelling we do either on holiday or business. But despite the enormous range of foods available to us, we do not necessarily choose a diet that is nutritionally balanced.

Many foods that we would never normally consider as part of our weekly purchases are not only nutritious but very satisfying and delicious too, as can be discovered by using specialist recipe books such as the *Foodwatch Alternative Cookbook*[3]. As an example, have you ever eaten millet? It is not just intended for budgerigars; in fact many millions in third world countries depend on it. As for whether it will improve your singing voice, you and your family will have to be the judge of that! But an explorer watching the weight of his backpack will vouch for the benefits of something like millet which, weight for weight, is one of the most nutritious foods known. There are some cereals which you may never even have heard of before which can be of great help on a restricted diet; how about sorghum, amaranth, or quinoa, for example? Supplies of commodities such as these are generally available only through specialist food outlets or ethnic grocers' shops, so you will have to search for them.

That the diet regime followed in many homes is of questionable value can be deduced by observation of the products that many supermarket shoppers put in their trolleys. The following scenario is probably enacted daily in millions of homes even today, even when many of us are becoming more enlightened in our food choices. Johnny comes down to breakfast, with not much time before going off to school, and wolfs down a plate of wheat- or corn-based cereal with sugar and milk. He then takes with him the packed lunch which his mother has provided, which includes sandwiches made of white bread, butter and jam, a packet of crisps or other savoury snack, and a piece of cake or some biscuits; if she is particularly thoughtful she will also provide an apple. When he arrives home after school, Mum gives him his

156 *The Last Straw*

favourite tea: sausages, baked beans and chips, followed by a large helping of ice-cream, all washed down with a large glass of orange squash. It is possible that this will be all that the child will eat all day, apart from perhaps a chocolate bar or portion of chips purchased from the school canteen or corner shop. This pattern of eating continues daily with minor variations.

If the contents of Johnny's diet are examined carefully, it becomes apparent that at almost every meal he is consuming wheat, corn, sugar, dairy produce, preservatives and colourings (though thankfully not so many artificial ones lately). So is it surprising that in a stress-laden society such as ours, the very foods which are implicated in a large proportion of cases of allergy include *just those foods?* And if you think that no family would feed their child in this way, it is sobering to note that, in a survey carried out on a council estate in Cardiff a few years ago, it was found that the most nutritious food that local children ate regularly was digestive biscuits, and this was only because the Health Visitor had recommended them to the parents because of their roughage content.

Reducing stress levels

And now to other sources of stress; what can we do about them? After consideration of the barrel illustration, many will reach the fairly obvious conclusion that the most important thing to be done to improve physical and mental health is to identify and then remove some of the major sources of stress in life, thus lowering the level of water in the barrel, as it were, and thereby causing the symptoms to subside. (This is a far more accurate analogy than that expressed in a recent television programme about alternative medicine, which misleadingly suggested that it was making the capacity of the barrel greater that would benefit the patient.) However reducing stress levels is often easier said than done: you may well find yourself worrying about what to do next or what to eat!

But there are several factors to consider which may contribute to an improvement, and probably most readers will be able to add to the list below.

1) Do you have a happy and lasting marriage? If so, you are privileged, as at least one third of all marriages fail throughout the world.

What else can we do? 157

2) Do you have a mate who is supportive of your problems? If so, again you are fortunate: as the saying goes, a trouble shared is a trouble halved. Some marriages mates only make matters worse when they tell their spouses to 'pull themselves together' without even trying to understand the basic causes of the problem.

3) Is there a chance that you are just too ambitious for your own good in a material way? A materialistic philosophy or a desire to 'get to the top' can cause immeasurable stress not only for you but for the rest of your family too.

4) If you have a job, are you happy there, and do you find it fulfilling? Difficult bosses or workmates and a poor working environment can be extremely debilitating over a period of time (see Chapter 5).

5) How much time do you spend every working day just in commuting to and from your place of work? Are you tired and stressed by the time you get to work because of traffic jams or train delays? When you get home in the evening are you so exhausted that you don't want to know your family and they don't want to know you? Although moving houses and jobs is itself very stressful, in the longer term that could be the best thing for you all.

6) Are your children happy at school? If you feel that it is not easy being a parent in today's troubled world, spare a thought for what the children go through. Try and get to know the teaching staff and see that they respect your wishes for the children as far as is possible.

7) What about your house? Is it old, damp, built over running water, or built on the site of an infilled rubbish tip? Does it have cavity foam insulation? Investigate for yourself as far as is possible and be prepared to move as a last resort.

8) Do you live in a noisy area? Perpetual noise, even well below the levels officially considered harmful, can cause stress. Sometimes moving is the only answer, but as we saw in Chapter 5, this in itself can be stressful! The quiet havens in this country are becoming few and far between as huge areas are devoted to industry and motorway building, and as an example the character of much of south-east London and Kent is due to be irrevocably changed with the coming of the Channel Tunnel and the necessary motorway links.

9) Do you live in an area of dense road traffic, with consequent air pollution by carbon monoxide, lead, nitrogen oxides, sulphur

158 *The Last Straw*

dioxide, etcetera? Or are there factories or power stations not far away which taint the surrounding atmosphere with fumes? And if you frequently have cause to complain about the poisoning of the environment with such fumes, stop and think for a moment if you could be contributing; for example, you may find the stench of the exhaust of the car in front of yours to be unbearable, but have you ever bothered to find out what *your* car's exhaust smells like?

10) Do you live near electricity pylons, TV or radar transmitters, transformer substations, or other powerful sources of electricity? Again, if your health is affected, moving may be the only answer.

11) Do you have troublesome neighbours? That may well be so in this society of ours, with its trends towards uncaring attitudes. But why not take a look at yourself? Is it possible that you are unwittingly doing something that irritates them, thus causing them to consider *you* as *their* troublesome neighbour? Seldom is any situation completely one-sided.

12) Is your food or water contaminated in ways that you do not understand, or find hard to control? There may be ways in which your local environmental health department or water company may be able to help; don't be afraid to approach them.

The main lesson to be learnt is really that we have to try to develop a positive approach to coping with stress. One of the most important steps we can achieve is to recognise the sources of it; identification of a problem immediately relieves the body of the necessity to keep in a state of constant alertness, so that, even if you cannot avoid the problem itself, you can cope better with it.

Awake![5] made some excellent suggestions, which can be summarised as follows:

(a) Try to adapt: make any changes to your lifestyle which are reasonable; these could include changing a job, organising your time better, and so on.

(b) Talk out stress: get things 'off your chest' by discussing your problems with someone sympathetic, perhaps your marriage mate or a trusted friend.

(c) Take exercise: stress prepares your body for strenuous effort (the 'fight or flight' syndrome). So go for a walk, dig the garden, have a swim.

(d) Balance work and recreation: it is good for us to be active and productive, both in our work and our other activities. Dr H. Selye

What else can we do? 159

recommended that 'in most instances, diversion from one activity to another is more relaxing than complete rest.' A life devoted solely to either work or pleasure is unbalanced.

(e) Get enough sleep: your body repairs itself as you sleep, so try and form a regular sleep pattern.

(f) Adjust your viewpoint: Dr H. Selye wrote: 'Rather than relying on drugs or other techniques, I think there's another, a better way to handle stress, which involves taking a different attitude toward the various events in our lives.' (See the end of Chapter 1). Re-evaluate your priorities; ask yourself as you consider taking on a new responsibility whether it is really worth the inevitable stress incurred, and whether you are prepared to go through with the consequences.

Conclusion

I hope that most people will agree from the evidence presented in this book that sensitivities to food and the environment have resulted largely from our failure to be able to adapt sufficiently rapidly to the changing world around us, rather as the confused animal described in Chapter 5 found itself unable to make decisions and consequently developed a recognisable nervous disorder. Regrettably the changes to our living and working environment have been initiated almost entirely by man, so we find ourselves in something of a Catch 22 situation. If we are affected (and presumably most persons who have read this book will be) we can take steps to change our lifestyle and thus remove some sources of stress, just as people may find partial relief from this world by emigrating, or tending a croft on the Outer Hebrides. But although we can ameliorate our condition to some extent, we still have to live with *ourselves* and also recognise that we do not get any younger. We still have to pay our taxes, and we need from time to time the services provided by doctors, hospitals, the fire brigade, schools, water, electricity and so on.

Recently there have been encouraging signs that we are waking up to the urgency to protect the environment before it is too late, and many will find fulfilment in working for 'green' causes. But we must learn to recognize that as individuals we cannot change either the world or our own inherited tendencies; we *can* learn to live with both in greater harmony by increasing our understanding of

160 *The Last Straw*

the world around us and the way in which our marvellously-designed bodies work, and that is the message that I have set out to put across.

Hopefully you will feel that this book has served its purpose in a practical and useful way; after all, 'forewarned is forearmed', or as the Bible puts it so succinctly[5]: 'Sensible people will see trouble coming and avoid it, but an unthinking person will walk right into it and regret it later.' If so, then you will be better equipped to help others who as yet have not reached the same level of understanding as yourself; after all, being unselfish with your time, your knowledge and your experience will benefit not only the recipient but you too as the giver. As an American psychiatrist once said: 'We are here to see what we can put into life, not what we can get out of it.'

REFERENCES
1. *The Food Labelling Regulations*, S.I. 1305 (1984), Section 16 (4).
2. Ibid., Section 18 (b & c).
3. Campbell, H.J., *The Foodwatch Alternative Cookbook* (3rd Edition), Ashgrove Press, 1989.
4. *Awake!*, 8 October 1980, pp. 8–13.
5. *The Bible (Today's English Version)*, Proverbs 22: 3.

Useful Names and Addresses

Food & Environmental Consultancy (operated by the author)

Peter G. Campbell
Cirrus Associates (South West)
Little Hintock
Kington Magna
GILLINGHAM
Dorset
SP8 5EW
Tel: East Stour (0747) 858165 (due to change during 1991 to 838165)

A Food & Environmental Consultancy service available to industry, clinics and the general public. Many services and products offered; information sent on receipt of a large SAE.

Supplier of Specialized Foods

Foodwatch International Ltd
Butts Pond Industrial Estate
STURMINSTER NEWTON
Dorset
DT10 1AZ
Tel: Sturminster Newton (0258) 73356

Worldwide Mail Order service for foods for special diets; information sent on receipt of a large SAE.

Suppliers of Nutritional Supplements

Green Farm Nutrition
BURWASH COMMON
East Sussex
TN19 7LX

162 *The Last Straw*

JH Products
33 West Way
Three Bridges
CRAWLEY
West Sussex RH10 1JY

Suppliers of Environmental Health Books & Equipment

Natural Therapeutics
25 New Road
SPALDING
Lincs PE11 1DJ

Cactus Nursery (for Cereus Peruvianus)

Abbey Brook Cactus Nursery
Dept. CP
Bakewell Road
MATLOCK
Derbyshire DE4 2QJ

Useful Organisations

Action Against Allergy
43 The Downs
Wimbledon
LONDON SW20 8HG

Association for Systematic Kinesiology
39 Browns Road
SURBITON
Surrey KT5 8ST

The Asthma Society
300 Upper Street
London W1 2XX

British Diabetic Association
10 Queen Anne Street
LONDON W1M 0BD

The Cancer Help Centre
Grove House
Cornwallis Grove
BRISTOL BS8 4PG

Useful Names and Addresses 163

The Candida, M.E. & Immune Deficiency Advice Group
P.O. Box 89
EAST GRINSTEAD
West Sussex RH19 1YB

The Coeliac Society of the U.K.
P.O. Box 220
HIGH WYCOMBE
Bucks HP11 2HY

The Food & Chemical Allergy Association
27 Ferringham Lane
FERRING BY SEA
West Sussex BN12 5NB

Foresight
The Old Vicarage
Church Lane
WITLEY
Surrey GU8 5PN

Henry Doubleday Research Association
National Centre for Organic Gardening
Ryton on Dunsmore
COVENTRY CV8 3LG

Hyperactive Children's Support Group
71 Whyke Lane
CHICHESTER
West Sussex PO19 2LD

M.E. Action Campaign
P.O. Box 1126
LONDON W3 0RY

M.S. Foundation
P.O. Box 772
Moseley
BIRMINGHAM B13 0AD

National Eczema Society
Tavistock House North
Tavistock Square
LONDON WC1H 9SR

164 *The Last Straw*

National Society for Research into Allergy
26 Welwyn Road
HINCKLEY
Leics LE10 1JY

Soil Association
86-88 Colston Street
BRISTOL BS1 5BB

Springhill Rehabilitation Centre
Cuddington Road
Dinton
AYLESBURY
Bucks HP18 0AD

Clinics (allergy, candida, homoeopathy, environmental sensitivity etc.)

This does not pretend to be a comprehensive list and apologies are due
to all those practitioners whose clinics are not mentioned below.

Allergy & Environmental Medicine Clinic
Breakspear Hospital
High Street
ABBOTS LANGLEY
Herts

Dr S. Birtwistle
66 Station Road
Fulbourne
CAMBRIDGE CB1 5ES

Dr A. Bramberg
17 Kings Street
BARNARD CASTLE
Co. Durham DL12 8EP

Dr H.J.E. Cox
The Clinic
46 St. Mary Street
HIGH WYCOMBE
Bucks HP11 2HE

Useful Names and Addresses 165

Mr T. Curtis
Thingley Firs Clinic
Thingley
CORSHAM
Wilts SN13 9DQ

Dr S. Davies
Biolab Medical Unit
The Stone House
9 Weymouth Street
LONDON W1N 3FF

Mr G.H. Davies
4 Calway Road
TAUNTON
Somerset TA1 3EQ

Dr B. Dawes
256 Brompton Park Crescent
Seagrove Road
LONDON SW6 1SZ

Dr D. Downing
Suite 3 & 4
Galtres House
Lysander Close
Clifton Moor Gate
YORK YO3 8XB

Dr K. Eaton
Cadley Mews
Cadley
MARLBOROUGH
Wilts SN8 4NE

Dr A.D. Fox
54 Barton Court Avenue
Barton on Sea
NEW MILTON
Hants BH25 7HG

Mr K.G. Grove
ASHA Manipulative Clinic
1 Victoria Avenue
CHARD
Somerset

Mrs J. Hampton
33 West Way
Three Bridges
CRAWLEY
West Sussex RH10 1JY

Dr M. Harrison
Ffynnonwen
Llangwyryfon
ABERYSTWYTH
Dyfed

Dr H. Howell
The Candida Clinic
93 Cheap Street
SHERBORNE
Dorset DT9 3LS

Dr R. Husband & Ptnrs
The Old Malt House
Main Road
Marchwood
SOUTHAMPTON SO4 4UZ

Dr J. Kenyon
51 Bedford Place
SOUTHAMPTON
Hants SO7 2DG

Dr P.J. Kingsley
72 Main Street
OSGATHORPE
Leics LE12 9TA

Mrs S. Lashford
The Sanford Clinic
15 Lake Road North
Roath Park
CARDIFF CF2 5QA

Dr J.S. Law
South Biggins
Newton
STURMINSTER NEWTON
Dorset DT10 2DQ

Useful Names and Addresses 167

Ms V. Lee
The Bournemouth Centre for Complementary Medicine
26 Sea Road
Boscombe
BOURNEMOUTH
Dorset BH5 1DF

Dr J. Lester
2 St. George's Close
St. George's Avenue
WEYBRIDGE
Surrey KT13 0DS

Mr J.G. Levenson
Flat 1   60 Welbeck Street
LONDON W1

Dr J. Maberley
Airedale Allergy Centre
High Hall
Steeton
KEIGHLEY
West Yorks BD20 6SB

Dr H. Manning
Musgrove Park Branch
Taunton & Somerset Hospital
TAUNTON
Somerset TA1 5DA

Dr J.R. Mansfield
The Burghwood Clinic
34 Brighton Road
BANSTEAD
Surrey SM7 3HH

Dr L.M. McEwan
London Medical Centre
144 Harley Street
LONDON W1

Mrs J. McFaull
'Edelweiss'
Studley
CALNE
Wilts SN11 9NH

168 *The Last Straw*

Dr K. Mumby
The Manchester Food & Environmental Allergy Clinic
Parkfield House
Parkfield South
Didsbury
MANCHESTER M20 0DB

Dr K. Mumby
18 Adelaide Road
DUBLIN 2
Eire

Dr S. Myhill
America Farm
Weavers Lane
ANNESLEY
Notts NG22 0AT

Dr F.T. Schindler
152 Bridgwater Road
Bathpool
TAUNTON
Somerset TA2 8BG

Mr S. Stock
The Medway Clinic
28 Rainham Shopping Precinct
RAINHAM
Kent ME8 7HW

Mr J.H. Varley
291 Green Lane
Palmers Green
LONDON N13

Dr D. West
Rutt House
IVYBRIDGE
South Devon PL21 0DQ

Mr M. Williams
Whitfield Farm
Colyford
COLYTON
Devon EX13 6HS

Useful Names and Addresses 169

Suggested Further Reading

Davies, G.H., *Overcoming Food Allergies*, Ashgrove Press, 1989.

Lashford, S., *The Residue Report*, Thorsons, 1988.

Budd, M., *Low Blood Sugar (Hypoglycaemia)*, Thorsons, 1984.

Butler, B., *An Introduction to Kinesiology*, T.A.S.K. Publications.

Jehovah's Witnesses and the Question of Blood, Watchtower Bible and Tract Society of New York Inc., 1977.

Chaitow, L., *Candida Albicans*, Thorsons, 1984.

Crook, W.G., *The Yeast Connection* (3rd Edition), Professional Books, Tennessee.

Mackarness, Dr R., *Not All in the Mind*, Pan Books Ltd., 1976.

Mackarness, Dr R., *Chemical Victims*, Pan Books Ltd., 1980.

Mackarness, Dr R., *A Little of What you Fancy*, Fontana, 1984.

Smith, Dr. C. & Best, S., *Electromagnetic Man*, J.M. Dent, 1989.

Brodeur, P., *The Zapping of America*, W.W. Norton Co., New York, 1977.

DeMatteo, B., *Terminal Shock*, NC Press, Toronto, 1986.

Mumby, Dr K., *The Allergy Handbook*, Thorsons, 1988.

Faelten, S., *The Allergy Self-Help Book*, Pan Books, 1987.

Lashford, S., *The Allergy Cookbook*, Ashgrove Press, 1983.

Petersen, V., *The Natural Food Catalogue*, Macdonald & Co., 1984.

Campbell, H.J., *The Foodwatch Alternative Cookbook*, (3rd Edition), Ashgrove Press, 1989.

Lewith, Dr. G. & Kenyon, Dr. J.N., *Clinical Ecology*, Thorsons, 1985.

The Biochemics Handbook, New Era Laboratories, 1969.

Hamilton, G., *Successful Organic Gardening*, Dorling Kindersley, 1987.

Harrison, S.G., Masefield, G.B. & Wallis, M., *The Oxford Book of Food Plants*, Peerage Books, 1969.

Morgan, Dr B. & Roberta, *Brain Food*, Pan Books, 1986.

Hanson, Dr. P., *The Joy of Stress*, Pan Books, 1987.

Valentine, Tom & Carole, *Applied Kinesiology*, Thorsons, 1985.

Index

Acid rain 48, 83, 91
Action Against Allergy 32
Acupressure 136, 137
Acupuncture 71, 137, 139, 146
Addiction 28, 47, 52, 70, 91, 129, 130, 132
Additives in food 25, 27–39, 69
Adrenal gland 129
Advertising 57
Advisory Committee on Pesticides 18
Aerosols 65
Aflatoxin 127
Ageing 118, 131
AIDS 1, 78, 81–82
AIDS & blood transfusion 75
Air conditioning 73
Aircraft 138
ALAR 124
Alcohol 4, 53
Alfalfa 134
Alice in Wonderland 87
Allergy 1, 6, 24, 52, 69, 156
Allergy clinics 20, 28, 30, 34, 119–120, 138
Allergy, definitions 67–69
Allergy, multiple 42, 77, 140
Allergy, reactions 67, 83, 89, 90, 102, 148
Allergy self-help groups 140
Allergy testing techniques 120–122
Allotments 15
Alternative medicine 118, 138, 156
Aluminium 46, 48, 87–88, 112, 129, 149

Aluminium in baby foods 124
Aluminium sulphate 44, 48
Alzheimer's disease 87, 130
Amalgams in dentistry 86, 133
Amaranth (cereal) 155
American Environmental Protection Agency 43
Americium 241 100
Anaemia 87
Anaesthesia 74, 76
Anaesthetic 71
Anger, Dr K. 84
Angina 120
Angioedema 68
Annatto 36
Antacid preparations 8, 134
Antibodies 68
Antibiotics 73, 76, 78
Antibiotics, sensitivity to 22, 33–34, 68
Anticipation 56
Antidepressants 70
Antigen 68
Antioxidants 28, 31, 131
Anxiety 71
Apples 17, 124, 127, 155
Applied kinesiology 136
Apricots 17, 128, 154
Ararat, Mount 96
Ark, Noah's 96
Aromatherapy 133, 134
Arthritis 5, 23, 24, 70 79, 98, 120
Asbestos 84
Aspirin 31, 134

172 *The Last Straw*

Asthma 17, 24, 69, 79, 90, 92, 120
Asymmetric exercises 142
Atherley, G. 104
Atherosclerosis 45
Athlete's Foot 77
Atom 138, 142
Atractosyl glycosides 130
Attitudes towards others 65
Autism 78
Awake! 2, 40, 43, 80, 83, 92, 158

Bacillus cereus 74
Bach remedies 133
Backache 70, 72, 120
Bacterial infection 72
Bananas 11
Baranowski Dr Z. 118
Barley sprouts 118
'Barrel' illustration 85, 152–153
BBC 105
Beans 12, 156
Béchamp 73
Becker, Dr R.O. 115
Beef 129
Begley, Dr. G.F. 119
Bender, Prof. Arnold 12
Benzoate preservatives 28, 31, 128
Benzoyl Peroxide 24
Benzpyrene 90, 92
Bereavement 144, 152
Best, S. 101
Beta-carotene 128, 131
Beta-glucuronidase 121
Betaines 125
BHA 31
BHT 31
Bible 5, 95, 160
Bifidobacterium 77
Biochemics (tissue salts) 146
Biological rhythms 115
Biscuits 125, 155, 156
Blank test 141
Block, E. 93
Blood 139
Blood pressure 60, 133
Blood transfusion 74–76, 118

Blood, volume expanders 76
Blue Baby Syndrome 47
Body language 137
Bonfires 91
Bonica, Dr. J. 71
Boston Globe 59
Boy's Own Paper 7
Brain waves 107, 134, 137
Bread 23, 132, 154, 155
Bread, alternatives to 132
Brilliant Blue FCF 34
British Medical Journal 6
British Museum Research Laboratory 97
British Nutrition Foundation 68
Brodeur, P. 103
Bronchial disease 90, 92
Brown, Prof. M. 117
Brown, R. 97
Brucella 73
Bruising 133
BSE 129
Buchu 133
Budd, Martin 79
Burleigh, Dr R. 97
Butane 89
Butler, B. 136
Butter 126–127, 155
Buttermilk 126–127

Cabbage 81, 88
Cacti 112
Caffeine 129–30
Cahan, Dr. W.G. 90
Calcium 45, 51, 87
Cancer 1, 5, 6, 8, 43, 45, 46, 47, 70, 79, 81–82, 84, 93, 98, 99, 100, 130, 131
Cancer, bladder 130
Cancer, pancreatic 130
Candida albicans 77
Candidiasis 23, 76–79, 127, 131–133
Cannon, Geoffrey 23
Car 147, 152, 158
Carbohydrates 132
Carbon dioxide 41, 85, 89, 92, 130

Index 173

Carbon monoxide 89, 90, 92, 157
Carbon filters 51
Carbon (radioactive, in atmosphere) 97
Carpets 85, 147, 148
Carroll, Lewis 87
Carson, Rachel 3
Casberg, Dr M.A. 119
Catarrh 120
Cavity foam insulation 94, 147, 157
Cereals 132, 155
Cereus peruvianus 112
CFCs 91
Challenge testing 120
Channel Tunnel 157
Charcoal tablets 133
Charging field 99, 150
Chemical Industries Association Ltd. 28
Chemistry on your Table, The 28
Cheese 73, 77, 124
Cheese, cottage 20
Cheese, vegetarian 20
Cheese whey 20
Chemical sensitivities 153
Chemicals in food 16–24
Chemicals in the home 84, 88–89
Chemicals in industry 43, 83, 84
Chemistry 83
Chernobyl 83, 127, 129
Chest pains 112
Chest infection 134
Child abuse 90
Children 58, 86, 152, 155, 157
Chiropractor 72, 136
Chlorine 45–46, 50
Chlorine dioxide 24
Chloroorganics 46
Chlorophyll (homoeopathic) 134
Chlorophytum (Spider Plant) 94
Chocolate 70, 146, 156
Cholesterol 117–118
Choosing remedies 117–135, 143
Choy, Dr R. 42
Chromium 49, 81

Churchill, Randolph 2
Churchill, Winston 2
Citric acid 17, 128
Citrus fruit 127, 146
Clapham Junction disaster 138
Climatic change 95
Clinical ecology 119
Clinics, alternative medicine 66, 79
Clothing 147
Clostridium 48, 73
Coconut 132
Coeliac disease 120
Coffee 70, 129, 146
Coffee, decaffeinated 130
Coliforms 20, 73
Colitis 120
Colours 148, 156
Colours, artificial 28, 29–30, 128
Colours, natural 34, 35–36, 128
Colours, nature-identical 128
Commuting 60, 157
Competition 58–59
Compost 92
Compound ingredients 125, 154
Computers 62, 85, 111–113, 148, 149
Conscience 69
Constipation 6
Contraceptives 49, 79
Cooking oils 118, 131
Cooking utensils 147
Coping 151, 153
Coping stone 151
Copper 48
Corn, 125, 156
Cotton 148, 149
Cottonseed oil 128
Credit Cards 58
Crocin 36
Cross-crawling 142
Cryptosporidia 50
Cultured skimmed milk 125
Customs & Excise 53
Cyanides 12
Cysteine 131
Cystitis 133

174 *The Last Straw*

Cytotoxic testing 121

Dairy produce 6, 19–22, 156
Damp-proof courses 110
Davies, G. 19
DDT 93
Death 63
Debt 57
Decision-making 59–60, 142
Delgado, José 114
Deltoid muscle 143
DeMatteo, R. 105
Dental care 46–47, 86—87
Department of Health 30
Depression 59, 69–70, 78, 99, 120, 144
Desperation 69
Diabetes 79, 120
Diarrhoea 69, 77, 122, 133
Diet 5, 79, 81, 132, 155
Diet (sugar-free) 131–133
Dioxin 91
Diphenyl 17, 127
Direction-finding (by animals & birds) 115
Disease, food-related 6, 7
Discharging field 99, 150
Diverticulitis 23, 120
Divorce 152
DNA 103
Doctors (also see under G.P.s) 118–119, 139
Double blind tests 138, 143
Doyle, Christine 120
Drinking water, quality of 44–55
Drinking water, purification of 50–55
Dry rot control 94
'Dutch Margarine Disease' 31
Dyke, Dr P.J.D. 70

Earache 70
Ear infection 78
Earthing, electrical 110, 149
Eczema 52, 120, 147
Eggs 36, 124
Electrical appliances 109, 148

Electrical emissions (ionising & non-ionising) 111, 148, 149
Electric blankets 109
Electrolyte 139
Electromagnetic fields 42, 87, 95–116, 123, 139, 142, 143, 150
Elimination diet 121
Emotions 65, 80, 81
Emphysema 92
Employment 61
Emulsifiers 28, 31
Endorphins 71
Energy balance 137
Energy meridians 137
Enkephalins 71
E numbers 27, 154
Environmental Protection Agency (U.S.) 43
Environmental sensitivities 119
Environment, physical 5, 84–85, 157
Enzyme potentiated desensitization 121
Enzymes 19–21, 81, 88, 118, 121
Ergot 13
Essential oils 134
European Community's Scientific Committee for Food 69
Exercises, asymmetric 142
Eye strain 85

Family supportiveness 61
Fasting 121
Fatigue 62–63
Fatigue syndrome 134
Fax machine 149
Fears 64–65, 70, 71
Feedback 140
Feet, aching 148
Field Strength Meter 108, 111, 113–114
Fibreglass 24, 94
Fibre, dietary 6
Field, charging 99, 150
Field, discharging 99, 150
'Fight or flight' 60, 158
Figs 74
Filter screens (for VDUs) 112

Index

175

Fitness magazine 49
Flambards 1
Flatulence 133
Flight simulator 62–63
Floor polish 147
Flour additives 154
Flour, bleaching of 24
Flour improvers 23, 24
Flour treatments 13, 28
Flour, unbleached 24, 125, 126, 154
Flour, unfortified 125
Flour, wholemeal 125
Flu-like symptoms, at office 85
Fluorescent lighting 85, 103
Fluoride 46–47, 88
Flying, fear of 65
Food, additives in 27–39
Food Allergy Workshop 68
Food aversion 68
Food & Agriculture Organisation 7
Food 'fads' 132
Food industry 27
Food interactions 146
Food intolerance 68
Food Labelling Regulations 27, 125, 154
Food poisoning 36–38, 122
Food, regular eating of 5
Food sensitivities 119, 124, 126, 141, 153
Football pools 57, 58
Ford, Henry 57, 138
Formaldehyde 92, 94, 131, 147
Fossil fuels 41
F-Plan diet 22
Freed, Dr D.L.J. 75
Fructose 125, 132
Fruit, ripeness 15
Fruit dried 18
Food For Free 11
Food labelling 14
Food treatments 16–24
Free radicals 117
Fruit juice 128
Fruit squashes 128
Fungicides 13

Furnishings 147

Gambling 58
Gardening, organic 15, 92
Garlic 132
Gas 89–90
Genetics 5
Geological faults 99
Geopathic stress 97–99, 134, 150
Getty, Paul 59
Ginger 133, 146
Girardet, H. 88
Glucono deltalactone 132
Glucose 132
Glycine 131
Goldstein, Dr A. 71
Goodheart, Dr J.G. 136
G.P.s 25, 30, 32, 67, 124, 133
Granite 99
Grapefruit 127
Grapes 43
Great War 1
'green' 3, 10, 83, 159
Greenhouse effect 83, 91, 92
Guilt, feeling of 69, 70
Gut, perforation of 77
Guy's Hospital 120

Hahnemann Society 122
Hair driers 109
Hamilton, G. 16
Happiness 59
Hate 65
Headaches 69, 85, 105, 110, 112, 134
Healing, natural 137
Health 5, 25, 38, 69
Health and Safety Executive 111
Health Food Stores 18, 25–26, 38, 124
Heart 60, 137
Heart disease 1, 5, 6, 45, 79, 90, 99, 130, 131
Heart murmur 33
Heart, open surgery 71, 76
Henry Doubleday Research Association 16
Hepatitis B virus 74

176 *The Last Straw*

Hepatitis C from blood 75
Herbs 133, 147
Herbicides 13, 49, 92–93
Hessian 148
Hewson, Dr A. 97
Here's Health magazine 52
Higham, T.M. 59, 60
Hill, Adrian 31
Hills, Lawrence D. 16
Hirayama, Dr T. 81
Histamine 68
Holistic medicine 120
Holmes, Dr T. 63
Homoeopathic hospitals 123–124
Homoeopathy 122–124, 133
Homoeopathy, side-effects of 123
Homoeopathic potencies 122–123
Honey 12
Hopelessness, feeling of 69
Hormone treatment 13
House, moving 64, 157
Hunzas 7
Hyperactive Children's Support
  Group 32
Hyperactivity 30, 34, 47, 52, 99, 120
Hyperglycaemia 79, 125
Hypersensitivity 68, 110, 112, 138, 147
Hypertension 99
Hypoglycaemia 79–81, 120, 132

Imazalil 127
Imbalances 136, 144
Immune system 67, 75, 81, 110, 117,
  131, 152
Indigestion 133
Ingredients lists 125, 126, 128, 154
Institute for Biokinesiology 138
Insulin 81
Interference (electrical) 105, 108
Iodine125 50
Ion exchange resins 51
Ionisers 112
Iron 48, 129, 139, 143
Irradiation 13–14

Jam 128, 155

Jam (sugar-free) 128
Jehovah's Witnesses 76
Johnson, Samuel 90
Journal of Clinical Gastroenterology
  134

Kaolin 133
Kee, Cynthia 102
Kenyon, Dr J.N. 138
Kettle elements 49
Kidney disease 87
Kinesiology 72, 114, 122, 136–150
Kinesiology, can you trust? 137
Kirlian photography 139
Kiwi fruit 128

Lactase 20
Lactobacilli 76
Lactose 20
Lamb 129
Lapachol 132
La Provincia 91
Lashford, Stephanie 16
Lathyrism 12
Lead 48, 84, 86, 94, 157
Lead nitrate 48
Lead in petrol 65, 86
Lead in solder 86
Legionnaires' Disease 73
Legs, aching 148
Lemons 17, 128, 132
Lethargy 99
Lettuce 12, 124
Leukaemia 90
Levin, Dr A. 78
Lewith, Dr G. 138
'Ley lines' 99
Life expectancy 5, 7
Lighting, fluorescent 85
Limes 128
Lines of force 143
Lipid peroxidation 118
Lips, swollen 20, 36, 73
Litter 65
Lockerbie disaster 138
Loneliness 69

Index 177

Love 65
Love affair 69
LSD 11, 13
Lung disease 60, 90, 92, 93, 94, 120
Lymph flow 136–137

Mabey, R. 11
Mackarness, Dr R. 30, 69, 91
Mackworth, N.H. 62
Macmillan, Harold 2
Magnesium 45, 51
Magnet 143, 149
Magnetron 107
Maize 6
Malic acid 17
Manganese 81, 129
Mangoes 128
Margarine 126–127, 154
Margarine (milk-free) 126, 154
Marmalade 128
McLaughlin, T. 11
Meat, cured 47–48
Meat, hormones in 128
Meat, infection of 73
Meat, organic 128–129
Media, sensationalism 27, 37
Medical Post 75
Mental symptoms 123
Mercury 86–87, 133
Meridians, energy 137, 139, 146
Methaemoglobinaemia 47
Methane 89
Methyl acetate 130
Methylene chloride 130
Microwave ovens 106–108
Microwave ovens, leakage from 106–107
Microwaves 95, 102–108
Microwaves, heating effects 104, 106
Microwaves, other effects 104
Mid-life crisis 61
Migraine 120, 144, 146
Milk, antibiotics in 21, 68
Milk, bulking of 21
Milk, cows' 19–22, 155
Milk, cows', sensitivity to 19

Milk, enzymes 20
Milk, evaporated 20
Milk, fluoridation of 46
Milk, goats' 20
Milk, human 88, 93
Milk Marketing Board 21
Milk, nitrates in 21
Milk, sheep's 20
Milk, skimmed 129
Milk, 'sniffer' 21
Miller, Dr K. 68
Miller's neutralising technique 121
Millet 6, 155
Milligan, Spike 65
Mineral oil 128
M.A.F.F. 24, 36, 37, 68, 108, 125
Miscarriages 111
Modern Maturity 63
Molasses 354
Molecules 142
Money 57
Monosodium glutamate 28
Monounsaturated oils 131
Moses 5
Mould 79, 127
Moving house 157
Muesli 128
Mumby, Dr K. 87
Multiple Sclerosis (M.S.) 5, 98, 132
Munro, Dr J. 42
Muscle testing 122, 136
Muscle rigidity 139
Muscle tone 136, 140
Music 60
Myalgic Encephalomyelitis (M.E.) 79, 132
Mycotoxins 74
Myristicin 11

Nalcrom 133
Naphthalene 93
N.A.S.A. 87, 94
National Association for Research into Allergy 32
Natural foods, toxicity of 10–13, 35–36

178 *The Last Straw*

Nervous attacks 120
Nervous system 142, 143
New England Journal of Medicine 86
New York City Department of
  Consumer Affairs 25
New York Times 43
Nickel 49
Nitrates 28, 47–48
Nitrates 28, 47–48
Nitrogen oxides 92, 157
Nitrosamines 47, 90
'Noah's Flood' 95
Noise 60, 157
North Pole 149, 150
Nuclear war, threat of 65
Nutmeg 11
Nuts 127

Oat fibre 81
Office, environmental hazards in 84
Olive oil 118, 131, 132
Oranges 17
Organic growing 10, 16
Organophosphorus compounds 93
Osteopath 72
Osteoporosis 45
Oxygen 139
Ozone 46, 85
Ozone layer 41, 83, 91

Pacemakers 108
Pain 70–72
Pain, in chest 33
Painkillers 134
Pallor 69
Palpitations 110
Pancreas 80
'Paper sickness' 85
Paracetamol 134
Paradichlorobenzene 93
Paraquat 93, 141
Passive smoking 90
Pasta 126
Pasteur 73
Pathogens 72–73
Pau D'Arco (Taheebo) tea 132

Peanuts 74, 127
Pears 17, 127
Pectin 81, 128
Penicillin 34
Pesticides 13, 26, 43, 49, 92–93, 131
Peterman, Dr T., 75
Photocopiers 85, 110, 149
Photography, Kirlian 139
Physical symptoms 123
Pineal gland 115
Pineapples 128
Pneumonia 120, 144
Polarity 150
Pollution 8, 83, 89
Polyphenols 129
Polypropylene 148
Polystyrene 91
Polyunsaturated fats 117, 131
Pomeranz, Dr B. 71
Posture 72
Potassium bicarbonate 13, 43
Potassium bromate 24
Potatoes 12, 18–19, 35, 124
Potter, Beatrix 12
Poultry 73
Power lines 100–102, 150, 158
Pregnancy 111
Preservatives 13, 17–18, 28, 29, 36,
  128, 156
Price, Dr J. 45
Probiotics 73
Processing aids 154
Propane 89
Psoriasis 120
Puff pastry 126
PVC 91

Quartz crystals 112
Quinoa 155

Radar 102–105, 158
Radiation (ionising & non-ionising)
  95
Radioactivity 95, 99
Radiocarbon dating 97
Radio reception 111, 112

Index

179

Radon 94, 99
Rahne, Dr R.H. 63
Railways 83, 138
Rainforests 41
Raisins 128
Randolph, Dr T. 83, 120
Rea, Dr W. 152
Reader's Digest 65
Redundancy 152
Remedies, choosing 143, 145–147
Remedies, homoeopathic 146
Remedies, simple 133
Rennet 20
Respiratory system 17, 93
Reverse Osmosis 53–54
Rhinitis 24, 69
Rice 6, 74, 118
Riley, Dr V.T. 82
Royal College of Physicians 68
Royal Family 10
Rubber 148
Russell, Bertrand 2
Rutherford 138
Rutin 133

S.A.D. 123
Salmonella 36, 73, 124
Salt 126, 139
Schizophrenia 123
'Science News' 87
Scott-Morley, A.J. 99
Screening, electrical 110, 149
Selye, Dr H. 65, 158, 159
Senile dementia 87
Sensitivity 153
Sensitivity testing 136
Serotonin 11
Sexual abuse 69
Seymour, J. 88
Shellfish 67
Shielding (electrical) 112
Shigella 73
Short circuit, bioelectrical 141
'Sick Building Syndrome' 85
Side effects, homoeopathy 138
Silent Spring 3

Skimmed milk 126
Skin rashes 68
Sleep, disturbed 53, 109
Smith, Dr Cyril 42, 107,113, 139
Smoke alarms 99–100
Smoking 28, 81–82, 89, 90–91
Smoking whilst driving 91
Smoking, passive 90
Society, demands of 5
Sodium 51
Sodium bicarbonate 133
Sodim cromoglycate 133
Sodium hexacyanoferrate II 126
Solanine 12, 19
Solar plexus 141
Sore throat 85
Sorghum 155
Sorrow 70
South Pole 149, 150
Soya 124, 128
Speer, Dr F. 90
Spices 146
Stainless steel 49
Staphylococcus 74
Starfruit 128
Static (electricity) 148
Sterilisers 13
Sterility 43
Stills 53
Stimulants 129
Stock, S. 90
Stomach ache 22, 120, 122, 133, 145
Stone Age diet 121
Strawberries 67
Stress, chemical 83–94
Stress, electromagnetic 95–116
Stress, general 5, 7, 8, 10, 37, 60, 80, 150, 151
Stress, geopathic 97–99
Stress and ill-health 67, 82
Stress, reduction of levels of 82, 117, 153, 156–159
Stress, social 57–66
Stress, triggering role in illness 152
Stress at work 60–63
Stressful situations 63–64

180 *The Last Straw*

Sucrose 124, 132
Sugar 6, 35, 47, 76, 79, 124, 155, 156
Sugar, beet 124
Sugar, cane 35, 124
Sugar, refined 35
Suicide attempts 70
Sulman, Dr F.G. 103
Sulphur Dioxide 17, 28, 31, 154, 157
Sultanas 17, 128, 154,
Sunday Evening Post 96
Sunday Telegraph Magazine 11
Sunday Times 85, 117
Sunflower oil 131
Sunlamps, ultraviolet 109
Supermarkets 25, 38, 124, 128, 144, 154, 155
Superoxide dismutase 120
Supplements 25, 44, 79, 81, 132
Sweeteners, synthetic 132
Switching 142, 154, 155
Synergistic effects 143
Systematic kinesiology 136

Taheebo (Pau D'Arco) tea 132
Tannin 129
Tartrazine 29, 31, 32–34
T-cells 121
TCP 46
Tea 46, 70, 88, 129–130, 146, 147
Tecnazene 18
Telephone extensions 108
Television sets 111, 137, 149
Tertiary butyl mercaptan 89
Theobromine 129
Theophylline 129
Thermosphere 96
Third World 3
Times, The 97
Tiredness 85, 120, 138
Tissue salts (Biochemics) 133, 146
Toilet paper 147
Tomatoes 43, 67, 88, 124
Tongue, white coating on 77
Toothache 70, 147
Toothpaste 47
Touch for Health 136

Toxic load on body, total 30, 85, 152, 153
Toxic wastes, dumping of 43, 44
Toxins, eliminating 133
Toynbee, Arnold 4
Tranquillisers 4, 70, 130
Transformers 101, 148, 158
Travel sickness 133
Truss, Dr O. 78
Trihalomethanes 46
Tswana tribe (South Africa) 6

Uhlenhuth, Dr G. 152
Ulcers 60, 130, 134
Ultra-violet light 46
Undulant fever 73
UNESCO 8
United Nations 7
United States Department of Health 98
United States Congress 100
Unrefined carbohydrates 80
'Upstairs, Downstairs' 1
Urinary infection 70, 78
Urticaria 31, 68
U.S. *News and World Report* 43

Vaginal discharge 77
Valium 49, 70
VDUs 111, 134
Vega electrical therapy 121
Vegetables 131, 132
Vibrio 73
Vicker, R. 8
Victorian Kitchen, The 14
Victorian Kitchen Garden, The 14
Vitamin A 131, 134
Vitamin B 131
Vitamin C 24, 134
Vitamin E 81, 131
Vomiting 69, 122

Washing liquid 147
Washing powder 88–89, 147
Water, analysis of 50
'Water arteries' 98

Index

181

Water, bacteria in 50
Water, bottled, spending on 44
Water, chlorine in 45–46
Water, EEC standards in 46–47
Water filters 45, 48, 51–55
Water, for drinking, quality of 44–55
Water, hardness in 45
Water, heavy metals in 48–49
Water, natural resource 40–41
Water, organic residues in 49–50, 51
Water, properties of 41–42
Water, pollution of 43–44, 88
Water, purification of 50–55
Water, as remedy 134
Water, sensitivity to 42, 44
Water stress 98, 134, 150
Water, taints in 51
Water, use in industry 40
Water, use at home 40
Wall Street Journal 8
Weather patterns, changes in 41
Wheat 6, 70, 118, 156
Wheat, residues in 23
Wheat flour 22–24
Wheat flour, additives to 23, 24
Wheat bran 22
Wheat, milling 23

Wheelock, Dr Vernon 37
Whey 126, 134
Which magazine 44, 120
'White noise' 111
Wilson, Dr C.W.M. 44, 52
Wintrobe, Dr M.M. 75
Witch hazel 133
Wood, Dr N. 90
Woodworm control 94
World Food Council 7
World Health Organisation 47, 82
World War I 2
Worldwatch Institute 43
Wright, Orville 138

X-rays 106
Xanthines 129

Yeast 31, 77, 131–3
Yersinia 74
Yin & Yang 99
Yogurt 7

Zapping 102
Zaret, Dr M 103
Zinc 81, 88, 129